SPACE CHASE

A Star Watch Novel

Written By

Mark Wayne McGinnis

Cover design by:
MWM

Edited by:
Lura Lee Genz
Mia Manns

Published by:
Avenstar Productions

Paperback ISBN: 978-0-9974514-5-0

To join Mark's mailing list, jump to:
http://eepurl.com/bs7M9r

Visit Mark Wayne McGinnis at:
http://www.markwaynemcginnis.com

FORWARD

Quick Tip:

For those using web-enabled e-readers, or who have access to the web via a PC, you can now refer back to the author's website for some pretty cool background information. In addition to illustrated floor plans of ships, such as *The Lilly's* and *The Minian's* various decks and compartments, as well as those of another vessel called the Parcical. Recently added, are beautiful—rotatable—3D diagrams of the Pacesetter II, the Consignment Freight Van, Sand-Crawler, and the ominous refurbished Paotow Tanker.

More ship diagrams will be added over time. Throughout this book, look for the various little icons (such as the one below) — provided as a quick reminder of this option—*simply click on the ship icon to jump to the* **Explore The Ships** *website diagrams:*

Quick Tip 2:

*After seven Scrapyard Ship books and five Star Watch books, there's a ton of character names, various alien star systems and planet names, not to mention all of the series-specific SciFi terms and phrases ... well, help is here! On the Mark Wayne McGinnis website there's a complete **Glossary of Terms** for your reference:*

CHAPTER 1

Jason entered the Jumelle's bridge and made a beeline for the captain's chair. Sergeant Major Stone looked back at him from her helm post. As usual, half her face was hidden behind long, one-sided, blond bangs. Recently, she'd added several new piercings—one over her exposed brow, and one just above her upper lip. She didn't need to say anything—her sad expression made her thoughts perfectly clear. As Rizzo's girlfriend, she believed she should be involved in determining such life or death decision-making for him. Maybe she's right, Jason thought. But in the end, he knew he alone would be the one most responsible. The mere thought made Jason sick to his stomach.

The young man's family had gotten back to him specifically, because of his long friendship with their son. How on Earth was he supposed to determine the right decision to make? Be the one to arbitrate whether Rizzo should continue on life support or ... not. Jason's thoughts flashed to a rundown New England farmhouse and a lone MediPod, installed in the middle of a once younger boy's bedroom. Was it necessary to determine the best course of action to take right away? *Oh God, Rizzo ... are you really going to make me pull the fucking plug? Wake up, buddy, you miserable son of a bitch!*

"What's on the agenda today, Cap?" Gunny Orion asked from her tactical station, behind him to the right. "An attacking star system warlord, or perhaps a fleet of attacking space Gorlicks?"

Jason smiled. "Not this time, Gunny. We have an old-fashioned missing person's case to solve."

"And how, might I ask, does that rate the attention of Star Watch?"

It was a fair question. Since the reorganization of Star Watch, there was kickback. Ten Star Watch captains had individually, or in combination with others, complained about their new district posts, by one means or another.

But change was necessary—even essential. Starting with the fact that most of the Allied worlds were fed up by the lack of attention—protection—they were receiving from the U.S. fleet's high command. Outright threats to leave the Alliance were becoming an issue. And then there was the dismal matter of the previous Omni's poor administrative skills—his own. It was amazing that Star Watch functioned as well as it had. Jason assigned to himself District 1, which included Sol, Alpha Centauri, Bernard's Star, Luhman 16, Wolf 359, Lalande 21185, Sirius, and about fifty other major star systems contained within a radius of about thirty light-years from Sol. Everyone wanted District 1. Some captains cried nepotism—Jason being the Omni's son—but the Omni was fine with Jason's selection. After all, Jason, in one way or another, was responsible for them having a job in the first place.

Jason said, "The missing person is a young man who works for Consigned Freight. He drives an interstellar delivery van. Apparently, he's a nice kid who just happens to be our previous president's nephew."

"Your ex-wife? Nan's nephew? I didn't know she had a nephew ... or even a sibling, for that matter," Orion said.

"Well, she does. She has both a brother and a sister. This is her older sister's kid. He's in his early twenties. I've never met him …Nan says he's a terrific young man."

"So what's the story? Any leads?"

"Just that he may have arbitrarily bumped into the wrong spacecraft and the absolute worst owner of such a craft."

The top of Ricket's head appeared as he moved along behind the front row of bridge consoles. Turning the corner, now fully in view, his attention was focused on his projected virtual notebook. He remarked, "Private commercialization of space within the Sol System has grown substantially over the last five or six years." He turned his attention to Orion. "One area in particular … mining. The need for new and rare elements has increased by a factor of three hundred percent in the last year alone."

"That's interesting, I guess, Ricket," Orion said.

"Based on dispatch records, the nephew plowed into the personal RV craft of one Orloff Picket," Jason said.

"Picket … I've heard that name before. Seen it stenciled on ginormous space freighters," Orion said.

"The Picket name carries a lot of weight when it comes to the mining industry in the Sol System. Especially in the mineral-rich Kuiper Belt … beginning at the orbital out-skirts of Neptune."

"So how does this Orloff Picket relate?" she asked.

"According to Nan, Orloff is a son of the infamous Mamma Picket. From what I understand, she's the family matriarch, also the company's general manager. A tough, no-nonsense old bird who is not to be taken lightly. There's an old saying in Appalachia … Don't mess with Mamma …"

"Appalachia!" Billy exclaimed, striding onto the bridge, bringing an apple up to his mouth. "That's one place you sure don't want to visit unless you absolutely have to."

"And why's that?" Orion asked.

"Tennessee … West Virginia … mountainous areas and

really rough terrain. There's still a crapload of peovils in that part of the country." Biting into the apple, his mouth full, Billy added, "Those things breed, you know ... like mangy rabbits."

Jason continued, "So anyway, prior to the infestation of molt weevils by that infamous Craing, Ot-Mul ... and the ensuing, near eradication of all human life on Earth—the name Picket was the most infamous in coal mining. Responsible for a large portion of surface mining in that part of that country. Tops of mountains were sheared off ... the landscape ravaged beyond recognition. At that time, coal mining was on its way out. Companies like Picket's were able to stay afloat only by cutting corners. Miners were given the barest minimum in the way of safety equipment; there was improper ventilation; long extended workdays below ground. You know, that sort of thing. Mamma Picket had long before run the unions out. Then, brought up on charges by the government, she was expected to go to jail."

Billy said, "Ot-Mul was the best thing to ever happen to her."

Orion ignored Billy's comment. "So we're going to see this Mamma Picket?"

Jason nodded. "Apparently, she keeps a very tight rein on her boys ... always knows where they are and what they are doing."

"Even Big Bubba up in space?" Billy asked.

"Orloff," Orion corrected.

"Even Orloff?"

"Especially those in space," Jason said.

Ricket, his attention back on his projected virtual notebook, said, "The Picket family makes little income from their earlier coal-based businesses. Whereas, their space mining ventures have proven to be enormously fruitful."

Jason added, "Yup ... we're talking billions of dollars. Mamma Picket, though she may not act like it ... or look like it, is one of the wealthiest women on Earth."

Billy said, "So what's next? We visit a bunch of hillbillies?"

"First, we'll meet up with Nan and go over how we're supposed to conduct ourselves. She's adamant that we must act and look like locals. Any whiff that we're Star Watch … space police … will screw up our chance to acquire information necessary in tracking down her nephew, Ryan Chase."

"I'm in," Billy said.

"I'd like to go, Captain," Ricket said.

"Sorry, Ricket … you'd stick out like a sore thumb in those parts. No, we need to keep this a tight-knit team." Looking over at Sergeant Major Stone, Jason thought, if anyone here needs a diversion, it's her. "Stone, would you be willing to lose the hardware for an away mission?"

She pursed her lips. "You want me along on this?"

"Yeah … I do," Jason said.

She smiled. "Definitely."

"Good. Then it's Stone, Billy, myself, and Nan."

"Nan is one of the most recognizable people on the planet," Billy said. "Add to the fact that she has a security detail lurking around her twenty-four seven …"

"You're preaching to the choir, Billy. She says she's reduced her service agents and she'll make sure she's unrecognizable," Jason said. "I'm not saying I like any of this … but the decision has pretty much been made. So it's Stone, Billy, myself, Nan and her security detail."

CHAPTER 2

Three days earlier …

The thundering base, *thump … thump … thump*, rhythmically pulsated from two fourteen-inch woofers—mounted high up on the small cockpit's rear bulkhead. With legs crossed at the ankles and propped up on the helm console in front of him, his boots kept beat to the Boss, singing *Boooorn in the USA … I was boooorn in the USA …*

Singing along, Ryan Chase took another oversized bite of his carne asada burrito and reached out for the open can of Mountain Dew. Feeling the lightness of the can—he shook it and felt, more than heard, the sloshing of what little remained of the liquid. He downed the last drops of Dew and chewed contently. Eyes closed, his thoughts drifted to another time—another place. In his highly opinionated twenty-three-year-old mind, there simply was no better era than the late 1980s, back on Earth. He knew everything there was to know about that particular time period. The music, of course, and also the styles of clothes back then. The awesome cars … like the Pontiac Firebird. *If only I'd been born forty years earlier*, he thought.

Ryan, allocated thirty minutes for lunch, knew he'd already spent close to forty. There were half a day's deliveries still to make, plus an extended run out to the glacially frigid Erass5B. He really hated making deliveries to that desolate crap-hole of a planet. Why would any species choose to live in a world where they had to wear thermal environ-suits twenty-four seven?

The strong abrupt jolt was enough to send the remainder of his burrito flying, and his empty can of Mountain Dew to fling, clattering, into the forward observation window. Thrown from his seat, Ryan found himself planted face down on the hard metal deck. In that same instant he knew exactly what had happened: *Space drift.* He'd forgotten to engage the RTM gyros ... again. *Shit Fuck! Shit!*

Ryan staggered to his feet, rubbing the goose egg now blossoming in the middle of his forehead. What he saw next out the forward observation window made his heart skip a beat. Paralyzed, he stared at a concave *dent* on a ... *what the hell is that?* He fired up the space truck's low-powered drive and eased the vehicle backward—goosing the reverse thrusters in small bursts—until he could see what he'd bumped into in its entirety. At fifty feet out, he shut down the drive and engaged the RTM gyros, which would keep his delivery van from drifting around in space, like it just had, unfortunately, only moments before. Why the hell hadn't the AI engaged proximity sensors—warned him about the drift—like she was supposed to?

"Music off!" he yelled over Springsteen's final verse.

The cockpit went quiet. What Ryan was seeing, his eyes open wide, was a true classic beauty. To most, the ship's rounded tubular, out of date dark-brown hull would simply look decrepit—like one of those rusted old Santa Fe tankers, or those Union Pacific cars, found back on Earth. But to him, the ship's coppery patina was simply magnificent—or had been, before he'd added a five-foot-diameter dent into it broadside.

It was, Ryan knew, a refurbished Paotow Tanker. The very first fuel tanker deployed to space. Only a few of those bad boys were made before the company went belly up. Anyone lucky enough to own one—or chance discovering one in a scrapyard somewhere—would do exactly what this owner must have done—refurbish it. Ryan, goosing the drive a little in order to maneuver around to the side of the spacecraft, noted, *Ah … he's added the Amersand-T20 conversion kit*, transforming the old propellant freighter into something pretty cool. Again, he stared at the big dent, now from a different angle, wishing he could rewind his life ten minutes. He'd inadvertently careened into the side of someone's multi-million-dollar RV conversion. *Crap … Shit! … Fuck!*

Ryan let out a breath and weighed his options. Sure, he could continue to simply back away. Within seconds, his little delivery van would be no more than a pinprick of light— far away in the vastness of space. Hell—accidents happen. Isn't that why companies carried insurance, for this kind of mishap? Three weeks ago, his friend, Gary Lomar, plowed into a house-sized rock, somewhere near the inside edge of the Kuiper Belt. Ryan had experienced some close calls there also. The nearly impassible remnants of the solar system's early formation—composed largely of frozen volatile ices, such as methane, ammonia and water. Yeah … but this was different, Ryan knew. He didn't mind pushing certain gray areas regarding rule bending, like taking forty minutes for lunch instead of the allocated thirty, but committing a Department of Space Compliance felony? That wasn't him. *Crap!*

Ryan, suddenly remembering, stomped his boot angrily down on the deck. He'd muted Bella, the onboard AI. Her bitchy voice was driving him crazy. He'd needed a reprieve—a few minutes peace while he sat and ate his lunch. He knew it was a big *no no* as far as Consigned Freight, his employer, was concerned, but everyone muted their AIs every now and then

… had to. He'd heard stories of drivers quitting for no better reason than to get away from hearing the superior-sounding, schoolmarm-ish, voice yak on and on. The problem now was that the delivery van's AI also controlled the proximity sensors. Mute one and the other muted too.

Ryan tapped the rapidly blinking red touch key on the console. Bella's voice, now unmuted, once again filled the small cockpit. "Collision! Collision! Collision! Safety protocols have been implemented."

"Put a sock in it, Bella. Just tell me what's going on with my van. Give me a damage report."

"Freight Van 412 has sustained forward hull buckling to panels A9, A10, and A11."

"Any breaches?"

"Negative, Driver of 412."

"Damage that affects environmental systems?"

"Negative, Driver of 412. My sensors indicate the RTM gyros were not properly set. A spatial drift occurred and the subsequent—"

"I already know what happened! I don't need you to recount events of the recent past, Bella. Why don't you make yourself useful and ping that ship's bridge for me?"

Ryan heard the melodic *ping-pong* sound as Bella hailed the Paotow Freighter's bridge. He waited but no response came.

"Are you picking up some life signs in there, Bella?"

"No, Driver of 412."

"So no one is onboard?" Ryan asked.

"There are not multiple life signs onboard; there is only one life sign, Driver of 412."

"You know, you could have just said that in the first place. Why do you have to make our conversing so difficult?"

"I do not answer hypothetical questions, Driver of 412."

He'd heard that same response back hundreds—hell, thousands of times before. The AI was fully capable of conversing since all modern AIs were programed to do so, but Consigned Freight saw fit to curtail the AI's conversational capacity. Something about drivers getting lost in nonsensical conversations, attributing to their distracted driving. So Bella, already bitchy and abrupt, was totally uninteresting.

"I want to leave a vid-message. Go ahead and access the freighter's HMS."

"The vessel's Hail Message System is currently not accessible."

"*Shit!* Then how am I supposed to let the owner know I'm the asshole who put a colossal dent in the side of his classic retrofit?"

"I do not answer hypothetical questions, Driver of 412."

Ryan lip-synced her standard reply and rolled his eyes. "Have you logged the freighter's DSCVID?"

The DSCVID—the vehicle's identification designation—was assigned by the Department of Space Compliance, which required all space-faring vessels to have a DSCVID to operate within the confines of the solar system, or within any of Alliance's connected provinces.

"No, Driver of 412. A valid DSCVID is not available."

That complicated things. With a valid DSCVID, Consigned Freight could at least attempt to contact the owner of the vessel via SpaceMail.

"Any suggestions, Bella?"

She didn't respond for several moments. "No, I do not have any, Driver of 412."

"Well, log it that I at least tried and that you didn't have any suggestions. Go ahead and initiate a course plot to the next delivery coordinates. I'm switching to manual helm control."

"Drivers are encouraged to utilize AI helm-controlled navigation whenever possible, Driver of 412."

"I know that. I'm taking the helm so spare me the lecture." Ryan was fuming. He'd just plowed into someone's spacecraft and was now leaving the accident scene. He could lose his job over this incident. *Shit, could this day get any worse?*

CHAPTER 3

"**D**river 412, you have an incoming hail from Central Dispatch. I can put that through to you now … if you like."

Ryan had just throttled up the van's propulsion system for what was to be a three-day-long jaunt. He turned and stared at the white, oblong AI-Pac—slotted into the same equipment rack—where similar, yet different, plug and play components were mounted. They controlled every aspect of the space van. The Environ-Pac system, the largest of the pacs, was nearly five-feet-high by two-feet-wide, while the Nav-Pac system was the smallest. There were various others, too—less essential, but still important components—plus the AI-Pac. Ryan specifically knew which pac was responsible for his present conversation.

"So you contacted CF without my knowledge?"

"It is my responsibility to notify the proper channels at Consignment Freight when one of their vehicles is involved in a collision. Especially a collision as egregious as yours, Driver 412."

Ryan had his suspicions about AI Bella. Not only was she far more capable than she let on, he was also certain she was out to get him. He'd shared such concerns with his friend and fellow driver, Two-ton, who didn't dispute that possibility, saying the damn things couldn't be trusted; that they were always lurking—spying on one's actions and listening—programmed to be both suspicious and duplicitous.

Ryan continued to stare at the AI-Pac. "Who is it … specifically?"

"Supervisor Tony Post. He is awaiting your response, Driver of 412."

Ryan squinted his eyes at the cold metal box and nodded, knowing that Bella's optical sensors would register the gesture.

"Chase! What in hell took you so long to pick up? You think I have nothing better to do than wait for your sorry ass to answer a hail?"

"How you doing, Tony? I was in the head … sorry."

"Bullshit! It doesn't take ten minutes to drop a duce. Why don't you talk to me about this collision of yours, and why you decided to leave the scene of an accident."

"What was I supposed to do? No one answered the damn hail and there weren't any provisions handy to leave a message. To top it off, the vehicle's DSCVID is nowhere to be found. Figured I'd keep hailing the ship, at least until I was out of range."

"You're an idiot, Chase! I don't know how you got this job; who you blew to get it. But I'm going to make sure you're one of the first sacked when the next set of cuts come along. Collisions mean paperwork … paperwork yours truly is responsible for!"

Crap! Ryan, already worried about his job, really needed to keep it. Work was extremely hard to find these days and he'd called in more than a few favors—requesting a Consignment Freight application, then getting it moved up to the top of the stack—*thank you, Aunty Nan*. He didn't have *to blow* anyone, as Tony so crudely put it, but he had bought more than his share of rounds at Bottoms Up—the dingy, ridiculously popular pub on space station CRW55.

"I have a mind to call you back in; have a replacement driver take over your route, at least, until a claim against CF has been entered and evaluated."

"Oh, come on, Tony, don't do that. Look, how about I take on an extra delivery route for the upcoming month ..."

"And why would I want you in the field any more than you are now? Everyone knows you're a train wreck just waiting to happen. Isn't that why that girlfriend of yours bolted?"

"Hey ... leave Wendy out of this, Tony. And our breakup was mutual, not that it's any of your business."

"That's not what she told me last night at Bottoms. Just saying ..."

Ryan imagined his fist delivering a quick jab to his supervisor's nose, followed by a *lights-out* upper cut to the man's nearly imperceptible chin.

Not hearing a response, Tony Post continued, "Maybe I'll get the rest of the story from her tonight, since it's almost quitting time and payday too."

Ryan was fairly sure Wendy, his very pretty, and far too intelligent girlfriend for all of nine months—*and now his ex*—had far higher standards than Tony. At least he hoped she did. What was Tony, thirty-five? Forty? Ryan cleared thoughts of Wendy away, like he had a dozen other times throughout the day—every day. The truth was his heart felt shredded without her—making it through one day at a time was all he could manage. And now he was on the verge of losing his job, too. *Unbelievable!* Dumped by both Wendy and Consignment Freight within the same few days.

"What do you want me to do, Tony?" Ryan asked, feeling more resigned to his fate.

The long silence following was agonizing. "Make that

delivery to Erass5B. And I better not hear a peep from you for at least a week. Keep out of trouble that long and you might keep your job ... No promises ... though."

"Thanks, Tony, I ..." Ryan halted mid-sentence, realizing the connection had already been severed.

CHAPTER 4

Ryan initiated a series of in-depth safety evaluation routines that he knew Bella had yet to perform. It might be overkill, but it had been a substantial collision. He'd heard of drivers becoming frozen icicle sticks; killed due to micro-cracked oxygen feed hoses, or misaligned hatch seals, or a handful of other critical life-ending catastrophes.

"Bella ... have you done an assessment of what's in our cargo hold? No sense heading all the way out to Erass5B, then finding we're delivering damaged goods."

"Container sensors are all showing green, Driver of 412."

Ryan was standing up at the helm—something he did fairly often on long-ass hauls such as this. "You know, saying *Driver 412* at the end of every sentence is totally unnecessary. I'm the only one on board. It's redundant ... not to mention ... super annoying."

"AI Speech Guidelines are pre-configured for every Consignment Freight vehicle, Driver 412."

The overhead alarm klaxon blared *Bwamp ... Bwamp ... Bwamp!* Ryan, worried that something related to the environmental systems had indeed failed, reviewed the console indicators before him. "Talk to me, Bella! What the hell's going on?"

"There is an emergency hail from a Consignment Freight vehicle. An incoming message from Driver of 211."

"That's Two-ton's van number, Bella. What's the intersect ETA for Coordinate 5899321?"

"Fourteen minutes and twelve seconds at our current—"

"Okay … got it." Ryan locked on to the coordinates and engaged the drive, quickly bringing the propulsion system up to redline limits. He staggered backward, as inertia-dampeners began to compensate for the increased speed.

"ETA?"

Bella said, "Eight minutes and forty-three seconds, Driver of 412."

"Bella, open a channel to Two-ton … Um, driver of CF vehicle 211."

"Channel has been established, Driver of 412."

"Two-ton! Do you read me? Don? Over …"

A fractured and distant-sounding voice crackled once.

"Come back on, Don. I did not understand your last transmission. Over …"

Ryan heard nothing.

"The channel has been lost, Driver of 412."

Ryan stared out the forward observation window, straining his eyes to see something, anything, resembling a spacecraft. His thoughts turned to Don, whom everyone, including himself, referred to as Two-ton. He was big, more than actually fat, like an overgrown Jethro. Twenty-four years old, the Kansas-born hayseed was a good guy and a good friend to Ryan. They'd planned to meet over the next few days. Two-ton was a technology genius, continuously modifying his delivery van in such undercover ways that biggies at corporate remained completely oblivious to any changes he'd made. Like improvements to the propulsion system, including removal of speed governors and, more importantly, changes to the onboard AI. All drivers named their AIs: In Ryan's van, the AI was called Bella; in Two-ton's, the AI was called Maggie, named after someone he knew in high school back on Earth. Two-ton wanted them to meet up; said he had a special present for Ryan—one that would put Ryan in his debt for the rest of his life.

The van's proximity sensors chimed and Ryan saw the familiar outline of the Consignment Freight van showing up on the console screen. Now, less than a minute out, Bella began reducing their speed. He continued to stare at the virtual representation of the space van. Something seemed *off* about it. Using his forefinger on the touchscreen, he manipulated the screen image 180 degrees, and the van's opposite side hull appeared, somehow dramatically distorted. He looked up and watched Two-ton's delivery van come into actual view. Sunlight reflected off the ship's exposed side.

Ryan adjusted his navigation joystick toward the right and began a slow arc around the rear of the small delivery ship ahead. He gasped. The forward third of the vessel on its port side was crushed in. Sparks flared up, then quickly dissipated in the vacuum of space. Atmosphere was escaping at various points, like spray from an old-fashioned aerosol can.

"Two-ton ... Don ... do you copy?"

No answer.

"Life signs, Bella?"

"Life signs for Driver of 211 are present, but weak. He is in need of immediate medical attention, Driver of 412."

"I'm going over."

"Negative. Spacewalks are not permitted without proper management pre-authorizations, Driver of 412."

Ryan ignored her. He engaged the RTM gyros, then headed from the cockpit hatch and down a short flight of stairs. Consignment Freight delivery space vans basically had three separate levels, or decks. The forward cockpit was positioned between the upper and lower deck. The top-most deck, commonly referred to as Cargo, or the hold, was where all deliverables were stored—either for delivery or for pick up. The lower deck, where the van driver lived, held a head, a kitchenette, and two bunks, as sometimes two drivers were assigned to a van. A tiny communal open space was at the rear of the lower level, plus a double, man-sized, air-lock. Spacesuits, by early twenty-first century, had progressed dramatically from their late twentieth-century counterparts. The influence of Caldurian tech—although a far cry from anything the U.S. Fleet or Star Watch possessed—allowed for lightweight spacesuits made of exotic materials. A highly durable tensile fabric, they were the latest environment suits of a non-military nature. Consignment Freight vessels were required to contain no fewer than three operational envi-ron-suits available for use at all times. One never knew when a hull breach would occur—something that happened with more frequency than many realized. At least, that's what Two-ton told him several weeks past, advising him to always keep a suit handy—stored inside a locker right within the cockpit.

Within the confines of the airlock, Ryan fitted his body into one of the hanging environment suits. Perfected over the years, they were designed for a rapid suit-up. Yearly, every driver was required to train for the possibility of a hull breach, which meant getting to the airlock and into an environment suit within sixty-seconds. Wearing the oversized suit—which would become more body fitting, more body conforming, once pressurized—Ryan reached up and unslung one of the three helmets hanging above him, which also held a pair of gloves inside. Using both hands, he stretched the helmet over his head and put on the gloves, pressure-latching them at the cuffs, then did the same to the environment suit pants, latching them at his boots. Lastly, he secured the helmet's neck-fitting latch and waited for the heads-up display, the

HUD, to come alive. According to the bright-violet display readouts—less than thirty minutes of compressed air remained stored within the three small oblong cylinders located around the back and sides of his helmet. Ryan momentarily considered retrieving an environ-pac from the adjoining compartment. Though it would give him several extra hours of breathable air, it would also take up valuable minutes. He just wanted to get over there as quickly as possible and help Two-ton. He double-checked, ensuring the inside hatch was secure before he hit the oversized, green-lit, vent pad button. Once it flashed red, he heard the air around him being sucked into storage tanks somewhere beneath his feet. The vent pad stopped blinking—remaining bright red.

Ryan, hurrying to unlatch his space van's outside hatch mechanism, waited for the door to slide up and disappear into the bulkhead. Thirty feet away, Two-ton's nearly identical-looking van sat damaged.

"Bella … get us in closer."

"Repositioning now, Driver of 412."

"Hey, Two-ton … you receiving?" Ryan listened hard to the still silent channel. "Hold on, buddy … I'm almost there."

Ryan watched as his own delivery van's thrusters, positioned both above and below the rear hatch, began to spit out momentary bursts. Though the other van seemed to be moving in his direction, he knew it was only an optical illusion. Bella maneuvered the van within three feet's distance of the other—close enough for him to reach over and strap a lifeline cable onto one of the metallic eyelets provided for just such an occasion. He swung his body over and onto the other van, briefly assessing his friend's ship's condition. He felt his stomach's contents go sour. There was horrendous damage—much worse than he'd first thought. It looked like a gigantic hammer had struck the van, leaving behind a huge, perfectly rounded indentation. *How could anyone survive such an assault?* His earlier fender-bender was nothing compared to what had happened here.

Bella said, "Driver of 412 … I am in communication with the AI of vehicle 211. Our systems are synchronized. Shall I open the rear airlock?"

"Yes, and hurry up," he said, mentally preparing for what he was about to see inside.

Ryan watched the rear hatch slowly open until it looked like a wide, gaping black mouth.

"Go ahead and open the inside airlock, too, Bella. I can already see where sections of the hull were breached so there won't be any atmosphere inside, anyway." He moved past the inside airlock's open hatch. Since the van's gravity generators were non-functional, he had to haul himself—hand over hand—into the lower deck cabin. Two-ton kept his ship far tidier than he did his own, he noted, even making up the bunk—something Ryan rarely, if ever, did.

The hatch entering into the cockpit was partially raised. Ryan swung underneath it and floated into what remained of the ship's cockpit. For several beats, he couldn't mentally process what he was actually seeing: He never expected to find Two-ton, wearing an environment suit and helmet, to be right there—facing him. But an arm and leg were missing. Crude tourniquets were tied—one at the elbow and one at the knee. In the dim light, his environment suit looked to be covered with a black substance that Ryan realized was blood. Two-ton's eyes were open—staring—but unfixed on any one thing—his lifeless body floating weightless five feet away.

Ryan, noting something substantial coming into view in his peripheral vision, didn't have time to duck away. The object smacked the side of his visor, leaving a gooey, dark red smudge behind, before bouncing off and twirling away. It was Two-ton's lower left leg, still attached to his size sixteen booted foot. Ryan, gagging, vomited into his helmet.

CHAPTER 5

Light headed, Ryan fought back the urge to throw up a second time. He lowered his eyes and let himself float for several moments within the wrecked delivery van's cockpit. He was dimly aware of Bella's voice, droning on and on inside his helmet.

Ryan steadied himself, grabbing ahold of a nearby partial bulkhead railing. He needed to get out of there. "Bella … you documenting? What's happened here?"

The AI's hesitation only underscored the gravity of what he'd just encountered. A cataclysmic space collision—the near-total destruction of the delivery van's cockpit—and his friend's unsuccessful attempt to stay alive, in spite of losing both an arm and a leg.

"Yes, Driver of 412. A vid-record has been stored and dispatched to Consigned Freight management."

"Make sure the proper authorities are notified. Hell … maybe even Star Watch. This looks like murder … whoever did this must be held accountable." Ryan mentally imagined the course of events: Two-ton's CF van, just moseying along in space, when suddenly struck by a much larger craft. The almost instantaneous cabin decompression, along with the crushing-in of the hull and metal struts—where Two-ton was situated in the cockpit—resulted in the severing of his limbs, the sudden loss of blood. But even with all that, his friend had tried; had attempted to stem the blood flow, in vain. No one could survive what happened there.

The AI's prolonged, pregnant silence set off warning signals in his head. But before he could pursue his present train of thought, something that happened several hours earlier reoccurred to him. There was no flipping way his little delivery van, having withstood only minor damage, could put a five-foot-diameter dent on that nearly-indestructible refurbished Paotow Tanker. Not from a mere space-drift impact. Far more likely, the true cause of that huge dent resulted from what he was seeing now. The first real hit and run was right here, and Two-ton never had a chance.

His visor, clouded with steamy chunks of vomit, prompted Ryan to get out of there before he was sick again. Authorities would have to make heads or tails of the two incidences. He gave Two-ton—Don—a final glance. *Sorry buddy … sorry this happened to you.*

Spinning back around weightless and heading toward the exit hatchway, something within the cockpit caught Ryan's eye—the van's plug and play component rack. Nearly identical to that in Van 412, he noted a secondary AI Pac floating weightlessly close to the deck, a crudely tied red bow affixed to its top. The gift Don was going to give him. Without further thought, Ryan grabbed up the X-Box-sized component and tucked it under his arm, then headed back out the same way he'd entered. Eerily, it seemed as if Two-ton's floating corpse was following him down the stairs and through the small living compartment. Even as Ryan hurried out of the van's rear hatch, he felt Two-ton's body beside him. Reaching his own van, he turned and saw the lifeless body, slowly emerging into open space. Tempted to go back, push the body back inside, he decided not to. Two-ton always had a mind of his own, so why should this moment be any different?

* * *

Once extricated from the soiled environment suit and stuffing it into a waste storage bin, Ryan, still in a haze, stumbled forward, plunking his body down at the compartment's cockpit controls. No matter how hard he tried to focus elsewhere—images of a floating, partially dismembered Two-ton returned to the forefront of his mind.

Hunched low in his seat, Ryan waited. He'd been instructed to stay on the scene of the accident—or whatever this was—until proper authorities arrived. Ryan wasn't sure who they would send. Most definitely an official, likely from CF. They needed to be on top of this—spin it in the right light. He had no idea who else would be sent—maybe someone from the Department of Space Compliance.

Bella's voice, a steady droning in the background, had pretty much been ignored since his return to the spacecraft, but there was an immediacy to her ramblings that sparked his attention. Raising his eyes from the Mountain Dew container still rolling around on the deck, he saw the approach of a vessel's running lights. *Wow, that was fast!*

Sluggishly, he sat up in his seat and assessed the myriad of readouts on the board in front of him. He furrowed his brow. "Huh … you may want to slow down there, dude."

Still too far away to make out the contours of the approaching ship, Ryan became conscious of a sudden tightness in his chest—the quickening of his breathing. "Bella … notify the approaching vessel to slow the fuck down!"

"The approaching vessel has ignored multiple hails already, Driver of 412."

"Well, who is it? The Consigned Freight rep?"

Ryan didn't need to hear her response. Rising to his feet, his eyes stayed fixed on the approaching tanker—one he'd recently come in contact with—literally.

"Bella! Hurry! Power up the drive. I need you to accept an unauthorized high-speed acceleration. Do it!"

The approaching Paotow Tanker was coming on fast. Headed directly toward his van's bow, at one hundred yards out Ryan could see the small concave section on the space tanker's hull, caused by the earlier collision. "Going manual!" Ryan said, pulling back on the controls. Immediately, he felt the delivery van's drive start to whine as the spacecraft began, sluggishly at first, to back away from Two-ton's wrecked van.

"Collision imminent ... collision imminent ... collision imminent," Bella announced.

"Shut up, Bella! Send out a distress ... " Ryan didn't get to finish his command.

The Paotow Tanker Retro Fit, with an approximate gross weight of 65,000 lbs., was nearly upon them. Ryan continued to throttle backward, bringing the drive indicator into redline territory. Unconcerned with the condition of his vessel's propulsion system, his only concern was surviving the next few seconds.

Ryan nervously watched the ominous-looking tanker draw closer, wondering if it was going to slam into the already crumpled delivery van. He pictured the van—struck again; a glancing impact that would probably obliterate it. Like a toy smashed with a hammer, pieces would fly off in every direction. But that didn't happen. The tanker, having slowed, came close to the damaged van then seemed to hesitate, allowing Ryan to gain a glimmer of hope. A half-mile distance now separated Freight Van 412 from the Paotow Tanker Retro Fit. Ryan needed to flip his van around—move forward—in order to achieve a higher rate of speed. He felt the barrel-hold on his chest loosen somewhat.

"Bella ... send out that distress call."

"Driver of 412, the CTB has been damaged; due, perhaps, from the initial impact with the tanker. Interstellar communications are not possible."

"What? Oh come on … you've got to be kidding!"

"Driver of 412, humor scripts were not initialized for this AI Pac."

Ryan knew the CTB she referred to was their Communications Transmission Beacon. Undoubtedly, the microwave oven-sized fixture, externally situated on the top of his van, was struck by some shrapnel-like pieces, blown off of Two-ton's annihilated van.

"We need to flip around," Ryan said aloud, bringing the overly heated ion-drive back into black. Engaging three consecutive bursts of the reverse thrusters, G-forces forced him up on his toes and pushed his thighs hard into the forward console. He spun the controls, forcing the equivalent of a three-pointed turn in space. Bringing the small spacecraft back up to speed, Ryan kept his eyes locked on the display. The tanker was still back where it collided with the other van. Maybe … just maybe … the son of a bitch was going to let him go. He pushed the propulsion system forward, just under redlining, and watched space between the two icons grow further apart. Ryan let out a steady breath.

First things first, he needed to find some means to establish communications with CF. That and have his van inspected for damage. "Bella, bring up the location of the closest space port. Someplace where I can get repairs and call dispatch."

"The closest space station is back in the same direction we came from, driver of 412."

"That is not an option. Hopefully, you're intelligent enough to know that."

Bella for once stayed quiet.

"So what's ahead of us? There has to be some kind of port, or base, in the relative vicinity … huh?"

"Driver of 412, three days at our current rate of speed will bring us to the fringe of the Kuiper Belt. From there, locating any of six local mining establishments would be possible."

"Go ahead and set the course, Bella, and you can now take back helm control." Ryan slowly sat back down. Settling in, he crossed his arms over his chest and stayed in that position for over an hour, never letting his eyes stray away from the display screen. Then he saw the icon—the Paotow Tanker was again on the move. *"Shit!"*

CHAPTER 6

Three days later …

Carl and Melissa Rizzo lived off Taconic—a winding two-lane country road on the outskirts of Greenwich, Connecticut. Captain Jason Reynolds, Master Sergeant Major Gail Stone, and Commander Billy Hernandez phase-shifted directly into the couple's expansive front yard. The threesome retracted their battle-suits and stood still, studying the colonial brick two-story mini-mansion. Jason figured the New England home was about as old as the country itself. But in spite of its once snooty zip code, the house looked to be run down and in need of repair. Like every other home on the street, there was a fifteen-foot-tall chain-link fence around the perimeter of the property. Atop it—loops of razor wire. There wasn't a town or city in the country, or around the word, that hadn't needed to safeguard against the ever-present peovils.

Stone wrapped her arms about her body against the morning's frosty chill. "Are we going to go ahead and do this or just stand around all day?"

Jason was fairly certain Rizzo hadn't returned home to visit in quite a while. His parents probably had no idea he had a girlfriend. A fact Stone was undoubtedly conscious of, and Jason attributed that to her nervousness.

Billy headed for the front entrance—his jaw set. There was no trace of humor in his eyes. For him, like Jason, the sad realization they were about to say goodbye to someone who was nothing short of a brother had fully set in.

Billy and Stone held up at the front door and waited for Jason. He stepped up onto the stoop and knocked. Nodding to them both, he wore a resigned expression—*let's just get this over with.*

He heard a commotion within the house—multiple voices talking at once. The front door opened and a heavyset woman, who looked to be in her mid-to-late sixties, looked back at them quizzically. "Yes … can I help you?"

"Mrs. Rizzo, hello, I'm Captain Reynolds. We met before … when …"

"Oh yes … Captain, of course!" Her face brightened as she swung the door all the way open. "Come in out of the cold, all of you. We have a fire going in the family room, so come in and get warm."

She led the trio into a circular foyer, then down a hall-way and into a large, well-decorated room with high ceilings and crown moldings. A comfortable-looking leather couch and two matching chairs were on one side of the room, a large sliding glass door on the other. Outside, rays of sun-light streamed through a distant row of red maple trees. At the far end of the room, within a broad flagstone fireplace, a well-established blaze was burning. Jason could feel its heat from twenty feet away.

Jason saw Rizzo's father, a silver-haired man, who looked about the same age as his own dad. Like his wife, he too was formally dressed, and talking with two other couples—perhaps friends or family members. There were ten or so people milling about the large room and probably more in other rooms of the colonial. Rizzo's father eyed them as they moved farther into the room, his gaze mainly fixed, Jason noticed, on Gail Stone. He pretty much ignored Billy's, and his own, presence.

What struck Jason most was the almost-jovial atmosphere in the room. Several folks entered the family room and, like everyone else, they too wore smiles, contributing to the home's overall aura of cheeriness. Jason and Billy exchanged a quick glance. Billy, leaning in close, said, "I guess this is more like a wake ... maybe they want to celebrate Rizzo's life."

Overhearing him, Stone grimaced. She looked ready to say something but held her tongue. Melissa Rizzo signaled to her husband with a high wave of her hand. He managed to extricate himself from the other couples and made his way over to them. She said, "Dear, you remember Captain Reynolds ... Ricky's C.O. and close friend." Billy and Stone raised their brows. Jason suspected neither had heard Rizzo's first name before, as he never went by anything other than Rizzo. Billy silently mouthed the words *Ricky Rizzo*, looking over at Stone quizzically. Jason, seeing her bite her bottom lip, knew she was stifling a laugh. A poor time for a case of nervous giggles. Quickly Jason said, "This is Commander Billy Hernandez; I think you've met him before, and this is Master Sergeant Gail Stone. Um ... Rizzo ... Ricky and Gail were very good ... close ... friends."

Carl shook Jason's hand, then Billy's. "Yes ... yes ... good to see you again." When Stone offered hers, he clasped it in his two large hands, sandwiching hers between his. "Oh yes, he's talked about you before."

"I think he's quite smitten," Mrs. Rizzo said.

That was a surprise to Jason, wondering how they knew about their son's relationship before he was killed. Their use of the present tense only emphasized that they were having a hard time dealing with the current situation.

Jason saw tears welling up in Stones' eyes—she was an

emotional mess. This whole party—wake thing—was a nice send-off for his friend, but Jason had already come to terms with Rizzo's passing. Jason now only wanted to get things over with—pull the proverbial plug and hightail it out of there. He suspected Billy and Stone shared the same sentiment.

"This is nice … all that you've done for Rizzo."

"Ricky," Billy corrected him.

"Sorry … Ricky. Unfortunately, we are on a bit of a schedule and …"

Both Rizzo's parents stared at Jason in confusion, not offering up the obvious *"Oh yes, we'll take you to his room now so you can do what you've come here to do."* In fact, they looked like they were on the verge of laughing.

"I'm sorry," Stone said accusingly, "but your reaction … your cheerful attitude … how can you be so upbeat when Rizzo is lying in there, about to have—"

"Hold on there, Missy!" Carl Rizzo said, suddenly serious. He looked at his wife then back at Stone. "You don't know? None of you know?"

Jason, only half-listening, was watching a small, gnome-like being move about the room. He had a drink in one hand and, although Jason had never seen him drink alcohol before, looked somewhat tipsy. He stood in front of the fireplace, tilting his over-sized head off to the side.

"Ricket!"

The room went quiet as all heads turned toward Jason. Conscious of his loud outburst, he said, "Oh … sorry," and signaled Ricket, now looking back at him smiling broadly. He swayed and staggered over.

"When did you get here, Ricket?" Jason asked.

Before he could answer, Billy asked, leaning down closer to him, "Have you been drinking?"

"Mrs. Rizzo offered me a … I believe she said it was a mimosa?"

Melissa Rizzo beamed. "We love this little man more than you can imagine, Captain Reynolds. I just want to pick him up and squeeze him!"

"What … the … hell … is … going … on … here?" Stone said between clenched teeth, clearly having enough of the craziness going on around her. She glowered first at Ricket, then at Jason and Billy, but they weren't looking at her. No one was. They were looking behind her.

Jason, his jaw dropping, was having a hard time finding his voice. He watched, stunned, as the tall and handsome Ricky Rizzo wrapped his arms from behind around Gail Stone. She stiffened for a moment—staring straight ahead—then a flood of tears began to fall and her body shook as realization slowly set in. Rizzo, leaning in behind her, softly spoke something in her ear. She laughed happily through her tears and spun around in his arms. She punched him in the chest then, hugging him, buried herself in his arms. Jason, Billy, and Rizzo all looked at each other. Rizzo was all smiles.

"Welcome back, my friend," Jason said.

"Thanks, Cap … good to be back among the living."

Ricket said, "You know, Captain, it was your idea."

"What was my idea, Ricket?"

"To use a newer model—one of the more advanced MediPod's on the *Parcical*. It was the only thing I hadn't tried. So I brought one down last night. It worked! Within two hours he was …" Ricket pointed a finger up at Rizzo, "… completely awake. An hour after that, he was up and moving around."

Rizzo's parents had drifted off to socialize with friends. He said, "Cap, I'm ready to get out of here … like as soon as possible."

Jason chuckled, "That's good, because we have some business to attend to about a thousand miles south."

Billy said, "Ever been to Dollywood … Ricky?"

CHAPTER 7

Just over five hours had elapsed. In the silence of the cockpit of Consignment Freight Van 412, Ryan studied the small console display. He'd done the calculations three times. Yes, for sure the tanker was gaining on him—but only marginally. At his current rate of speed, Ryan's van would be well into the Kuiper Belt before being overtaken. After that, it would still be a concern, but only if that lunatic, whoever he was, hadn't lost interest in him and changed course before then.

Ryan checked the time. Wendy would be ending her shift about now—heading over to Bottoms. Ryan wondered if she'd look for him. Or would Tony Post make good on his promise? He couldn't imagine Wendy being interested in Tony. Apart from being almost twenty years older, he was a douche bag. Ryan was well aware he would drive himself crazy thinking about her over the next few days, especially with his comms down. No, he needed to find … something. Some diversion.

Ryan stood. Stretching his arms over his head his fingertips almost touched the overhead bulkhead. Then, shaking the tension from his arms and legs he followed up with a series of circular head/neck rolls. His eyes caught sight of a splash of color. On the deck lay the crumpled, bright-colored bow atop his gift from Two-ton—the AI-Pac.

To even contemplate doing what he was considering was crazy. An infraction that could not only get him fired—it could get him killed. Piloting rule number one: Don't fuck with your onboard AI while traveling across the cosmos at nearly the speed of light.

Checking the time again he noted all of four minutes had passed, and rechecking the display, he saw the tanker was still following his course. An unbearable couple of days lay ahead.

Ryan sat down, casually turned in his chair and looked at the plug and play device. He reached over and touched the crudely made bow, wondering where Two-ton had found the ribbon.

At that moment, Ryan was very conscious of Bella's presence. She was watching him—his movements—even analyzing his micro-facial expressions. *Does she suspect what I'm contemplating?* he wondered. He brought his attention forward and gazed out at the countless stars before him.

"I'm putting you in slumber mode," he said aloud, before he had time to think about it—talk himself out of it.

Bella's voice answered with measured and firm resolve. "Placing a Consignment Freight vessel's AI into slumber mode while traversing space is a violation of CF protocol."

Ryan waited for the expected … *Driver of 412*, but it didn't come.

"You've been damaged. First in that impact with the tanker then by the debris exploding off Van 211," Ryan said, getting to his feet. Standing, hands on hips, he looked at the tall rack of system components. "You need a cold reboot, Bella. You're damaged and don't even know it. Do you want to be responsible for endangering my life—the life of the pilot of this spacecraft?"

"Placing a Consignment Freight vessel's AI into slumber

mode while traversing space is a violation of CF protocol."

Ryan said, "What is protocol when a CF Van's AI is functioning erratically?"

"Driver of 412, you must bring the vehicle to a complete stop, engage RTM gyros, and conduct a complete systems diagnostic."

"Uh huh … are you even aware we are being chased, Bella?"

Ryan waited for her to respond. She didn't. "Are you aware that the refurbished Paotow Tanker was responsible for the destruction of Van 211, and the driver killed its pilot? Is that what you want to happen to us too, Bella?"

"Driver of 412, you must bring the vehicle to a complete stop, engage RTM gyros, and conduct a complete systems diagnostic."

"Okay … that's fine, Bella. Please log my protest. Van 412's AI is obviously malfunctioning. The AI has recommended that I totally ignore the fucking murderer now chasing us … that I stop this CF van in the middle of nowhere … and start conducting a series of ridiculous tests. Do you have the protest logged, Bella?"

"What are your alternatives, Driver of 412?"

For the first time, Bella was sounding … almost *human*. Ryan snatched up the AI-Pac from Two-ton. "I have a backup."

The ensuing silence was consistent with an AI processing complex information having life or death ramifications— billions, maybe trillions, of variables being considered. There were inherent self-preservation sub-routines built into all AIs, which were understandable and necessary. A completely altruistic AI would be dangerous dealing with the near-constant perils of space. Right now Ryan strongly suspected Bella was coming face-to-face with her need to survive versus her first directive to keep her pilot breathing. Did he present a strong enough case that she'd been damaged? And being damaged, she was capable of making that determination?

"Driver of 412, proceed with the insertion of the auxiliary AI-Pac. I will configure it for an in-parallel configuration."

Ryan thought about that for a moment. Bella continued, "I will need to determine the validity of the replacement AI-Pac … that it has not been modified from factory presets and is fully compliant with Consignment Freight programming protocols."

"Yeah … well that's not going to work, Bella. Based on the way you are processing information … all the nonsensical things you are saying … you shouldn't be involved in any decision-making. Unfortunately, you wouldn't know that since you are obviously damaged. You probably don't even realize what you're saying half the time. We'll get you reinitialized later, after we've reached a station within the Kuiper Belt. I'm sure you'll be repaired … be as good as new in no time."

"Driver of 412, you must run a full diagnostics package on the auxiliary AI-Pac. Ensure it fully conforms to standards."

"I'll do that. Now release the software blocks you've placed on the temporary replacement Pac. You're taking way too long to act on something that should have already been done."

"Driver of 412, software blocks have been suspended. You may proceed with the temporary component swap."

Ryan tore the ribbon off the unit and inserted it into the slot directly to the right of the other AI-Pac—Bella's AI-Pac. He felt it click into place, seated snugly into its motherboard slot. Immediately, the new AI-Pac's green access indicator LED began to flash, then it stayed brightly on. Without a second thought, he yanked Bella's AI-Pac from her positioned slot and placed it on down the deck. "And adios to you, Bella."

Ryan stood back and looked about the small cockpit. He'd just completed an emergency AI-Pac swap. Dangerous and probably stupid. Again, he contemplated on the dismissal offenses he was racking up. Checking the status LEDs on all the other rack components, he found everything operational. Only then did he consider several potentially negative repercussions. One, Two-ton may not have completed the necessary reprogramming of this AI unit. Two, it may be a joke.

Two-ton was a habitual prankster—one of the things Ryan liked most about him. But *this* would not be funny; not when a properly functioning AI-Pac corresponded directly to his very survival. No, Two-ton was a lot of things, but dangerous, treacherous, wasn't one of them.

Ryan's left foot began to tap nervously as he chewed the inside of his cheek. By now, Bella would have barked off any number of observations or complaints about his actions. *Shit! Something must be wrong.*

Only by chance did he happen to glance toward the helm console and the small display panel. A shiver ran down his spine. *That's impossible!* The Paotow Tanker was almost upon his van.

CHAPTER 8

Three days later ...

Originating from the worlds of the Mazzett—a cruel war-mongering race destroyed by the Craing seventy-five years earlier—the *Goliath*, with its dramatic, angled-back downward curvature wings and its swooping, boomerang-shaped nose, had become the *Jumelle* pilot's most preferred shuttlecraft. The craft's cockpit sat four comfortably and had a separate forward entrance. The vessel also possessed expanded rear cabin space, an advanced defense system and weaponry, and—most importantly—incredible speed and maneuverability. The *Goliath* basically was a badass *hotrod* shuttlecraft, outfitted with the ability to phaseshift as well as to call up an interchange wormhole.

The three sat inside the *Goliath's* cockpit—Jason, at the controls, was enjoying the opportunity to pilot again. As a Star Watch captain, navigating small crafts—such as fighters or shuttles—typically wasn't part of the job description, but then Jason was hardly a typical Star Watch officer. He loved the *hands-on* level of control that piloting such crafts afforded, and since Sergeant Major Stone was currently in the rear cabin—catching up with Rizzo—Jason had gladly volunteered for the job. They had one other quick stop to make before continuing on to Tennessee.

Madam President Nan Reynolds, the former acting President of the United States of America, and Jason's ex-wife, now resided in Franktown, Colorado, within a sprawling, tree-studded but hilly compound of twenty acres. The nearest neighbor was two miles to the south and that was a seventy-five-year-old rancher who'd been fully vetted years earlier.

The trip from Greenwich, Connecticut to Franktown, Colorado would normally take the shuttle about ten minutes, but Rizzo had personally asked Jason to ease up some, stay light on the throttle. He'd taken a more scenic route, dragging the voyage out to twenty minutes instead.

"We're coming up to the compound," Jason announced.

Bristol used a fist to hammer on the cockpit's rear bulkhead: "Time's up, love birds!" he yelled.

Jason and Billy exchanged a glance. Billy pulled the stogie from his mouth and said, "I remember those days … young and wild; life was all about getting naked with someone special."

"Yeah," Bristol said, "too bad you blew it with Gunny Orion. Heard she's into the new captain of the *Pisces*. What's his name? Baxtor? Jack Baxtor?"

Billy, refusing to acknowledge Bristol's comment, kept staring out the forward observation window.

"John," Jason said.

Billy looked at Jason, his brow raised.

"Not Jack … it's John. John Baxtor. And Bristol … maybe it's best if you keep ship gossip down to a minimum."

Banking the craft, Jason circled the sprawling compound below, while looking out the side window. There was the main living structure—a modern, ten-thousand-square-foot timber lodge—along with eight or ten smaller structures situated elsewhere around the grounds. At the bottom of the property was a large, freshly painted white barn. Alongside it was a corral, holding several grazing horses. Their heads came up as the *Goliath* passed by overhead.

"I count twelve secret service agents, and that's only those in plain sight," Billy said.

"Having the title of former madam president comes with its share of encumbrances, I suppose," Jason said.

"You're being waved over to that plateau over there."

Jason followed Billy's outstretched finger and saw two agents dramatically gesturing for them to head in a certain direction, toward the flattened, and cleared, hillside beyond them. He slowed the craft—positioning the *Goliath* over a painted white X—and engaged the landing thrusters.

* * *

With the rear gangway extended out, they hurried down the ramp—except for Stone. Jason looked back over his shoulder, and said, "Stone ... need you to stay with the *Goliath*."

Away teams typically don't leave their crafts unattended. A relatively new regulation, which judging by Sergeant Major Stone's glum expression was not sitting well with her. She looked at Rizzo with an expectant expression—one urging him to dispute the order—but Rizzo only smiled at her affectionately and shrugged. Stone's blank expression back at him appeared far chillier. She engaged the closing of the hatch with a loud slap and turned away.

A six-seater ATV pulled up, carrying two agents. Both the driver and the agent riding shotgun wore green camos and protective vests, and carried a side arm; the one who rode shotgun held a familiar-looking multi-gun rifle.

No sooner had Jason, Billy, and Bristol piled into the ATV's back seats than the driver gunned the little engine, causing dirt and small rocks to spray out from under all four wheels.

"What the fuck, dude … where's the fire?" Bristol yelled, nearly catapulted from his seat.

Jason looked intently at the driver—holding similar sentiments.

"Former President Reynolds has requested no dilly-dallying … there's a young man's life at stake and too much time's been wasted already."

Billy spat something out the side of his mouth. About to say something, Jason beat him to the punch: "You're secret service, right? What is your name?"

"That's right … originally from the Marines. I'm Pope … Colonel Stephen Pope. Everyone calls me Pope."

"Well, Colonel, if you can … do your best to get us there in one piece, will you?"

"Oh … sorry!" he said. "Didn't mean to scare you." The second agent snickered.

Billy's head spun toward the colonel, his face already turning red. Jason didn't like the guy either, but he didn't want to go to war with the asshole. He shook his head at Billy, pointing a finger instead at the now nearing structure. "Nice place."

* * *

Nan, walking out through the ten-foot-tall double front doors as they pulled up, carried a military-issue duffle bag over one shoulder. She wore snug-fitting faded Levi's, which hugged her slim curves, and a button-down, faded, red plaid flannel shirt—the sleeves rolled up to her elbows. Her once auburn-colored hair, now dyed black, was tied back into a long ponytail. She'd aged well since their divorce and, thanks to MediPod technology, she'd never look a day older the rest of her life.

The colonel jumped out of the ATV and hurried over to her. They were talking in low tones as Jason got out and walked toward her. When she looked up she half-smiled and Pope took a step backwards.

"Damn it, Jason … you're late!"

"Sorry, got a little held up. We'll make up the time."

"You're right … we will!" She brushed past him and assumed the driver's seat of the ATV. The agent, sitting shotgun, got up and let the colonel take his seat.

Both Nan and the colonel looked up at Jason expectantly.

Jason said, "Um … I'd like to see Michael. Haven't seen my son for a few weeks."

"And whose fault is that?" Nan answered sharply. "Anyway … he's at summer camp. We need to go. Get in."

Jason stared back at her, "He's five … isn't that a little young for camp?"

He looked at Billy, Bristol and Rizzo, still sitting in the backseat.

Nan shrugged. "Michael's fine … you can see him after we complete our mission."

Billy mouthed the word *mission* and made a face.

"Fine … let's go," Jason said, climbing in beside them.

Nan glanced back. "Hi, guys." She got the ATV underway and drove even faster than Pope had. Looking behind him, Jason noticed there were two duffels in the cargo bed—Nan's and the colonel's.

Nan spoke over the high whine of the ATV's engine. "Pope can go over the mission parameters once we're in the air."

"Why is he coming along?" Billy asked. The same question Jason was about to ask her.

"Madam President doesn't go anywhere without a trained secret service agent present."

Bristol said, "And you're a colossal ass clown! I don't even know you, and I can tell that."

It was worth bringing Bristol along if only for that one comment. "Look," Jason said, "I understand you want to protect Nan—"

"Madam President," Pope corrected.

"No, I meant Nan, and correct me like that again and I'll throw you ..."

Nan quickly looked over her shoulder. "Jason! Stop with the machismo bullshit! And Pope, he's my damn ex-husband ... he can call me whatever he wants."

As the *Goliath* came into view up ahead, Jason instructed Stone, via his NanoCom, to fire up the shuttle's drive and open the rear hatch.

Only then did he notice Pope's arm, so casually draped around Nan's seat back. Shit ... there *was* something going on between the two. *Why should I even care?* I'm married ... he questioned himself.

CHAPTER 9

Ryan stood at the helm console and tried to figure a way to eke out an increase of speed from the van's ridiculously low-powered propulsion system. "Come on!" he said, stomping a foot down onto the deck. He watched the ever-present, significantly larger, display icon steadily gaining on his current coordinates.

A familiar voice said, "You're an idiot!"

Staring straight ahead Ryan froze. *That's not possible.* Ryan looked at the comms section of the board in front of him. The Communications Transmission Beacon, the CTB, was still demolished—no signal present. *Then how?*

"Two-ton?" Ryan said tentatively—his voice barely audible.

"Don't be stupid, kid ... I'm an AI ... nothing more ... nothing less."

Ryan stared down at the the newly inserted plug n' play component. Ryan smiled and then, just as quickly, felt the tears welling up in his eyes. Two-ton was dead and hearing this voice only compounded the sadness he'd been trying to shelve over the last few hours.

"Hey ... if you want ... you can always plug Bella back in. Ain't going to hurt my feelings ... I'm an AI."

"No! I was just taken by surprise … hearing your voice."

"Uh huh."

"Two-ton … are you aware that …"

"That my namesake is toast? Yup … I've processed that information … by accessing the van's memory module. Not sure how I feel about that …"

"Really?" Ryan asked.

"No … I don't feel emotions. I'm an AI."

That brought a smile to Ryan's lips. Well, the AI certainly captured its namesake's smart ass personality. Ryan knew Two-ton had been an amazing coder but he didn't think this level of humanness in an AI was possible.

"Are you also aware of the situation with the pursuing tanker?"

"I am."

"And?" Ryan said.

"And the Paotow Tanker Retro Fit is a fast mother … I calculate it will be upon us within the next three hours. To make things worse, we won't reach the asteroid belt for another couple of days."

"Any options?"

"I'm working on it," the AI said. "There's only so much I'll be able to do at a systems' level. There'll need to be hardware modifications made. Much the same as were made to Two-ton's van."

"Whatever I need to do … just tell me," Ryan said feeling a glimmer of hope.

"Right off the bat I can see the van's spare parts bin hasn't been refilled in like forever … you know you're supposed to check that and have it maintained every so often."

"Yeah … sorry."

"Let me check something … hold on."

Ryan waited for the AI while watching the tanker's icon move ever closer.

"You may need to cross over to the dark side, buddy."

"What do you mean?" Ryan said.

"First ... I'm obligated to tell you that tampering with customer packages is not only a fireable offense ... it's totally illegal."

"Yeah ... all drivers know that," Ryan said.

"Well ... it just so happens three of the cartons up in the hold just may help you get out of this mess."

"What do you mean?"

"Cartons designation 71392, 71393, and 104339 each have a variety of things that may allow you to nearly double the propulsion output of this little craft."

"Double? How is that even possible?"

"Do you really want me to go into the technical aspects or do you want to try to outrun that pursuing Paotow tanker?"

"Right. Let's open up those cartons."

"Fine ... two of them, designations 71392 and 71393, are Consignment Freight inter-station transfers. Basically, parts transfers. You may not get into as much trouble for opening those two packages."

"And the other one?" Ryan asked.

"Designation 104339 is a whole 'nother story. It's insured for $5,000,000."

"Two-ton ... I could go to jail for even looking at that package."

"Yeah ... CF would pretty much throw away the key for that one."

"How important is it?"

"If the contents of that carton are what I think they are ... very important."

"But at the end of the day ... what? ... you're pretty much just guessing?" Ryan asked.

"My guesses are based on fairly stringent calculations ... including both sending and receiving parties ... previous shipments between the two parties, the carton weight and size, and something else."

"What's that?"

"The accompanying paperwork says what's in the box."

Ryan rolled his eyes. "So what is it?"

"Scientific experimental equipment … a *Tominacco* micro-reactor. Sent from a Star Watch ship's Chief Engineer … the guy's named is Bristol … sent by way of Liberty Station. It's headed for—"

Ryan cut the AI off, "It's headed for the Alpha Centauri system. I remember logging that carton in."

"Correctamundo," the AI replied. "So what do you want to do? Get trapped by the nutcase chasing you or spend a decade or two lounging within one of the three sector penitentiaries?"

"Why don't we start with CF cartons … see if those parts make a difference," Ryan said.

"Sorry, man … wouldn't make enough of a difference. It's all or nothing."

Ryan said, "How much time do we have?"

"Calculating the current rates of speed and the inevitable intercept vectors … two hours and ten minutes."

"What are the odds he's coming to do to me what he did to … you … to Two-ton?"

"It's a guess but I'd say eighty-three percent, that whoever that crazy fuck is … is coming to destroy this delivery van with you along with it."

"And you have no idea who it is?"

"I'm working through a database … making calculations … assumptions. I may be able to narrow it down to a few individuals … in time."

Ryan suspected the AI already had those names. Had made those calculations in a fraction of a nano-second. Truth was, knowing who it was chasing him wouldn't do him much good, anyway. Especially with his communications equipment on the fritz.

* * *

The cargo hold area of CF Delivery Van 412 was approximately fifteen feet long, ten feet wide and eight feet tall—with the hold somewhat wider toward the stern. Three rows of shelves lined the bulkhead and hundreds of cartons filled the space. The van had a full load. Delivery cartons were reusable and comprised of lightweight tensile strength materials. They came in a variety of sizes from a few inches square to the size of a standard dishwasher—and each CF carton was software coded into a locked state until delivered to the confirmed proper recipient.

Ryan had three CF cartons sitting in the middle of the hold. "These are them," Ryan said.

"You still haven't broken any Consignment Freight regulations or Department of Space Compliance felonies," Two-ton said.

"Wait … I can't open these. Don't have the unlock codes."

"Would I have suggested opening the cartons if I couldn't unlock them for you?"

"I guess not," Ryan said. "Um … I'm having second thoughts about this, Two-ton. The whole felony aspect. I like my freedom."

"That is understandable, Ryan. Perhaps I should tell you a little about the individual pursuing you … pursuing us."

"So you do know."

Two-ton was silent.

"Well, tell me!"

"The owner of the refurbished Paotow Tanker is Orloff Picket."

"Okay … is that supposed to mean something to me?" Ryan asked.

"I guess not. Orloff Picket is one of four sons of one Abigale Picket … most commonly known as Mamma Picket.

She is the family matriarch and general manager of Picket Mining. Once one of North America's oldest and largest coal mining outfits from the nineteenth and twentieth centuries … Picket mining is now a substantial mining organization of a variety of rare elements mined within the Kuiper Belt."

"So that's a good thing … right? This Orloff … he's some kind of businessman."

"No, Ryan. He is not."

Ryan waited for more. "Well … go on."

"Although Orloff Picket has indeed worked within the family mining business from time to time, he has been relegated to living in space for very specific reasons."

"Uh huh."

"He is bat-shit crazy. Once referred to as a sociopath … now the politically correct reference to that is anti-social personality disorder. Orloff, institutionalized on three separate occasions on Earth, has very violent tendencies. And since he does not exhibit any sense of guilt or remorse … it is my opinion … he has been misdiagnosed. It is far more likely he is a raging psychopath … a vicious nut-ball."

"What's he done? Like … why was he institutionalized?"

"Two of those were juvenile instances. But I peeked into his locked case file. Apparently, Young Orloff liked playing with animals. Animals of all sizes and species. His particular interest lies in the taxidermy side of things."

"Like the mounting of dead animals? The kind of thing hunters do?"

"Yes. Although Orloff's particular interest lies with the capturing of living creatures. He displays them … while still alive … that is after he's done … working with them."

Ryan made a face. "That's who's coming after me? Someone who does that to … animals?"

"He progressed past animals in his early twenties."

"How old is he now?"

"Orloff Picket is forty-three years old. His formal education level is the third-grade. He is six foot five and three hundred and three pounds. He is missing two fingers—both pinkies—believed to be the results of self-induced anatomical experiments."

"I need to get these cartons open ... fast."

CHAPTER 10

Once provided the codes to unlock them, Ryan quickly opened and unpacked the three cartons; their contents now lay on the hold's deck. According to the Two-ton AI, what they first needed to do was convert the onboard ion drive to a fusion drive—basically, making Mickey Mouse into Mighty Mouse. What they were attempting wasn't that much of a stretch. Consignment Freight already provided a similar fusion-drive vehicle. Among the contents strewn about on the deck was an Aldo-Pack, designed by Dr. Aldo Wreck, of MIT fame, five years earlier. An Aldo-Pack was a self-contained two-foot by three-foot by four-foot polished metallic power plant module—basically a small nuclear reactor—that was presently totally inert and not dangerous in the least.

Ryan lifted the highly reflective module off the deck. "It's surprisingly light ... for the size of the thing. What's it do?"

"Basically, fusion reaction occurs when energy is released by a couple of light atomic nuclei being fused together to form another, much heavier, atom. The same energy that powers a star ... the sun. This is where hydrogen nuclei are combined to form helium," the Two-ton AI answered.

"This thing does all that?"

"And more. But there is a problem."

Ryan looked up, unsure where to put his attention since the AI was viewing him via a multitude of integrated cameras located throughout the ship—specifically the hold area. "What problem?"

"The ion drive module is roughly the same size as that thing you're holding. Both are controlled by the same systems controller located within the cockpit systems rack. And I can provide any missing code."

Ryan, tired, was on the verge of stifling a yawn. If it weren't for the simple fact that the Paotow Tanker was barreling down on them, he'd be climbing into his bunk for a few hours' nap. "So what's the problem?"

"The output thrust coming from an ion drive is miniscule compared to that of an Aldo-Pack self-contained drive module. This freight van does not have the most robust main rear thruster, or numerous directional thruster nozzles situated along the outer hull."

"What … they'll burn up?"

"Bingo."

"So why then are we doing this? Why waste our time?"

"Because I think there's a MacGyver."

Ryan had seen every episode of the mid-1980s TV show. The action hero could create amazing things from duct tape, a pencil, a ball of string, and a can of Coke. "I'm almost afraid to ask … what is it I have to do?"

"There are three environ suits on this craft, correct? One you discarded into the recycle bin."

Ryan's mind flashed to the copious amounts of blood present on his suit when he returned from Two-ton's mangled freight van.

"You want to use that one?"

"It's never a good idea to get rid of your backup suits. We'll have to use that suit, as its material is practically impervious to heat."

"Even to heat equivalent to that of the sun?"

"Almost. It will serve our purpose," the AI said.

"So … how do I …"

The Two-ton AI said, "I believe there are scissors on board."

* * *

Ryan discovered there were twelve cone-shaped *conoid* thruster nozzles situated around the vessel. Most opened into a three-inch-diameter orifice. The larger main rear thruster, spherically-shaped, was approximately thirteen inches wide by eight inches tall. Cutting out linings for the three-inch cone thrusters simply meant he needed to cut out three-and-a-half-inch diameter circles then add another radius cut to the center of the circle. According to the AI, they didn't need to fit perfectly.

The largest cutout on the environ suit would come from the back of the suit. Two-ton's voice guided Ryan on how to make the cutout for that oddly shaped thruster.

"Um … don't mean to be a Debbie Downer here, but you do know these little cutouts won't stay put. They'll pop out as soon as I engage the drive … if not before."

"Oh ye of little faith, I have taken that into account. You'll need to use an adhesive, one that can withstand a radical amount of heat."

Ryan, sitting on the deck with his legs crossed Indian-style and scissors in hand, looked up again.

The AI said, "One of the few things still left within your spare parts bin is a container of Starlite."

Ryan, and anyone from Earth traversing the cosmos, was familiar with that miracle secret sauce. Painting it on the torn areas of an environ suit it became almost as good as new again. Actually developed by an English inventor—back in the 1980s—a former hairdresser named Maurice Ward. A guy with no real scientific education or training, he put the various ingredients together at his kitchen table using a food processor. The sticky, viscous liquid could be painted on virtually any kind of surface.

"Why don't we just use the Starlite to coat the thrusters?" Ryan asked, flicking a dried flake of blood from the current circular cut out he was currently working on.

"As fantastic as that stuff is, it wouldn't last. Would be too thin a coating. But used as an adhesive with the cutouts you've made, I think we have a winner. We have one hour to attach the cutouts … and install the module."

"We stop and the tanker will overtake us," Ryan said, coming to the same conclusion.

"You'll need to spacewalk this task for us to maintain our current speed and velocity."

"Of course, I do. But … if I get separated from the ship …" Ryan let his words trail off.

"You'll be tens thousands of miles away in the blink of an eye. So don't do that."

* * *

By the time Ryan got suited up, equipped with a makeshift carryall container strapped across his abdomen, he'd burned another fifteen minutes. It took another few to make the progression through the airlock to reach the outside of the ship. The ion drive was off and the temperature, at −454 Fahrenheit, cooled the individual thruster nozzles down in no time. The AI had told him to start first with the largest and most difficult rear thruster.

There was no sensation of speed, although the freight van was traveling at thousands of miles per second. The rear thruster was positioned directly below the rear hatchway—along the bottom hull at the stern of the vessel. Weightlessly, Ryan moved forward—hand over hand—clipping his lifelines onto the various metal eyelets positioned at key hull locations. Never did a moment pass when at least one of his two lifelines wasn't attached to something. With only the slightest push off, he dropped down to the underside of the ship and found the vessel's primary thruster.

"Okay ... here I go," Ryan said. He listened for Two-ton's voice but the AI was being uncharacteristically quiet.

Finding the jar of Starlite right where he'd put it in his strapped-on carryall, Ryan opened it and watched the lid immediately flip free of his fingers and drift away into the blackness of space. "Oops ... shit."

He used his gloved index finger to scoop out an ample portion of the thick liquid, liberally coating the inside of the thruster. That done, he snatched up the largest cut up piece of environ suit and positioned it into the spherically shaped cone. Giving it a tug, it still held firm. "Two-ton, you know it's not a great fit."

"I can see that via your helmet-cam. It's fine ... move on to the next one."

Ryan did as told and, one by one, repeated the same process with the next ten smaller thruster nozzles. Now at the bow of the freight van on the port side, he said, "Kinda running low on Starlite."

"Do you have enough for the last nozzle?" the AI asked.

"Yeah ... I think so." He gave the inserted cut out a little tug, and, like all the others, it too held firm. "I'm moving on to the last one." Ryan unclipped one line from the closest eyelet and transferred its clip to the one four feet to his left. Reaching back to unclip the second lifeline he heard Two-ton's voice. And something in it not normally present—Could it be fear?

"Leave it ... get back inside."

"I'm almost done. One more—"

"No. Now!"

At that same moment Ryan saw a glint of light reflecting

off a metallic surface. A ship was approaching. *Seriously?* It was Orloff's tanker, of course.

CHAPTER 11

West Virginia folk music filled the space—the rhythmic strumming of an old banjo echoed down from somewhere overhead. The cavernous, dimly lit, central cabin—with its wide-plank paneling and hardwood decking—looked more like a 100-year-old timber-built home than a space-faring vessel. The Paotow Tanker Retrofit had been accomplished with a meticulous eye for detail.

Orloff Picket's schooling may have ended with the third grade, but he wasn't stupid. Not by a long shot. In fact, in his own peculiar way, he exhibited borderline genius characteristics. Unfortunately, as with many geniuses, those traits become actualized in certain individuals, Orloff included, as OCD—*Obsessive Compulsive Disorder*. So in addition to being a raging sociopath, he was also a stickler for the arrangement of objects and the order in which things were to be accomplished.

Orloff was relentlessly hard on himself, like the current project he'd immersed himself into. He readjusted the spring-arm table lamp to better illuminate the area of the wood-topped workbench and what lay upon it. Orloff grimaced. The work was not up to his typical impeccable standards. This was nothing more than a hack job. *Literally.*

MARK WAYNE MCGINNIS

As a boy, Orloff spent countless hours with his father and three brothers traversing the hilly terrain of the Southern Appalachian Mountains. In the beginning hunting was far more than a recreational weekend pastime; it was a necessity. First to provide food stocks for the days and weeks ahead—wild boar, elk and whitetail deer, black bear—but later, as the infestation of molt weevils, and their later emanation, peovils, spread throughout the territory like a raging torrent—hunting became more about survival than sustenance.

Orloff, a long, curved sewing needle sticky with viscous blood poised between thumb and index finger, stopped and looked up at the bulkhead across from him. He let his mind wander back to those earlier days when his father would awaken him at three in the morning and together they'd get the equipment and vehicles ready for the morning's excursion into the wild. That was their special time: father and son. Only then, with the prep work completed, would his father awaken his three older brothers. The hunts could last for days. The five of them, the men of the family, dressed in camo and carrying high-powered rifles, were highly competent bringing down a six-point bull at two, even three hundred yards. Toward the end his father, when black lung disease took a firm hold of him—no longer capable of field dressing the kills—supervised. The four brothers were highly adept in the preparation of wild game—it all started with a knife. The knife needed to be incredibly sharp or you could mangle the job.

Starting at the back end—the anus—called the vent, and working fast and sure, a proficient hunter *rarely* needed to touch the slain game's hide at this point. Following the crease between the legs—then up through the abdomen—careful not to cut so deep you slice through the internal organs, you cut right up to the breastbone. Thereafter, your hands will certainly get bloodied. With the abdominal cavity spread wide, you reach in and find the last rib on both sides and slice away the thin wall of muscle that separates the abdominal organs from the chest cavity—the diaphragm. Once that's severed, you reach inside the chest cavity and grip the heart and lungs.

Orloff felt himself stir—felt the hardening of his manhood within his jeans. He thought about the intricacies involved in field dressing elk, then of working on full-grown peovils. He thought of the molt weevils—those spidery alien creatures that devastated the land and the life they had always known. They were faster, far more cunning, than the typical Appalachian game. There was real sport at bringing down a five-hundred-pound alien. And those sons of bitches could still spray you—even after they'd been killed. Wrap you up in a cocoon before you had time to flinch. *Fucking things.* Orloff chuckled to himself, recalling the time his oldest brother, Brent, was wound up so tightly he nearly suffocated up there in the trees. Uh huh, molt weevils were good hunting—real good sport—but there was no sense field dressing the damn things. Insectile—not much left to work with once they were dead—their paper-thin skin practically turning to dust in no time at all. But peovils … *oh boy* … that was a different story. They'd lost their father to peovils. Too sick to run, a band of those zombies had overtaken him, eviscerated him in seconds. Orloff didn't feel emotions like most others did, but he'd appreciated his father, perhaps even missed him. Perhaps not. Orloff's mind turned back to the peovils. Yeah … sure … they looked like people. Had once been people, but they weren't human anymore. Field dressing a peovil, the brothers discovered, was an acquired talent. He felt his erection returning as he reassessed the work he'd accomplished thus far. His need for perfection was conflicting with his need to hurry and add to his collection.

Orloff's father once said there was no sensible use to *cape* an elk. The term referred to saving the horns and/or hide— for mounting trophy heads on a wall. Notwithstanding ridicule from his siblings, along with that of Mamma Picket after his father's demise, Orloff had taken a keen interest in the ancient art—the art of taxidermy. Again, his eyes lifted to the top of the adjacent bulkhead and its row of mounted heads and shoulders. He admired his perfection. No one captured the realism, the life—dare he say *the spirit*—as he had done. Glistening eyes stared down at him from above. He often wondered if they were judging him—condemning him to eternal hell—for what he'd done to them. It wouldn't matter if they did. Orloff Picket did not have the emotional bandwidth for such sensitivity.

He had to lean forward and crane his neck to see the first of the ten mounted heads and torsos—some forty feet down the row—a male peovil with a long face, hollow-looking cheeks, and alabaster-white flesh. Even now its eyes seemed cold and calculating. Orloff smiled at the mounted trophy—inhaling deeply, he let air escape from his lips with a sigh.

Making eye contact with the rest of the trophies—one after another—he started with the seven-point elk, an old bull hunter, called an *Imperial*. Then came the great rhino-warrior—this one was a Black with two fully intact horns. An impressive beast of almost unimaginable strength, Orloff had nearly lost his right leg in bringing the beast down. His collection of trophy mounts was a mismatch of Earth and alien beings. He had his favorites, like the peovil and the rhino-warrior. But the Craing twins, females mounted together on one platform—their small heads and torsos so identically alike that even Orloff had a hard time telling them apart—held a special place in his dark and demented psyche.

Orloff dipped his fingers in a small water bowl, rubbing and swooshing away the congealed, jelly-like globules of blood, tissue, and fat, then continued with the intricate work of sewing on a human ear. The stitching—called a blind stitch—would never be seen; he took far too much pride in his work for that.

A display screen came alive off to his left. Mamma Picket's face impatiently glared back at him. She couldn't see him. Leaving him a vid-message—was it the seventh or the eighth? He didn't want to talk to her … or anyone else, right then, only trying to enjoy a moment to himself. He would call her back when he was good and ready.

He concentrated on the intricate folds along the inside earlobe. Here the stitches needed to be ever so small. Mamma Picket's voice had risen an octave or two and he looked back up at the display.

"Damn it, Orloff, answer my hail, you hear me? Answer it right now! You been taken your meds, boy? What's going on with you? You had one simple job to do. You take care of that … take care of that business?" Mamma went quiet and the display went black.

Orloff already had tuned her out—his attention fully back on his work. He began humming along with the music, recognizing the tune. *What was it called?* Oh yeah … Dueling Banjos.

An alarm tone rang out—disrupting the music.

Feeling his irritation grow, he said, "What the hell is it now, AI?"

"As directed, this is notification that we are nearly upon the Consignment Freight delivery van."

He felt the tanker dramatically slowing down. "How close?"

"One point eight miles."

He completed the final set of stitches on the ear, then sat back, appraising his handiwork. Just as he'd done with all his trophies, he would need to place a brass placard beneath this latest mounting. It was important, in addition to the name of the species, to use the subject's real name. His quandary was whether to use the name Don—Donald—or use his nickname … Two-ton?

Orloff felt depressed. His personal hobby time was just

about over. Rousting himself off his stool, he knew there would be others. Some worthwhile hunting was coming up—adding more wall trophies. *Taking care of business didn't have to be all work, did it?* He thought of the small delivery van and almost smiled.

CHAPTER 12

Three days later …

As the ATV approached the *Goliath*, Jason hailed Stone. "Go for Stone."

"Extend the gangway, Sergeant Major … we're almost there."

"You got it, Cap."

Up ahead, the *Goliath*'s rear hatch began to open and the gangway extended. Jason watched as Colonel Pope did a double take seeing the odd-looking craft.

From the back seat, Jason asked, "You ever been in a spacecraft, Pope?"

He shook his head—almost imperceptibly.

Nan said, "Not everyone's life revolves around space travel, Jason."

Now she was defending him. *It must be serious*. "You're right about that," he replied.

Nan said, "Once we're situated, I want to talk to the group. What we'll be walking into will take a lot more diplomacy than you're accustomed to. This won't be about brute force, Jason. Got that?"

Jason raised his palms in mock surrender. "Hey … this

is your show, Nan. Star Watch is here to support you—your needs."

Jason, seeing Pope glance back at him in his peripheral vision, turned and gave him a quick wink. Looking irritated, Pope turned back to what was now looming above them—the *Goliath*.

* * *

They assembled in the rear cabin of the *Goliath*, some taking seats while others, like Jason and Billy, remained standing.

Nan stood in the hatchway to the cockpit and waited for everyone to quiet down. "So I wanted to say a few words before we get going."

Bristol dramatically huffed and made a pained expression.

"You have a problem, Bristol?" Nan asked.

"I don't know why I'm here. It's not like I don't have a shitload of stuff to do back on the *Jumelle*. I'm Chief Engineer … how does this fit into my job description?"

Nan didn't answer, looking blank-faced toward Jason instead.

Jason said, "You've become what is commonly referred to as a *space worm*."

"I know what a space worm is," Bristol said, looking annoyed.

"Then you know that space worms have a tendency to lose perspective … to forget that life is more than what's inside the hull of the ship that's up there in orbit. Plus, since Ricket wasn't a good fit for this operation, you're our de-facto science officer. So why don't you just try to enjoy the experience."

"I don't get it. Since when does Star Watch handle missing person issues?" Bristol asked.

"Since the issue is my nephew," Nan replied. "This is personal. Look, I haven't asked a lot from any of you over the years. But I can remember a few times when I pulled strings for most of you sitting here, including you, Bristol. Anyway … things are relatively quiet in your district right now … yes?"

Nan's reference to their district referred to that sector of space in which the *Jumelle* was assigned. Star Watch no longer moved through space as a combined fleet—answering calls for assistance on a first request, to a first to respond, type basis. At present, there were ten separate districts within Allied space—each assigned one of the Caldurian technology Star Watch vessels. Jason got first dibs, grabbing the district containing the Sol System along with other nearby star systems. There had been more than a few cries of nepotism directed toward Omni Reynolds, Jason's father.

Nan continued, "When we arrive, we'll be out of place; we'll stick out like sore thumbs. There'll be mistrust and a good amount of animosity toward us. Roll with it. We're coming onto their turf."

"I can do that," Billy said.

"Yeah … with a name like Hernandez you'll fit right in to their hillbilly culture," Bristol added.

Even Nan had to smile at that. "The people we're meeting with are indeed locals and somewhat backward. But don't forget, they are wealthy and have their own space mining operations going on. Don't underestimate anyone."

Jason asked, "Couldn't a phone call have sufficed? You don't think this is a bit over-kill?" He gestured around to the others and at the ship.

"We tried that … numerous times. These people don't respond well to anyone associated with the government. You need to remember how things were right after the invasion. There was no more *America*, per se. Hell, most government officials were wrapped in cocoons. It's why I was brought in as the interim president from a lowly Secretary of Interstellar Relations. As far as the Pickets are concerned, the part of the country we're headed for is a nation unto itself. No, if we're going to get answers … it'll be on a one-to-one basis."

"How did they ever get up in space in the first place?" Jason asked. "Going from backwoods coal miners to space-faring entrepreneurs seems a bit of a leap."

Colonel Pope stood and said, "In the foothills of Tennessee at the end of the Craing war, a parked alien craft … I think a heavy cruiser … was preparing to leave. I guess to head back into space. The whole story's secondhand, incomplete, but word is the Picket brothers … armed for bear with automatic weapons … entered the nearly deserted ship and captured the bridge crew. Apparently, the Craing had left the gangway extended and the boys took the opportunity to inflict some good ol' boy *whoop-ass* retribution."

"So what? They commandeered the ship?" Rizzo asked.

"That's right. Thirteen Craing crewmembers were, and still are as far as I know, their hostages. They've increased their holdings by pirating three more Craing warships over the last five years. Since mining is all they really knew, it was a natural turn of events to continue with that same vocation up in space. Their operations are mostly somewhere within that asteroid belt around the solar system."

"The mineral-rich Kuiper Belt," Jason added.

"So what's our cover story? Why are we dropping in on them?" Billy asked.

"We need to have something they want and I'm guessing the doubling or tripling of their operations would be a good enticement," Nan said.

Jason exchanged a glance with Billy.

"We're going to proposition them. I'm Tanya Pope—the Pennsylvania-version of Mamma Picket—and the Colonel here will play my husband. He keeps his name, Stephen Pope. His family, on his father's side, were miners from way back, so he knows the lingo."

"So what are you offering them?"

"Like the Pickets, we've also made the transition into space. Our mining operations are far smaller but we have an opportunity. Clients of ours, the Mau, are hard up for Tanzamine. I know the Pickets are currently one of the few mining operations that excavate that rare mineral. The Mau have given us a first order for a billion tons of the stuff."

"And you've already set this conspiracy up with them … the Mau?" Jason asked.

Nan smiled. "Thanks to what the infamous Captain Jason Reynolds did for the Mau during the war, you're a hero in their star system. They were glad to help. Any inquiries by the Pickets to double-check our story will be verified by them."

"You think they'll go for it? From what you've said … they seem pretty reclusive," Jason countered.

"I'll sweeten the deal. Tell them the Mau will pay in gold bullion. The Pickets' preferred method of payment."

"So who are we?" Rizzo asked. "We don't all look like family members." His eyes settled on Billy.

"We're not all in the same area of operation. Billy and Rizzo, you are our security chiefs. Bristol, you're our mineralogist, so you may want to bone up on the subject matter over the next hour."

"Seriously? I have an hour to sound intelligent about fucking space mining?"

"Probably less," Nan replied, giving an indifferent shrug.

"And me?" Jason queried. "Like you … I'm fairly recognizable."

"That's why you'll need to shave your head. I think Ricket once told me our nano-devices will allow us to change our eye color."

"Yeah … we can do that," Bristol commented unenthusiastically.

Nan said, "Jason, you're our broker … the deal-maker. You're the one bringing the parties together to make this deal happen."

Bristol said, "And you'll be the first one they'll skin alive if they smell a rat. Screw this up and we'll all end up lynched or something."

Jason gave Bristol a weary look, though he knew he was speaking the truth. He too needed to bone up on both space mining and deal-making over the next hour.

Sergeant Stone stuck her head out the forward hatch. "We ready to head out yet?"

"Give it an hour, Sergeant Major," Jason said, as he activated his virtual notebook.

CHAPTER 13

Jason, seated to the right of Stone at the *Goliath*'s controls, scanned the lush green horizon. An endless blanket of trees and rolling hills. This was beautiful country. Pigeon Forge was situated between the Smokey Mountains National Park to the East and South, with Jefferson City to the North and Knoxville, Tennessee to the west.

Jason had needed an hour and a half to bone up on various subject matter, then another half hour to speak quietly with Nan and Bristol. In the end, he instructed Stone to phase-shift the craft directly to the Virginia-Tennessee border.

It took them less than a minute to reach Sevier County, and then Pigeon Forge. As Stone banked the shuttlecraft in a tight circle, Jason took in the landscape below. The word that came to his mind was *overgrown*. He'd heard of Dollywood—the famous country singer's theme park and resort—a tribute to Dolly Parton's humble beginnings in the Smokey Mountains many years before. Seeing it now, he was certain the buxom singer would be horrified. He wondered if old Dolly was still alive or, like so many millions, had succumbed to the molt weevils. Perhaps she was a nearby peovil, moving about outside the miles and miles of twenty-foot-tall fencing topped with concertina wire. He whipped the ugly vision from his mind and looked straight down.

"There … right on that main street below should work," Jason said.

Stone leveled out the *Goliath*, engaging the landing thrusters. Only then, off in the distance on a hillside, did Jason see the distinctive bug-like outline of a Craing Heavy Cruiser.

The shuttlecraft settled onto the pavement and Stone cut the propulsion system. Nan, seated directly behind Jason, leaned forward so he could see her. "This is one scary-looking place."

Jason had to agree. Looking merely overgrown from above, it was downright *jungle-like* up close. "You said you let them know we were coming?"

"Talked to the oldest brother … Brent. He wasn't exactly accommodating, but he agreed once Mamma Picket gave him the OK."

Nan was laughing.

"What is it?" Jason asked.

"I'm sorry, you look so … different."

Right before leaving Franktown, Colorado, Nan foraged through her bag and came up with a battery-powered electric razor. Jason, surprised how reluctant he'd been to have his somewhat longish hair reduced to a quarter-inch stubble, grimaced.

"It'll grow back … I hope," he said defensively.

"It's your eyes … too. Blue. It suits you. And you do look a whole lot different."

Bristol had instructed Jason how to navigate the multitude of nano-device menus and sub-menus until he'd landed on the one that allowed for optics and pigment color options for irises. The others in the group found the process so interesting that most experimented with their own eye colors. Jason had to admit—the process was fun, and a welcome break.

Nan also chose to become blue-eyed, and with her long black hair—a wig—she looked like a different person. There was something exotic about her appearance now. He had to admit—the new look was enticing.

"Looks like the welcoming committee has arrived," Billy said, seated next to Nan.

"Go ahead and open the rear hatch and extend the gangway, Sergeant Major," Jason said, rising to his feet. Outside, he caught sight of six big strapping men dressed in jeans and plaid work shirts, all armed with various energy weapons. Several he recognized as multi-guns.

"Let me guess, you want me to stay with the ship."

"Sorry, Gail, but yeah. Be ready. If things go tribal, we'll need to get out of here … fast."

* * *

One by one they headed down the gangway onto the main street, with Nan and Pope taking the lead. Jason noted Stone had set the *Goliath* down in front of a three-story building. A burgundy sign out front said Palace Theater. Another sign below it, in a handwritten font, exclaimed *Dollywood*. The W was a rusted, somewhat off-kilter, butterfly.

Surrounded now by the mountain men, Jason turned around and took in the rest of the surroundings. A town, similar to Main Street at Disneyland—that probably once had quaint little shops and various boutiques and parlors—now had all the charm of a ghost town. In the distance was rollercoaster scaffolding. He saw intermittent train tracks with gaping sections missing.

As the six armed men closed in around them, separating the three brothers out was easy. They were standing in front of the Dollywood sign and they were all over six-five, packed with two hundred and fifty pounds of muscle, bearded, and looked like Jethro from the old TV show *The Beverly Hillbil-*

lies. Brent, Payne, and Larry.

Nan, taking the initiative, stepped forward with her hand out, ready to shake, but suddenly halted, hearing the roar of a big V-8. The distinct profile of a 1959 Ford Fairlane was fast approaching down the town's main street. As the old automobile approached them, Jason noticed two front-seat occupants—one large and one small.

Bristol looked nervous, seeing the old car barreling down on them and not slowing. "That bitch is out of control."

Jason heard him, but barely, and doubted the three brothers had, due to the engine noise. The classic car abruptly skidded to a stop, five feet in front of Nan and Pope. The driver-side door flew open on rusty hinges and an immense woman hauled herself out.

"At least we know where the juniors got their girth," Billy said, leaning close to Jason.

Wearing a formless cotton dress the size of a small circus tent, dotted with some kind of flowery print, Mamma Picket was an imposing figure. Easily six foot three and weighing no less than two hundred and fifty pounds, probably a lot more, she strode up to Nan and Pope with her hand raised—a finger pointing straight at Nan like a Smith and Wesson six-shooter.

"You're late! That's disrespecting me and my boys. If this is how you and your kind do business, well, you can scamper your skinny ass back on that space vehicle of yours!" She came to a stop well within Nan's personal space. Hands on hips, the woman towered over Jason's ex-wife. If Nan wasn't terrified, Jason certainly was for her. He wasn't exactly sure why, but the whole situation suddenly seemed somewhat comical and he was having a difficult time keeping a smile from his face. He glanced to his left and noted Billy wasn't smiling, but was certainly captivated.

The pregnant silence dragged out to the point things were getting uncomfortable. Finally Nan said, smiling as though the huge woman had greeted her with hugs and kisses, "Mamma Picket, it's a pleasure to meet you. I have a gift for you." She back-handed Pope's chest and said, "Don't just stand there! Give it to her."

As if awakening from a dream, Pope said, "Oh … yeah. Here." He held out a gift bag—colorful tissue paper sticking out through its top opening.

Mamma Picket looked from Pope to the bag then to Nan. "You brought me a gift?" Sounding more than a little surprised, her face morphed into an expression of guilt.

The passenger car door opened with a painful squeal. The young woman emerging was the exact opposite of Mamma Picket—as far as stature. Also wearing what looked to be a homemade cotton dress, her hair was long and stringy, and oily as if it hadn't been washed in days … maybe weeks. She slammed the car door—putting all her eighty to ninety pounds behind her two-armed shove. Turning back, with all eyes upon her, she said, "Sorry." She wrapped her thin bare arms around her body then leaned against the front quarter panel of the car.

Nan, grabbing the handles of the gift bag from Pope, held the gift bag out to Mamma Picket. "Open it …"

Mamma Picket stole a quick glance over at her boys and snatched the bag from Nan's outstretched hand. Head bowed, she dug through the tissue paper with one hand and came to an abrupt stop. "No. Um … this is … Oh my, Tanya Pope! No no no!"

Nan, a bemused smile on her lips, glanced back over her shoulder at Jason. Her confident expression said, *Go ahead … watch this …*

Mamma Picket's hand came out, holding a bright yellow brick. Obviously gold—there was some kind of inscription engraved on the brick's top. Jason was no expert but that bar of gold—especially post-Craing war—was easily worth $100,000.

"What's it say on it … Mamma?" one of her boys asked, raising up his chin in an attempt to get a better look at the yellow brick.

Mamma Picket pursed her lips, continuing to stare at the gift in her hand. "It says … it says …

I hoped I wouldn't miss you long …
but I still can't believe you're gone
and I still miss you just as much as always.
I hoped I'd get you off my mind,
It's been a long time, but I find
that I still think of you as much as always …"

While the big boys nodded with confused appreciation, Mamma Picket was speechless. When she looked at Nan her eyes were moist and she seemed to be having difficulty breathing. "Lyrics from *As Much As Always*; Dolly had released that song back in 1982."

Nan tilted her head then lowered it in such a way that seemed familiar. She'd used that same look on him, too, years ago. It was always effective.

Billy leaned in: "Here it comes …"

It came as fast as a freight train. Mamma Picket's sequoia-sized arms came around Nan's waist, pulling her up and off her feet. A bear hug like none Jason had ever witnessed. He caught a glimpse of Nan's startled face, squished beneath Mamma's *fleshy* mammoth-sized arms. Wide-eyed, Nan looked concerned for her very life.

CHAPTER 14

It seemed as if everything was happening in slow motion. Ryan knew the refurbished Paotow Tanker was nearly upon him, but he couldn't seem to get his arms and legs moving fast enough to get away from it—to get back inside the van. Locomotion in the weightlessness of open space was problematic to begin with. Without gravity, and the ability to push off something else, there was a lot of gyrating around that had little or no effect.

Ryan, now nearly at the midway-point of the vessel, clipped and unclipped his safety lines as fast as his gloved hands could manage. He tried to avoid looking at the approaching vessel, knowing even that small moment of hesitation could, potentially, cost him his life. But it was there in his peripheral vision—dark and looming—like doom itself approaching. He clipped then unclipped the lines to the eyelets—each spaced three and a half feet apart—one following another. He felt as much as saw the tanker vessel moving closer. Fumbling the clip at the stern corner eyelet, he missed getting it secure three more times. *Shit! Shit! Shit!*

Ryan heard the familiar voice in his helmet. "Your heart rate's jackhammering, man."

"I already know that," Ryan said, swinging around the

stern of the van and awkwardly thrusting his body through the open rear hatch. Immediately, his makeshift carryall got caught on the hatchway cowling. Repositioning it, he cursed aloud while worming his way inside—pulling his legs in tight so they'd clear the van's obstruction sensors.

Ryan yelled, "Close the damn hatch!"

It descended agonizingly slow. *Come on, come on …* The hatch finally locked into place and he heard the rush of atmosphere enter the airlock. He decided to keep his suit on, leave the visor portion open, and he wanted to scream at Two-ton to get them the hell out of there. But the propulsion system—not converted—remained only partially disassembled—he still needed to swap reactors.

Ryan's eyes were glued on the still-blinking red indicator when it suddenly illuminated to bright green. He opened the inside hatch and hurried through the cabin, then up the steps, past the cockpit, and up a second set of steps to the cargo hold area. Everything was laid out just as it was before.

"What's going on with the tanker out there, Two-ton?"

"Not much. I'm reading one occupant. A quite large occupant. He's moving."

"What do I do next with the fusion drive module?" Ryan asked, staring at an open panel on the bulkhead where he'd previously patched thirty to forty wiring harnesses.

"Go plug in the Aldo Pack—the fusion module. Easy-peezy … everything's plug n' play."

Doing his best to ignore the presence of the nearby tanker, Ryan hefted up the shiny rectangular module. "It seems bigger than the other one. The fusion reactor that's in there … no?" he asked.

Not waiting for a reply, he made his way down both sets of stairs and entered the main living cabin. He had to turn sideways in order to move past the small dining table in the kitchenette section. He set the Aldo Pack down near the stern, just to the side of the airlock hatch. He then grabbed a portion of the metal deck grating and pulled it straight up. Swinging it around, he placed it on the deck behind him. He stared down at the van's integrated propulsion system and what he saw made him want to punch something. Fists clenched, he looked up. "Just as I said, they … are … different … sizes!"

The AI took a beat before answering. "Yes … an Aldo Pack is a far more complex piece of equipment, Ryan. That kind of technology takes up some serious real estate."

Ryan, wishing Two-ton was alive just so he could beat him silly with a wrench, or perhaps the fucking Aldo Pack, said, "If you're screwing with me …"

The AI cut him off: "Look … yes they are different sizes. But this will work. You'll have to leave the removable deck plate off. The Aldo Pack will stick out a half-foot into the cabin so be careful not to trip over it."

Ryan reached in, finding the three separate thumb-latches that secured the ion reactor module in place. While two came away easily, the third was giving him a problem.

The van shook. Ryan stopped futzing with the latch and waited. *Had he caused the van to shake or* … the van shook again. This time far more violently.

With his head and upper torso immersed below the living cabin deck, Ryan yelled, "What is that, Two-ton?"

"Keep going … continue what you're doing."

The thumb-clamp was beyond stuck. He repositioned his hands so he could get both thumbs positioned on top of the thing. Straightening out his arms, he put all his weight down on the clamp and pushed. The clamp stubbornly resisted until, finally, it sprang free. He grabbed the sides of the grimy box and pulled it upward. He felt the unit's card edge connector disengage first, then the module became loose, sitting within four metal guides. With a groan, he slid the box all the way out and looked around for some free space on the deck to place the ion unit. He leaned it up, length-wise, against the left-hand bulkhead, then reached back for the Aldo Pack. Picking it up, he flipped it around so the card edge connector was facing down as he positioned the thing over the open section of the deck.

"You sure about this? We're not going to blow up or anything … are we?"

"I don't think so. Perhaps you can ask Orloff Picket."

That was not the answer Ryan was looking for, but at least the van had stopped shaking. Carefully, he lowered the module and was encouraged when he saw that the metal guides did in fact line up with the four edges of the Aldo Pack. The unit was the same size for width and height … only its length was different.

He let the fusion reactor module slide all the way down until he felt its card edge connector come to rest on its receiving connector, directly below it. If the Two-ton AI was correct, the contacts would be a perfect match. He put slightly more weight on the box and felt the connector seat itself.

Quickly, he repositioned the three thumb latches into place and exhumed himself from the sub-compartment. He was in the process of reaching for the deck plate behind him when he remembered the Aldo Pack module was now sticking out of the opening. He left it *as is* and stood up.

"Done. What else do I need to do, Two-ton?"

"Get to the cockpit … we have a problem."

* * *

Standing at the helm console, Ryan's view through the forward observation window was completely blocked. The rusted orangey-brown hull of the refurbished Paotow Tanker sat mere feet in front of the bow.

"Why haven't you gotten the propulsion system online, Two-ton?"

"The process has been initiated. There's a twenty-minute

self-test. Fusion malfunctions are best to be avoided, since they typically result in a vessel, along with its occupants, being atomized."

Ryan was beyond the point of losing patience with the AI. It doled out information only as it saw fit while here he was—mere feet away from some kind of psychopath.

"What's he doing in there ... can you tell?"

"The sensors on this van are rudimentary, at best. Even with the beefed-up AI functionality. The van is being held securely to the tanker by some kind of docking clamp."

Ryan looked downward out the window and saw *something* there—an extended section of the tanker that could very well be a clamp of some sort. Swaying suddenly, he was forced to take a step backwards due to sudden, increased, inertia. "What just happened?"

"We're moving ... a whole lot faster," the AI said.

"I thought you said our propulsion system was conducting self-tests?"

"We're moving along with the Paotow Tanker. Orloff Picket must want us along for the ride. I'm sorry, buddy. There's nothing more I can do at this point. I have no idea what his intentions are; what he wants with you."

"What do we have in the way of weapons on board?" Ryan asked.

"Consignment Freight does not provide, nor sanction, its drivers to be armed. With that said ... together ... we might be able to come up with something moderately effective. I suspect we'll need to do that task prior to him reaching whatever intended destination he has in mind for us."

CHAPTER 15

With the forward observation window blocked, Ryan watched the console display. The two vessel icons—one small, the freight van, and one large, the Paotow Tanker—were right on top of each other. He manipulated the settings, broadening out the spatial reference area around them to one light-year's distance. The closer fringe of the Oort Cloud now came into view. They were moving in the same general direction Ryan had intended to go—where he'd look around—make contact to be rescued. Orloff Picket, driving the tanker, obviously had his own reasons.

"Hey ... I may have an idea," the AI said.

"What kind of idea?" Ryan asked.

"I don't want you to dismiss it ... just because it sounds crazy," the Two-ton AI said.

"Bring it. At this point I'm open to any and all suggestions. It's not like there are many options. Who knows where this guy is taking us? Nowhere good ... I can tell you that."

"Good, you're being receptive. I like that."

"Uh huh. Why don't you just spit it out," Ryan urged.

"You're already suited up ... right?"

"You know I am."

"There may be a way to get away from that spacecraft."

Ryan was already shaking his head no. "If you're thinking I'm going back out there, with that lunatic clamped onto this van, you're crazy … or malfunctioning."

Ryan stood up and paced the small cockpit for several minutes. Nothing could be worse than this—having no control over his own destiny. He always prided himself on the fact he was his own man. When his parents were killed, during the Craing molt weevil invasion, he was sixteen and he'd run away. His famous aunt wanted him to come stay with her, even pleaded with him. But he was angry and needed to deal with the inner rage he was feeling in his own way. So Ryan joined what was left of the U.S. Navy. All military branches were devastated by the invasion. Millions of soldiers were either killed or cocooned—later to become peovils. Tall for his age, Ryan looked somewhat older than his years. Requirements for potential pilots to hold a Bachelor's degree first went by the wayside. With lots of training and plenty of testing, he took to flying like a duck to water. He spent the next three years piloting virtually everything—from helicopters to fixed-wing fighters—then on to an assortment of spacecraft. That was how he'd qualified for his current job.

He stopped pacing. "Fine … tell me your idea."

"I've determined the clamping mechanism on the tanker is a Strom & Lewis 569 retractable clamp."

"So?"

"Well, Strom & Lewis 569 retractable clamps are used throughout the mining industry. Tankers, raw material space-trucks, and freighters all use this clamp, or a derivative of this same model clamp."

"Again … so?"

"So I have the disengage instructions. Surprisingly simple. These same clamps are often used for space station docking berths and are typically programmed for remote activation. That's not an option for us but we can do things manually. The only problem is … you'll need to go outside and open a small maintenance panel on that tanker. It's situated near the extended area of the clamp."

"You want me to just stroll over there and start screwing with his ship? He'll see me."

"My sensors inform me he's plopped down mid-ship. Sitting at some kind of desk or workbench. He appears to be engrossed in what he is doing."

"How about our van ... is it ready to go? Will the swapped reactor work?" Ryan asked.

"It's fairly far along in its systems test and there are zero errors so far. Things are looking good."

"I can't believe I'm agreeing to this. Tell me what to do with that maintenance panel."

* * *

Once free of the airlock, Ryan came around the starboard side of the freight van, which was slightly less in view of the tanker. Becoming more proficient at the clipping and unclipping of his safety lines onto the hull eyelets, he moved steadily forward at good speed, then slowed as he moved toward the bow.

"Is the guy still sitting where he was?" Ryan asked.

"Still there."

Ryan slowed his advancement on the tanker. "I don't see the maintenance panel you were referring to."

The AI said, "You will ... keep going."

Ryan, now at the van's bow, was ready to step over to the Paotow Tanker. He looked along the hull for a place to clip his safety lines. *There it is.* It was fairly close to the clamping mechanism, so that, at least, was one positive. He unclipped both safety lines, which made him more than a little nervous, and was about to take the long step over to the tanker when the AI said, "Ryan ... you'll want to keep your head low. The vessel has an oblong porthole positioned relatively close to where you'll be standing."

"Terrific. Of course it does." He stepped across—his knees bent—which did absolutely nothing since there was no gravity to tug his body downward. Arms outstretched, he immediately opened his palms wide when his fingers came in contact with the tanker's hull to absorb his advancement. He gently pushed his hands upward—bringing his body down—but not before he got a momentary view through the porthole into the refurbished Paotow Tanker. What Ryan viewed didn't quite register—not completely, anyway. He did see someone sitting within at a workbench, along the same side of the hull he was currently crouching at outside. He attached one of his safety lines to the one eyelet he'd spotted earlier. So far so good.

"Do you see the small maintenance hatch by your left foot?"

Ryan looked down and saw the nine-to-ten-inch square panel, with an eighth of an inch groove around it. "How do I open it?"

"Checking …"

Ryan let another full minute pass before asking, "What's the holdup?"

"I'm still working on a solution … keep your pants on," the AI said.

Waiting, the fleeting mental image of what he'd seen inside the tanker began to take form in his mind. It made no sense … it was nonsensical. The interior of the ship was like no other spacefaring vessel he'd ever encountered. The compartment was wood paneled—about twice the width and length of a typical school bus. Along the opposite hull were mountings—mountings of animal heads. One was a rhino-warrior—of that he was certain. But it was the one closest to him, mounted at the very end, which perplexed Ryan the most. Somehow familiar, why was he having such a hard time placing … *oh … my … God.*

Paralyzed, Ryan stared at the closed panel. "Two-ton?"

"Yes, Ryan."

"Did my helmet-cam pick up the interior of the tanker?"

"Oh yeah."

"So you saw what was mounted on the bulkhead?"

"Yup. Disconcerting."

"I'm sorry, it must be …" Ryan didn't know what to say.

"Don't sweat it … remember … I'm an AI. I'm actually more concerned with your state of mind."

"We need to get away from this crazy fuck as fast as possible."

"You think? The good news … I've figured out how to access the panel. Simply press down on the two opposite sides of the panel simultaneously."

Ryan did as instructed; using both index fingers, he applied pressure evenly and pushed down. The square panel recessed inward about an inch before springing back out and stopping about six inches above the hull.

"Ryan … there are four touch pads within the now-exposed control mechanism. One set opens and closes the clamp, while the other set extends and retrieves the extension arm. I would suggest you not touch the extension arm touch pads. The hydraulics associated with that big arm would, undoubtedly, be loud enough to alert that menacing-looking dude inside."

Ryan, having a hard time breathing, couldn't get Two-ton's distorted, waxy-looking, face out of his mind. The eyes … *so life-like. So incredibly real!*

"You need to concentrate, Ryan."

Ryan leaned in closer and found the touchpad switches that Two-ton described. It took him another few seconds to figure out which touch pads controlled which function. If he hadn't been so nervous, so distracted, he would have seen right away that each was marked. With his forefinger he pressed on the touch pad marked CLAMP OPEN and then simultaneously heard the nearby clamp *clank* open.

"Get going, Ryan! Go now."

The tension in the AI's voice was enough to scare the bejesus out of him. He leapt toward the van, only to be abruptly halted in mid-flight. *Damn!* His safety line was still attached to the tanker. He hand-over-hand reeled himself backward toward the Paotow Tanker. He unclipped the safety line and, as his eyes came up, he again found himself staring into the tanker's porthole. Only this time it was blocked. Blocked by the face of a crazed-looking bearded man.

CHAPTER 16

As it turned out, much of Dollywood had burned to the ground seven years before. With the high concentration of peovils in this part of the Smokey Mountains, the resort hotel, vacation cabins, and several roller coaster rides were destroyed by what remained of the U.S. Government. Now, from what Jason understood, most of Timber Canyon, Wilderness Pass, and Craftsman Valley—both the north and northeastern sections of the park—were gone, leaving only Show Street, Owens Farm, Country Fair, Rivertown Junction, and The Village. Surprisingly enough, the Dollywood Express steam locomotive was not only still around—but operational. A fact Jason was very aware of since he was sitting in one of the moving tour railcars listening to Mamma Picket explain everything there was to know about the ill-fated theme park, with a surprising level of detail.

Mamma Picket, standing between two vertical railings, had her hands wrapped tightly around them for support. The open-air car pitched and swayed as it followed behind the laboring steam engine. They were all getting the royal tour treatment, including a tour of what remained of the park.

"I met Dolly once. I was a child ... no more than eight or nine. I thought she was the most beautiful creature on God's green earth. Still do. Now, coming up here on the left, you'll see Grist Mill, and just beyond that ... Owens Farm."

She'd positioned Nan and Pope before her—providing them both a front row seat to her presentation. The rest of the team—Billy, Bristol, Rizzo and Jason—were scattered about in the seats behind them.

The small, waif-like woman was sitting next to Jason, and he'd become immediately aware of her distinct, rather unpleasant, scent—unwashed and downright gamey. She looked up at him and attempted a shy grin. What little remained of her smile consisted of several missing teeth; the few still there—precariously clinging to blackened gums—were mostly crooked and brownish-gray in color.

"Mamma knows everything there is to know about this park. Heck, she can tell you the names of the carpenters that built that water tower over yonder."

"That so?" Jason politely queried.

"My name is Eleanore Hatfield ... of the Hatfield and McCoy fame. Everyone calls me Ellie." She put out a small hand for Jason to shake.

Shaking her hand, he said, "Glad to meet you, Ellie. Tell me, what's your relationship to Mamma Picket?"

"She's my cousin ... and my aunt," she said with a sideways look.

Jason quickly ran through the mental gymnastics, trying to figure out how that could even be possible, then quickly gave up. "You live here ... at the park?"

"Oh yes, we all live here. Mamma lives at the Dreamsong Theater ... it's very grand. I live right back there, in the Grist Mill. Got a cot set up and everything."

Jason slowly nodded, not knowing what more to say.

"Mamma's going to let me go up in space, she promised, on their next excursion to the mining camps."

"Asteroid belt?"

"Uh ... I guess so. I don't know for sure, anyway."

"Where are we going now? Where's this train headed?"

She smiled, her expression implying it was a ridiculous question. "Are you daft? We're going to the train station. It ain't far up ahead."

"After that?"

"Oh ... probably going to Mystery Mine."

"Isn't that one of the areas that burnt down?" Jason asked, remembering something Mamma had said earlier regarding Timber Canyon.

"No. That's still there ... didn't burn down. Mamma says it was a miracle. Anyway, we usually take people there."

Jason took the opportunity to glance around the railcar and the one trailing behind them. The three Picket brothers were sitting together four rows back. He could see their rifle barrels sticking up behind the seat back in front of them. In the training car were six other armed mountain men—all wore beards and had bored, expressionless faces.

When Jason caught the eye of Bristol, seated a row behind him on the other side of the aisle, Bristol leaned forward and said, "I'd throw myself off this train if I thought it would kill me."

Ellie looked back at Bristol, then over at Jason. "That's a strange thing to say."

Jason nodded. "Bristol has a unique sense of humor. Takes a bit getting used to."

"Does he have a girlfriend?"

"Um ... well ... I don't think he does." Jason didn't want to get into it. Especially down here in the southland where Bristol's sexual orientation might not be all that popular. "We're slowing."

"We're here. Good thing, too ... I have to pee."

* * *

Mystery Mine was everything Jason expected it to be.

On the outside, it was a rustic timber and corrugated metal structure, designed to look old and ready to fall down. The adjoining roller coaster was nothing more than a heap of metal tracks atop a small mountain of charcoal. They were ushered inside, where it was dark and, Jason assumed, pretty much looked the same now as it did during the park's heyday. An empty roller coaster car that sat eight—two rows holding four passengers each—sat on a track that entered and left this concourse for Mystery Mine on opposite sides.

He heard Mamma Picket continuing her tour narrative. Both Nan and Pope turned, looking around at the various things Mamma was pointing out to them. Every so often Nan would ask her a question or two, but Jason couldn't hear more than an occasional word said. He wondered if she had asked about Orloff … Mamma's son? The whole reason they were there—to find the woman's son and, hopefully, track down Nan's nephew, Ryan.

Jason stepped in closer and asked, "Is this a good time to talk about our proposal?"

He was, after all, supposed to be the business broker here. "My Mau contacts await my answer. They want availability and pricing information for raw Tanzamine as soon as possible."

Mamma looked annoyed. In the middle of a lengthy description of the song, *Coal Miner's Daughter*, she loudly expelled her breath between red, puffed-out, cheeks. "I suppose. We can go in there," she said, pointing toward what looked like the entrance to a mineshaft tunnel. With Mamma Picket in the lead, the group followed. Dark as the main room had seemed, inside the tunnel was even darker. Jason had to adjust his nano-devices in order to really see. He then noticed that the three brothers had brought their weapons up, where before they'd hung loosely down at their sides. Eventually, the tunnel opened wide into a large circular area. Here, too, the walls were only compacted dirt and, if he hadn't known better, he'd assume they were hundreds of feet below ground. He noticed in the center of the room a large hole—easily twenty feet across and obviously deep, since he couldn't see the bottom.

"Gather around, please," Mamma Picket said, gesturing to the dark void in front of them. Jason and Billy exchanged a look that read … *be ready for anything*.

Jason stepped up to the lip of the hole and looked down. If it weren't for his nano-devices he wouldn't be able to see down, to the thirty or so feet to the bottom. There was movement down there—something alive milling about.

Mamma signaled to one of her sons with her chin. A moment later, a high-up spotlight came on directly over the hole. Jason heard Nan's quick intake of a breath.

"What's that?" Nan asked, her eyes locked on the five creatures moving about below.

"Those are molt weevils," Brent said, the oldest of the sons.

"I know what they are. Why are you showing us them and why are they here?" Nan asked.

Mamma smiled—looking at her three sons like it was some kind of inside joke. She began walking the perimeter of the hole, moving behind the group. Considering her huge girth, it wouldn't take much to shove any one of them over the edge. The spidery-looking molt weevils were now flittering around—agitated. Having a body the size of the average dishwasher—along with eight thick and hairy legs— the creatures seemed to be anticipating something. One molt weevil in particular was taking a special interest in Jason. Its cold beady eyes locked on him, as it tried to climb up the steep dirt walls only to slide back within seconds.

Mamma continued her slow trek around the group's perimeter. "You want to do business with the Pickets, that's good. Understand … we don't tend to work with outsiders; we like to keep to ourselves." She stopped behind Nan and

Pope. "But I like you, Tanya. We are kindred spirits, I'm sure of that." She placed a hand on Nan's shoulder and leaned in, whispering something in Jason's ex-wife's ear. As casually as he could manage, Jason let his right hand find the SuitPac device hanging at his belt. His thumb and forefinger found the two inset spring tabs. He was ready to activate his battle-suit should it become necessary.

Mamma stepped away from Nan and continued on her way around. "I myself do not travel much into space. I manage things from here. My boys … they do the heavy lifting up there … in space. You'll be working with them, but probably with Orloff, mostly. He's not here. On vacation right now."

Jason saw Nan and Pope nodding their heads. *Progress.*

Mamma halted again, three people down from Jason. He watched as she joined them, now standing at the lip of the open hole. She closed her eyes, as if saying a silent prayer, and looking as if she had the weight of the world upon her shoulders.

Suddenly, thick and muscular arms wrapped around Jason's upper body. It was Brent. Jason smelled the giant man's warm foul breath—a mix of coffee and chewing tobacco. He noticed that Billy, Rizzo, Bristol, and Pope were held also in a similar fashion by two of the other brothers, and two guards. Jason didn't resist … not yet. With his nanite-infused physiology, breaking Brent's grasp wouldn't be difficult. But first, he wanted to see what this was all about. Once their cover was broken, there would be no turning back and they still didn't have the answers they'd come for.

Mamma's eyes popped open and, moving incredibly fast for a woman her size, she reached to her left, grabbing the back of Eleanore Hatfield's loose-fitting dress in her hand. The little woman's body tilted forward horizontally—her arms and legs frantically gyrating.

"Put me down, Mamma … please … please! Oh god, Mamma … I'm scared!"

The molt weevils below were squealing now, two starting to hop about. But Mamma's eyes weren't on her niece-cousin—or whatever she was—they were locked on Jason, preparing to let go.

"Put her down!" Nan shouted, her eyes wide as saucers. "Don't do this, Mamma …"

Her words were cut short when Mamma released her hold on the small woman, who then fell screaming into the hole.

CHAPTER 17

Startled at seeing the lunatic inside the porthole—the face that must have belonged to Orloff Picket staring back at him—Ryan kicked out with both feet. A knee-jerk reaction which, on reflection, might cost him his life. In that moment, he realized both safety-line clips were still clutched in his hand; that he was no longer tethered to either ship. Frantically, he reached to grab ahold of something, anything, on the tanker, but he'd already drifted several feet away from it. His only hope was that his backward momentum would send him toward his own freight van. Ryan watched in horror as it slid by, mere inches from his outstretched fingers.

"Dude … you're hyper-ventilating."

"Yeah … well, I'm floating off in space with no way to get back to the van … so yes, I'm hyperventilating."

"Try to stay calm. We'll think of something."

Ryan did his best to relax. Either he'd suffocate as soon as his air supply ran out, in twenty-minutes or so, or … *more likely* … that bearded maniac was going to come after him. He briefly pictured his own head and upper body mounted on a bulkhead inside that Paotow Tanker. That would be worse than dying. Better to simply die out here, floating amongst the stars. His mind turned to Wendy, as it often did in times of distress. He briefly wondered if she would miss him? Who would be the one to tell her of his early demise? Probably Tony Post. He'd enjoy that.

Ryan's thoughts turned to the last night he'd spent alone with her. Neither had slept—neither wanted to. The next morning she was called into work two hours early, undoubtedly Tony's doing. She was in and out of the shower in two minutes flat as Ryan watched her from the bed. Naked, her hair wet and hanging in her face, he caught her eye in the still steamy mirror.

"Don't look at me like that," she said.

"Like what?" Ryan replied innocently.

She leaned forward over the counter—unabashedly giving Ryan a front row seat to view her amazing bare bottom. She brought her face closer in toward the mirror as her left, then right, eyelashes got a few rapid strokes of mascara. Their eyes met again and she stifled a giggle. "Don't you work today too?"

"Yeah … later this morning. What time is it?"

She said, "Six-thirty." Rubbing moisturizing lotion over her toned upper left thigh, she stopped mid-motion. "I think you work at seven."

"Ten."

"Uh uh. Tony changed the schedule yesterday."

"Shit!" Ryan flung back the covers, jumping out of her still warm bed, but the sheets got tangled around his ankles and he fell face forward. He heard her laughing, which made him laugh too. Finding his pants in a crumpled heap on the floor where he'd dropped them, he searched for his T-shirt in the semi-darkness and found it lying on the other side of the compartment. Bending over to retrieve it, he felt her arms come around his waist. As he straightened, he felt her soft face pressed up against his back.

"I don't want to wait a whole week before I see you again," she said, her voice muffled and barely above a whisper. "Tony keeps giving you these long runs."

He turned around in her arms and found her gazing up at him. Placing his hands on either side of her face, he gently kissed her lips—feeling himself stir.

Then came that wonderful giggle again as she pushed him away. "Oh no, that's not going to happen. I'm already going to be late … and so are you."

"Ryan!"

Instantly bringing his attention back to the here and now, he was only partially aware of Two-ton's AI voice in his helmet.

"What? What's happening?" Ryan asked, turning his head both left and right. He saw the Paotow Tanker in the distance. Three quick bright-yellow tongues of flame emanated out from the ship's stern thruster. The tanker slowly moved forward, increasing its speed. Ryan watched, unaware he was holding his breath. *Just keep going … you're done here … nut ball … keep going.*

At five hundred yards out—the bow of the tanker slowly turned in his direction. He pushed the feeling of dread away. "Ideas? Two-ton, are you there?"

"I'm here, working on a few things, but my options are limited. I'm sorry, Ryan."

Ryan checked his rudimentary HUD readings. He had about ten minutes remaining of breathable oxygen. There was only one option he hadn't really considered. If it came down to it, he could vacate the air tank early. *Am I prepared to do that? Kill myself?* he wondered.

The tanker was almost upon him and with it came a feeling of doom—of inescapable dread. As it passed by him, the hull no more than ten feet away, he felt dwarfed by the vessel's enormity.

Reverse thrusters came alive at key positions on the vessel and the ship shuddered to a complete standstill. Ryan found himself staring at the Paotow Tanker's substantial stern section—its tight grouping of three main thruster nozzles. Around the tanker's outer corner, on the starboard side, was an arched hatchway. As Ryan watched, the hatch slowly slid open, first seeing feet, then legs and body and then his helmeted head staring back at him. Though his visor was highly reflective, Ryan felt the man's glare even if he couldn't actually see his cold dark eyes.

Ryan, only ten feet from Orloff Picket, and incapable of moving away, simply waited for what the man would do next. He was holding something in his right hand. *Is that a weapon? Is he going to fucking shoot me?* As the weapon lifted higher, Ryan noticed it was different—not a weapon. Pointed directly at him, he pulled the trigger and a misty plume of debris scattered out from the muzzle—a projectile emerged. Unlike a bullet fired from a gun, the projectile moved relatively slow and purposeful. It took a full two seconds to reach Ryan, before thumping against his chest and sticking there. Ryan grabbed for it with one hand and tied to pull it away, but it held fast. Then, using both hands, he tugged even harder, but it had somehow become embedded into his environ suit.

"What the ..." Ryan said aloud. There was also a line attached to the projectile he hadn't noticed against the blackness of space. He was being reeled in. Ryan stopped struggling. At five feet out, he now could more adequately assess the man's size. He was a giant—at least six-five, maybe taller—and very broad. His shoulders were immense. The next course of events seemed clear: This crazed lunatic was going to kill him, dismember his body, and stick his head on a fucking plaque. No other two ways about it.

Ryan's decision to empty his oxygen tank was, by that point, a simple one. An environ suit, such as the one he was wearing, had numerous built-in safeguards against the type of action Ryan was preparing to undergo. One by one, he scrolled through the menus, defeating each safeguard as it appeared. Proceeding through four separate warnings, he affirmed after each that he did indeed want to vacate his air tank. At the final prompt, he hesitated. This was it … the end of his life. As the big man's gloved hand reached out for him, Ryan selected YES—dump the damn air!

The rush of air spewing from the back of his environ suit was constant and loud—like a waterfall—the sound of a life venting freely into the cosmos. Again, he thought of Wendy. *Damn … I really like her.*

There was movement in his peripheral vision. Ryan turned his head just in time to watch something that didn't seem possible—the fast approaching stern of his own delivery van.

The roar of oxygen leaving his air tank stopped as suddenly as it had begun. Everything turned quiet and he knew he was taking his final breaths.

Orloff Picket stopped reeling Ryan in and watched in apparent confusion as Delivery Van 412 continued backing toward his pursuer.

Struggling—feeling the first effects of oxygen deprivation—Ryan heard Two-ton's voice say, "Wait for it …"

In a blur, something shot out from the back of the van. Whatever it was, it missed Orloff Picket's head by mere inches. Retracting, it again shot back out—this time nailing him in the upper torso—momentarily flattening him against the tanker's outer hull. Like a piston—in and out—striking the huge man again and again, Ryan realized it was the van's metal gangway, being used now as a battering ram. Obviously, the Two-ton AI had somehow modified the deploy-and-retract timing mechanism. Ingenious!

Unfortunately, Ryan found himself quickly suffocating. Tunnel vision and spasmodic convulsions were sure indications the end was near.

The violent pounding movements ceased suddenly and all became still. Lightheaded, Ryan had already come to terms with his own fateful end. At first, the ongoing shouting in his helmet was difficult to comprehend, the AI was upset with Ryan's decision to vacate his oxygen tank.

He recognized the gangway as it floated near him—right up to him. And there … just beyond it, the open hatchway— as if beckoning him into the van's awaiting airlock. *Eight feet away and it may as well be one hundred miles.*

CHAPTER 18

Eleanore Hatfield landed on the back of a molt weevil and just as quickly slid off and toppled to the ground. Amidst a blur of skittering legs, she screamed bloody murder and curled into a ball, her arms and hands covering her head.

Jason broke from Brent's grasp as easily as if he were a child and jumped away. Since he'd already depressed both tabs on his SuitPac device, by the time he landed within the dirt pit his battle-suit's segments nearly covered his entire body. Surprised to see both Billy and Rizzo arriving below too—their suits nearly initialized—the trio raised their arms up simultaneously. Jason aimed his integrated wrist plasma cannons at the molt weevil closest to the fallen woman.

"Stop!"

Ready to fire, Jason, Rizzo and Billy hesitated and looked up at Mamma Picket as if they were peering up the pinnacle of a mountain. Her expression was hard to read—perhaps a cross between bemusement and confirmation. Clearly, she had fully expected their attempt to rescue the fallen woman.

Sounds of muffled laughing broke Jason's gaze away from Mamma. On the ground, Ellie peeked up at them through crossed arms and oily strands of hair. "Don't shoot them, … they're just pets. Won't hurt nobody." Uncurling herself, she got to her feet. One of the molt weevils nudged her gently with, Jason surmised, its head. She gave it a couple of pats, fearing it no more than if it were a golden retriever.

Jason kept his wrist cannon pointed at the molt weevil. He looked up and found Nan staring down at him with wide eyes. He knew there were very few things she hated more than molt weevils. She and Molly had endured more than their share of encounters with the awful beasts in recent years. Tentatively raising a hand, she said, "Hold on, Jason … for now." She looked across the pit to where Mamma Picket stood. "What the hell is going on, Mamma? Those things have killed millions of people. Why on earth would you keep them as pets?"

"Relax, they've been … modified. Pinchers cut off and they can't spew anything. Brent took care of that. He's real good with that knife of his." Jason saw Brent smile back at his mother.

Apparently a molt weevil moved in too close to Billy, and he kicked at it with a solid blow to its mid-section. Squealing, it hopped backward. Jason saw black nubs emerge below its eyes where once pinchers, long and sharp enough to sever a man's leg—before Brent mutilated the molt weevil.

"Hey! No need for that!" Ellie yelled. "Dory won't hurt nobody! That was just mean." She looked up at Mamma, and said, "He's a mean man."

"Okay, this is beyond a fucking freak show," Bristol said, standing on the lip of the pit above them.

Ellie turned her attention up to Bristol. As quickly as though a switch were flipped, she smiled up at him. "You want to come down here and pet 'em?"

Bristol stared down at her with revulsion. "I think I'll pass … as tempting as your offer is."

"What's going on, Mamma?" Nan said. "What's this all about?"

"I wasn't expecting to see the technology you all possess,

but I needed to know if you were good people. Like I said before, we don't usually work with outsiders."

Jason asked, "A test?"

She nodded. "Thank you. The three of you didn't think twice about your own wellbeing. That says a lot about who you are." Her eyes left Jason's and came to rest on Pope and his men and finally on Bristol. Her expression turned to less than warm.

"I'll get a rope," Brent said.

"No need," Jason said. He took ahold of Ellie's small arm and phase-shifted them up with Billy and Rizzo following suit. They immediately reappeared several paces behind the onlookers above.

Ellie yelped and ran toward Mamma's side.

Startled, Brent said, "That's Caldurian shit, Mamma. Only military has that kind of tech."

"That true … Mr.? You military? Or associated with the government somehow?"

Nan interjected, "You won't tell anyone, will you, Mamma? Stolen battle-suits could get these boys five to ten in a U.S. fleet brig somewhere."

Mamma continued to study the three outsiders. She smiled, exposing several gaps teeth once filled. "Look at them, boy …" her eyes fell on Billy. "This one's some kind of Mexican, and that one over there looks like some kind of skinhead."

Jason unconsciously ran his hand over the stubble on the top of his head.

"No, those three ain't no military men. Maybe that one is … though," she said, pointing a finger in the direction of Colonel Pope, then gesturing with her chin toward his three men.

This time Jason spoke up first: "They're ex-military. Mercenaries … guns for hire. As you probably know, space mining is a contact sport. Turn your back and space pirates will slit your throat for a carton of coffee grounds." He continued,

"The Mau. Ever work with them before?"

Mamma shrugged. "No."

"Takes a while to get used to them. But they're honest … won't screw us if we don't screw them. Like the deal they're offering for the Tanzamine. They'll pretty much buy as much as we can deliver and that's good for all of us. Your operation's already up and running within that section of the Oort belt, and it just so happens there's a whole lot of Tanzamine right there. Ready to be mined. All we need to do is verify purity and quantities. Run a few tests."

"That's not a problem," Brent said. "What are those Mau willing to pay per standard gravity-free barge?"

"Not delivered?" Jason queried.

"I suppose. Yeah … not delivered."

"All depends on the purity of the mineral. But I would guess five million dollars per barge … payable in gold bullion."

Brent and his mother exchanged a quick look.

"Make it eight and we have a deal," Brent said.

"I'll make it six and we'll pay your delivery costs," Jason said. "And the Mau's paying our commission."

"That's a fair deal," Mamma said. She turned to Nan. "Tanya … that work for you?"

"Like my broker said, we need to verify the product as well as your operations. Make sure your outfit's up to the task. That's going to be a lot of Tanzamine."

"Oh we're up for the job, don't worry about that," Brent said.

"Excellent!" Jason said, holding out a hand for Mamma Picket to shake on. She stared at his outstretched hand for several beats before taking it in her own and shaking it.

Jason turned to Brent. "You'll be joining us, then? We're heading out there, directly."

"No," Mamma said. "I have another son … one you haven't met yet. Orloff. He's in charge of our mining operations there in the belt. Problem is, he's on vacation right now. Taking some personal time away from the mines."

Jason rubbed his chin, looking concerned. "The Mau … are looking at other suppliers in the area too. The timeframe was a primary concern for them. Maybe this won't work after all."

Mamma looked at Brent first then at her other two sons—Payne and Larry.

Payne said, "I'll take them. The *heavy* is again operational."

Both Jason and Nan looked toward the youngest brother. Payne must be referring to the Craing heavy cruiser situated up on the hillside. What they really wanted was a clue where Orloff could be found, bringing them one step closer to finding Ryan—if Orloff hadn't already killed him.

Jason said, "That sounds fine. But I'm sure your boys are as much an expert on the Tanzamine mining process as … I'm sorry, what's your other son's name again?"

"Orloff. No, Orloff is the one you probably should talk to," Mamma said, sounding frustrated. She exhaled and appeared to be pondering her options. "First things first, we'll need to find him. Whether he's here in the Smokey Mountains, or out in space, when he goes hunting … he's unreachable."

"Hunting?" Nan asked.

The three sons smiled. Brent said, "There's some good hunting up there. Orloff is just about the best tracker … hunter … anywhere. He lives for it."

"What in hell would he hunt for within our own solar system?" Billy asked.

Mamma's face became serious. "Whatever he wants … I suppose."

Brent said, "He checked in yesterday; I have those spatial coordinates. He went dark again after that."

Jason raised his brows. "We're not bad tracking people down ourselves. What do you say we go find your brother so we can all make a shitload of money."

CHAPTER 19

Ryan awoke inside the freight van's airlock. His head was pounding and he could smell vomit—undoubtedly his own. When he turned from his side to his back he felt the soupy mess flow down both sides of his face and collect at the back of his helmet. His visor was open and he didn't recall opening it. For that matter, he only partially remembered making it safely back inside the van. His last memory was of floating in space—resigned to dying. Running out of oxygen, he was on the verge of losing consciousness. Then, suddenly, an open hatchway appeared close by. At some point, he'd obviously made it to safety, somehow getting back inside. But that part he didn't remember.

"Rise and shine, Cupcake, there's things to do. That is, if you want to stay alive."

"Ugh. You saved my life."

"More than once, but we can celebrate my wonderfulness later on. Get up and head to the cockpit," Two-ton's AI voice commanded.

Slowly, Ryan began to stir and sit up, but his throbbing head—added to the rank smell within the confined space of the airlock—was too much for him. A series of dry heaves ensued that only relented after several breathless minutes.

"You should have let me die," Ryan said, meaning it.

"That just might happen, anyway. We're not out of trouble yet; not by a long shot."

Ryan remembered the Paotow Tanker and its crazy owner, Orloff Picket. He also recalled the merciless beating the bearded man underwent from the relentless jack-hammering of their gangway into him. "He lived through that?"

"Yes, although he's injured. Multiple fractures … his clavicle, two ribs, plus three fingers. He also suffered a concussion from two solid smacks to the head."

Ryan swayed as he rose to his feet and removed his helmet. Next off was his environ suit. He opened the inside airlock hatch and breathed deeply in the wonderful fresh air. "How do you know all that? His specific injuries?"

"Once he climbed back inside, he queried the SpaceNet. Searched various medical conditions for what he could do without a doctor's presence."

Ryan, stopping at the small sink in the kitchenette, leaned over and drank directly from the faucet. Upon straightening, he used his sleeve to wipe his mouth. "Again, how would you know all that?" Though Ryan, entering the cockpit, suspected he already knew the answer. The Paotow Tanker was still there—right alongside the freight van. "I'm betting we're close enough to pick up his SpaceNet link. Even with our van's Communications Transmission Beacon gone, at this close range I'm betting you're tapping in."

"That's right! You'd be surprised at what I picked up about Orloff Picket. Remember when I told you he was batshit crazy? Well, there's even more. I delved into his Space-Mail account. He's suspected of murdering three people over the past year. Perhaps his hunting hobby eclipsed his day job. And now that Orloff's been injured, be assured he'll chase you until one of you is dead."

"So why are we still sitting here? We need to go … while he's nursing his injuries."

"Can't."

Ryan moved to the side observation window and looked out along the starboard-side outer hull. "We're not clamped together like we were before," Ryan said.

"No, but the van's gangway at the stern is jammed into the tanker's port-side hatchway."

"Seriously?"

"I wouldn't joke about such a thing."

"Then how did Orloff get back into the ship?"

The AI said, "There's another hatch on the far side of the vessel. With his injuries, it took him forty minutes to access the other entrance."

"He must really hate me."

"Understatement."

Ryan asked, "Have you tried firing up the thrusters and yanking the van away?"

"No. Consignment Freight vans are flimsy, inexpensive craft. The probability of separation of the stern airlock cowling is far too great. The van would lose atmosphere and you'd most likely be killed, although I'd be fine."

"And if he engages those big rear thrusters? The same effect, right?"

"Undoubtedly. To be honest, I'm somewhat surprised he hasn't done that already."

Ryan made the determination—right then and there— to suit up in the van's remaining environ suit as soon as he had a moment to spare.

"Can the ramp assembly be uncoupled ... somehow? Preferably from inside the van?"

"I don't have any records indicating that that procedure has actually been attempted other than within a dry-dock situation," the Two-ton AI said.

* * *

The prospect of removing the gangway turned out to be a beast of a problem. The living compartment's stern area deck plating was removed first then stacked in the kitchenette. Lying on his stomach and holding an electric socket wrench, Ryan—hot and tired—lay below the living compartment's deck. He was covered from head to toe in grime and grease. Above and over the more than two hundred various sized-bolts holding the retractable unit in place would be a new, gaping, forty-two-inch-wide by thirteen-inch-tall opening at the stern—just below the rear airlock hatchway that would be left behind—resulting in the cabin losing pressure. No amount of Starlite goop was going to fix something like that.

"I'm down to the final four bolts, Two-ton. Did you come up with something to cover this opening?"

"Yes, well … sort of. You'll need to drill matching mounting holes and install a replacement sealant, like weather stripping."

"Uh huh … okay. And where do I get that?"

"Promise me you won't shoot the messenger?"

"Damn it, Two-ton … I'm way too tired to play games."

"Let me put it this way: it's actually a good thing the gangway is still attached."

* * *

Changed into his last environ suit and standing within the confines of the van's airlock, Ryan secured his washed-out helmet. The AI confirmed Orloff Picket was indeed fast asleep within his cabin, near the bow of the Paotow Tanker. Apparently, he'd taken enough painkillers to put even a Budweiser Clydesdale out for twenty-four hours. Two-ton had easily hacked the vessel's onboard AI, which provided them a complete listing of the tanker's inventory of spare parts.

The AI assured Ryan that the parts he needed were quickly accessible from the partially opened rear starboard hatch. And although too tight a fit for someone the size of Orloff, Ryan—far leaner and with a bit of maneuvering— would be able to squeeze into the tanker's airlock just fine. Once inside, it was simply a matter of hurrying into one of the stern holds.

"Two questions: First, if I'm going back over there anyway, why can't I also disengage the gangway from the tanker's hatch? Second, with the hatch jammed open like that, once I open the inside airlock, won't the tanker's atmosphere begin venting out to space. And won't that kill *sleeping beauty* snoring away in his cabin?"

The AI said, "You can attempt to disengage the gangway. Have at it, but from my analysis of the situation, it won't come away without hours of disassembly. Both stern hatchways access the same rear airlock. As far as showing concern for Orloff, remember he's tried to kill you several times now. Fuck him."

Ryan laughed out loud at the AI's frank disregard for the crazed lunatic's well being.

The AI continued, "He's up on the top deck where the bridge and living compartments are. Those compartments appear to be adequately sealed off from the rest of the ship by hatchways at the top forward and aft stairways. As long as they remain sealed, he'll keep breathing. With that said, he was forced to completely depressurize the ship because of the wedged-open airlock. His remaining supply of breathable oxygen reserves is approaching a dangerous level."

"So eventually he'll run out of air, right?" Ryan asked.

"Let's hope it's sooner rather than later."

Ryan, thinking about what the AI relayed, was still nervous. His earlier spacewalk hadn't gone well. "And you're certain I'll find what I'm looking for in that hold? That I'll be in and out ... fast?"

"Yup, like shit through a tin horn."

CHAPTER 20

Fortunately, both the freight van and the Paotow Tanker's running lights were on—offering adequate illumination of both ships. Ryan pulled himself along the extended gangway, vowing that this would be the last spacewalk he'd undertake for the rest of his life. Attaching the two safety lines as he had before—clipping on to anything that was sized appropriately—he proceeded toward the tanker.

"You'll tell me if he moves, right?" Ryan asked.

"Hey … if he farts in his sleep you'll be the first to know."

Ryan, on reaching the rear of the Paotow Tanker, assessed the gangway and the partially open hatch. The two vessels, not in alignment with each other, were canted at a ninety-degree angle, causing the now sideways ramp to extend into the top portion of the hatch. The hatch door opening was no more than fifteen inches wide. Ryan, studying the gap, thought, *I should be able to squeeze through there okay … maybe.*

He unclipped the end of his safety line from an outer flange on the gangway and was suddenly aware he was floating unsecured in space. Keeping a tight grip on the underside of the ramp, he pushed headfirst through the gap. Reaching in further, he found a section of the mangled gangway to grab on to and pulled himself inside. A snug fit—his chest and back rubbed against the partially open hatchway. Halfway in, with the exception of several blinking indicator lamps, Ryan had difficulty catching much detail within the tanker's dark airlock compartment.

"You'll need to turn on your helmet light, Ryan."

In the process of doing just that, he silently wondered how it had gotten turned off in the first place. He said in a whisper, "It's not working. It's not coming on." Perhaps he'd done too vigorous a job earlier, cleaning out the vomit from all the nooks and crannies inside his helmet. His decision to save the spare helmet for future use, he realized in retrospect, was stupid.

The tanker's gravity generators were operational and his body was pulled downward toward the deck. Once his legs and feet cleared the hatchway, he dropped into a kneeling position. As his eyes adjusted to the space, he realized that the faint glow emanating from the indicator lights did provide him sufficient illumination to see by. "I can sort of see ... I think it'll be okay."

"That's good, Ryan. I see that you are approximately midway into the airlock. You'll need to pivot around clockwise fifteen degrees."

Ryan did as instructed and squinted into the semi-darkness. "Okay ... I see the closed inside airlock hatch in front of me." Taking several tentative steps forward, he noticed a flashing red touchpad to the left of the hatch. Below it was a multi-digit keypad. Now, unquestionably the brightest illumination in the compartment was coming from a rapidly blinking message displayed over the hatchway:

WARNING — REAR AIRLOCK NOT SECURE!

"Will the inside hatch open?" Ryan asked. "Even the freight van has safety protocols that won't allow both hatches to remain open at the same time."

"Orloff would have dealt with the same problem," the

Two-ton AI said. "There's a touchpad override code … let's just hope it's still in place."

"I'm betting this will make a lot of noise," Ryan said, his hand poised before the large release pad.

"Undoubtedly so. You'll need to move fast. Once the latch releases, the hatch will raise upward into the bulkhead. You'll then be fighting the lower level expulsion of atmosphere, so hang tightly onto something. And it's not like Orloff can come running down the stairs. First off, he's injured. Second, he won't jeopardize losing any upper compartment oxygen."

Ryan pushed the square touchpad. Nothing happened. Just as he was about to complain to Two-ton, a shrieking alarm blared all around as the hatch began to rise. The strong burst of atmosphere that entered beneath the hatch knocked Ryan off his feet, forcing one hand to lose its grip on the strut. Only barely, with his arm extended, was he able to maintain a grasp with his other hand. Feeling his fingers ready to lose their grip on the vertical bulkhead strut he was clinging on to for dear life, he looked back at the narrow gap opening of the outer hatch. About to be sucked back toward it—so fast it would surely kill him—he forcibly used his arm and fingers to haul himself closer yet to the bulkhead strut. Mustering his last vestige of strength, he reached out with his free hand and managed to close his fingers around the same vertical strut. He held on tightly, eyes closed, and waited. A full minute passed before he felt the tension in his arms subside, his outstretched legs lower to the deck. Then only silence.

"You need to get moving."

* * *

Ryan stepped into the Paotow Tanker's primary compartment, the same one he'd peered into before when he was outside one of the tanker's forward portholes. From his present angle, he could see Orloff's workbench. Everything that was strewn atop it earlier was gone—now drifting out in space somewhere. High up on the right were the gruesome mounted heads. This time, Ryan managed to avoid looking over at Two-ton's, hanging some fifty to sixty feet away.

"As expected, Orloff is on the move up on the upper deck. Listen, on this level … on the starboard side of the ship … are a series of small compartments. Turn to your right and you'll notice an open passage."

Ryan, seeing it ahead, hurried in that direction. The passageway quickly forked into two directions. The passage on the left continued down the length of the ship, while the one on the right led to a closed hatchway.

"That hatchway leads to stairs, which go to the upper level and the bridge, so keep left and find the second hold compartment."

Ryan ran. It struck him as strange, seeing the regular, old-fashioned, hinge-type doors. He passed the first compartment and came to a halt outside the second. Turning the knob, he swung the door inward. Sure enough, it was a storage hold, equal in size to the one on the freight van. The shelved bulkheads were filled with containers of varying sizes.

"Okay … what am I looking for?"

"To your right. The bottom shelf has an assortment of outside hull patching materials. Orloff's records show there's a slew of loose panels—"

Ryan cut him off: "Okay, I see 'em." There were several stacks of both quarter-inch and half-inch-thick sheets of a composite material. "Huh … this guy is organized." Stacked in order of size—the largest sheets were arranged toward the bottom. Realizing this was taking too long, he quickened his efforts and found a rectangular sheet almost the perfect size to patch up the freight van's hole. "Will this one do?"

"Yes, now grab the box on your right that's on the middle shelf. Within it is a spool of insulating material and a full canister of Starlite. Hurry … get going!"

Since there were three boxes, all similarly sized, Ryan peered into them all in order to select the right one. Grabbing on to it with his free hand—the other holding the composite sheet—he stopped mid-step, feeling a series of vibrations come up through the deck.

"He's awake … isn't he?"

"Yes."

"I thought you were going to tell me if he moved."

"You needed to first find what you came for. I hadn't accounted for the aft stairway sealing off from the rest of the ship … for hatchways at both the bottom and top of the stairs. He can use that stairway as an inter-ship airlock. In retrospect … that makes sense. He's wearing an environ suit."

"Does he know I'm in here?"

"Considering he's headed for the starboard passage, I suspect so. One more thing, Ryan … he has a weapon."

"Crap, what kind?"

"A pistol … perhaps something like a like a Glock 17 semi-auto. On the positive side, he *is* badly injured."

Ryan looked about the hold for something he could use as a weapon. In the dim light, he spun full-circle, then quickly turned back. Looking for something long, like a broom handle to swing at him, he almost missed the gun rack, hanging on the bulkhead. There were three vertically mounted rifles. "You see what I'm seeing?" Ryan asked.

"Those weren't listed on the hold inventory," Two-ton's AI replied defensively.

The rifle on the left, the largest of the three weapons, was a Barrett .50 caliber—capable of hitting an extreme long-distance target. One of the most expensive sniper rifles available, it meant Orloff was indeed a serious hunter. In the middle hung what looked like a standard issue AR-15 assault rifle; on the right was an older model Tavor TAR-21—bullpup assault weapon … developed by the Israelis. Ryan was familiar with the small compact weapon from his stint in the Navy. Since he'd spent his years in the service sitting on his ass flying aircrafts, he only had a passing knowledge of guns. Even so, he knew he could hit whatever he aimed at with any of these weapons. Tavor would be the best choice for close-in combat. Fortunately, none of the weapons were locked down. Putting down the box and the sheet of composite, he lifted out the Tavor; releasing the clip into his palm he then checked the load. A full magazine. He replaced the clip and chambered in a round. Nothing he did made a sound—not with a present lack of atmosphere. He knew the way modern ammunition was manufactured—containing its own oxidizer, a chemical that triggered the explosion of gunpowder—that firing off a round, even in space where there was no oxygen, would still be just as lethal.

Ryan looked toward the partially open door. Orloff had probably figured he'd discover the weapons, and maybe that was for the best. Truth was, things didn't have to get too Western: *Just go back upstairs, nutball … and I'll be on my way.*

Ryan had left the passageway door partially open. Positioning the stock of the weapon tightly into his shoulder, he aimed forward, slightly increasing pressure on the trigger.

Ryan said, "Tell me when he's halfway down the passage."

"He's there now."

Ryan stepped into the passageway and leveled the muzzle of the weapon at Orloff's head, some ten feet away. A gesture that spoke *Hold it right there. Make a move and I'll put a hole between your eyes without giving it a second thought.*

The bearded man looked even more imposing than he remembered. Wearing a new environ suit in dark-gray, he stood favoring his one side—obviously in pain. Behind his helmet visor was an expressionless, badly battered, face. He looked as if he'd gone twelve rounds with Mike Tyson. Ryan, recalling the repetitive battering from the gangway, almost felt sorry for the man. *Almost.*

Orloff's eyes were on the gun. "Two-ton ... can you patch me in to his helmet comms?"

"Done."

Ryan gestured with his weapon and said, "Place the Glock down on the deck, then step backward. Do it now!"

Orloff said nothing. After several moments, he did step back—the gun still in his hand, though not aimed directly at Ryan. Keeping a safe distance apart, Ryan followed him all the way back to the still-open hatchway. Behind him, he saw the rising stairway, which led to the second level.

"Don't make me kill you. This is over. You understand me? I'm disabling your ship ... then I'll be on my way."

Orloff backed toward the stairwell and paused. He filled the space—his shoulders nearly touching both sides of the hatch threshold. For the first time he spoke—his voice was calm and contained the same lack of emotion as his expressionless face. "You should kill me now, delivery man."

"He's right about that," the AI said.

Ignoring Two-ton's voice, Ryan said, "Yeah, well ... I've had enough killing for one lifetime. Why not chalk this experience up to bad luck. What do you say we just forget about this ... crazy situation? Go close the hatch and get back up those stairs. But do know this ... the next time I see you, I will kill you, I can promise you that."

Orloff Picket's face instantly transformed into a menacing sneer. In that moment Ryan knew, beyond all doubt, he should empty the full magazine into the sick fuck. Then the hatch swung closed. As Ryan watched the latching mechanism engage he let out a long breath of relief.

Backing away, Ryan headed toward the hold, needing to grab the items he'd selected to patch up the freight van. He scanned the compartment until he found what he sought. Perhaps even older than him was an oversized, green and brown, camo backpack. Peering inside it, he found a small folded tent, along with aluminum support poles, rope, and ground stakes. Ryan spilled the contents onto the deck and replaced them with the patching sheet and sealing materials. Slinging the pack over one shoulder, and holding the Tavor in both hands, he moved back out into the passageway.

"Talk to me, Two-ton."

"He's back on the top level. And Ryan, there's something else. Remember when I said he was the only one on board?"

Ryan, waiting for the AI to continue, heard strange sounds of heavy breathing. Apparently, he was still connected to Orloff's helmet comms. "Wait … what is that?"

"You need to understand the freight van's sensors are crap … just the basic motion detection and infrared. So when I stated Orloff was the only one onboard, I meant no other warm-blooded beings were detectable. He has initialized two mechanical dog-sized bots. I recognize them as Tromian technology … used for security purposes. I assume Orloff has modified them to make them his personal hunting canines. They would work well in that capacity."

Through the open comms channel, Ryan heard the clattering of metal hitting metal. They were descending the aft stairway.

"Ryan, you need to get out of there …"

CHAPTER 21

Ryan, approaching the end of the passageway, kept his eyes on the still-secured hatchway. He knew that each time it opened precious, breathable air voided out to space. He only hoped Orloff was aware of that trade-off too whenever he opened it. After all, how important was revenge when your very life hung in the balance?

As he passed by it, the hatch opened up several inches. Inside, there was a blur of frenetic activity—something wanted out. Ryan ran faster, making it to the air lock before coming to an abrupt stop.

There were two of them. Somehow, one managed to race up ahead and now stood four feet from him, while the second one stood behind him, four feet back. What his eyes were seeing was beyond chilling. Ryan's mind instantly pictured an old-fashioned bear trap. Each design aspect of these knee-high bot-creatures supported their snapping, jagged, twelve-inch-wide jaws. He had little doubt that a single bite could take off an arm—perhaps even a leg.

Almost forgetting that he was armed, he fired the Tavor—distributing rounds between the two vicious-looking attackers. Momentarily stunned, they skittered backward. Within seconds, the Tavor's magazine was spent.

Apparently not damaged seriously, the bot-dog behind lunged, and Ryan reflexively moved his legs away, placing him closer to the forward bot. It too lunged. By some miracle when its jaws clamped shut, it merely clenched a mouthful of environ suit, not flesh and bone. Though Ryan used the weapon's stock to hammer the bot it didn't let go.

"You need to get out of there, Ryan."

The bot-dog's jaws remained mercilessly clamped on Ryan's environ suit, as the second bot circled him, angling for its own line of attack, cautiously leery of the Tavor's hammering blows. Adrenalin pumping, Ryan screamed, "Get off me!" as he swung his leg around, the bot-dog still attached, and smashed it hard into the bot circling him. His leg was suddenly free, though his environ suit showed puncture holes in multiple places. Warning alarms rang in his helmet as strobe messages flashed onto his HUD:

ENVIRON SUIT COMPROMISED!
OXYGEN LEVELS DEPLETING!

Ryan caught a break, noting that both dog-bots' jaws were enmeshed—as if one was attacking the other. In that moment as they viciously tried to free themselves, Ryan unhesitatingly dove into the airlock. Still in mid-air, he slapped the touchpad inside the bulkhead. Crashing onto the deck, he spun around, keeping his eyes locked on the two bots outside. As the airlock hatch slowly descended, Ryan noticed Orloff emerge from the stairway hatch. Behind his visor, Orloff's expressionless face stared back at him as he slowly raised the Glock gripped in his right hand. Instinctively, Ryan spun around. Bringing his legs in tight, his body formed into a ball.

Though the sounds were not heard in the vacuum of space, Ryan *felt* the fired rounds—like blows from a sledgehammer—strike his back, one after another. Hit five times before the hatch fully descended and provided a protective barrier, he slumped onto his side, waiting to die. Waiting for blood to drain from his body and all oxygen seep from his punctured environ suit.

"Are you going to just lie there?"

"I'm waiting for the end to come. The pain … how can anything hurt so much?'

"There's duct tape and Starlite in that box."

"Box?" Ryan repeated dully.

"The box, along with that sheet of composite material, which just saved your sorry ass. You know … in your backpack."

Ryan had forgotten all about the pack, still slung over his shoulder. The AI was right; the sheet of composite material tucked inside it most assuredly had saved his life. Yet, holy mother of God, he still felt like he was dying.

He lowered his shoulder, letting the strap droop low enough to pull his arm through. Every movement seemed to bring more agony than the one preceding it. Tugging the pack forward, he opened the top flap and peered within. The sheet of composite material was dimpled in multiple places and he knew his life had been spared thanks to that simple quarter-inch sheet. Reaching his hand inside, he opened the flap to the box and found the roll of duct tape and the canister of Starlite.

Ryan spent the next three minutes liberally coating the suit's punctured holes before wrapping his leg with duct tape. Another thirty seconds passed before the blaring alarm in his helmet ceased, and the HUD's flashing message disappeared.

He repacked the backpack then crawled toward the rear of the airlock and the open gap below the tangled end of the van's gangway. Ryan knew he needed to push the pack through separately, that it wouldn't fit kept on his back. He attached the safety line that still hung from his waist onto the pack's shoulder strap and pushed the pack through the gap. Then, head first, he angled his body through it. Outside, and halfway across, he had to stop—the pain in his back was too intense. He asked, "Two-ton, what is he doing? What's going on in the Paotow Tanker?"

"You need to keep moving. He's heading off, but I suspect he'll be back."

Ryan knew the AI's assumption was correct. He then remembered he'd left the Tavor behind. *Screw it … it was out of ammunition, anyway.* He reached outward with both arms until he found something solid to grasp on to.

* * *

Not until safely back in his own craft, with the airlock re-pressurizing, did Ryan realize something. When he was in the tanker, Orloff easily could have opened the hatchway from inside the main compartment. And he also probably had ten or more bullets available in the Glock's magazine. So why hadn't he? Did Orloff purposely let him escape? That didn't seem likely. Ryan had seen the look in his eyes—so cold and calculating. *No, this scenario was far from over.* Seeing again in his mind's eye the mounted upper bodies and heads, hanging high up on the bulkhead, Ryan knew Orloff Picket lived for one thing—the hunt.

Taking care not to further damage his semi-functioning environ suit, he carefully folded it then placed it, along with his helmet, inside a storage locker. Standing there, he got a good whiff of his body. *Ugh.* His clothes reeked—dried vomit, sweat, smeared grease and grime covered the entirety of his Consignment Freight jumpsuit. But there wasn't time to deal with that.

Moving like a 90-year-old man, Ryan dragged the backpack over to the same area he'd worked at before on the extended gangway. His plan was to finish separating the internal hydraulic mechanism from the extended ramp, which lay outside the craft. After he removed the last four bolts, the ramp outside the van should come away. He considered retrieving his patched environ suit and helmet for what was to come next but knew they'd likely become damaged when he was beneath the tight confines of the deck—among its sharp mechanisms. With that thought in mind, he first needed to vent the cabin's oxygen into the van's storage tanks.

A small oxygen-breather unit, stored in the medical supply cabinet, would suffice for the few minutes he needed to complete the job. But environ suits did more than sustain oxygen levels; they maintained constant temperature readings against the frigid outer space environment. It should only take a few minutes. Bundling up … he was sure he would manage okay.

* * *

With an oxygen mask secured over his nose and mouth, an elastic band around his head, the small—twelve-inch-long by two-and-a-half-inch-diameter—air tank hung down his face like some kind of alien proboscis. Earlier, while digging through his limited supply of clothes, Ryan found a Navy skullcap, sweater, windbreaker, blue jeans, and a pair of thin gloves. Pulling the jeans up over his jumpsuit pants, he added five pairs of socks atop the ones he wore. Next came the sweater and jacket. He then covered the thin gloves with six pairs of latex gloves he'd pulled from a dispenser inside the medical supply cabinet. He felt like the old Michelin Man.

"Two-ton … would it be possible to leave a tiny bit of air in here … enough to maintain some heat?"

"What you are planning to do is ridiculous. -454 degrees. That's how cold it is outside. You think the extra latex gloves will help? Really?"

Ryan said, "That's why you'll need to leave some atmosphere in the cabin. As long as the cabin is depressurizing the cold will stay outside … right?"

Not waiting for an answer, Ryan eased into the space

below the cabin deck and, finding his movements far more restricted with the added clothing on, wiggled his arms. His tools lay within easy reach, along with the patching kit of supplies pilfered from the tanker, and he felt as ready as he'd ever be.

"Two-ton ... start storing the cabin atmosphere in the reserve tanks. And crank up the heat as hot as you can make it."

"You need adequate atmosphere. Heating a near-vacuum space won't do much," the AI replied.

"And the upper levels are sealed?"

"Yes, Ryan ... for the fifth time."

Ryan waited until he heard then felt the cabin pressure change. He picked up his powered socket wrench and began loosening the first of four bolts. Seconds later it spun free as the nut securing it to the other side of the bulkhead floated away outside. The bolt held firm due to the difference of inside/outside pressure. He next went to work on the second bolt, choosing to loosen the one placed diagonally across from the first bolt. Again, it soon spun freely.

"Two down, two to go," Ryan said. Upon seeing his breath—it quickly had become very cold—he turned the valve, which produced a steady flow of oxygen into his mask. *Ah, that's better*, he thought.

Ryan, unaccustomed to the AI being quiet, went to work on the third bolt. As it loosened, the gangway mechanism shifted. What atmosphere still remained in the cabin was being sucked out through the edges of the mechanism plate. The socket wrench spun freely, indicating the third nut had fallen off too and was, like the others, drifting out in space.

The cold was way beyond what Ryan expected. He stared at the final bolt—the socket wrench poised above it. Things were about to get a whole lot colder. Placing the wrench over the bolt head, he triggered the power button. As it whirled, sounds emitted by its small motor could scarcely be heard. The bolt spun free.

Ryan wasn't looking forward to the next step. He needed to physically manhandle the hydraulic ramp mechanism toward the bow of the van. There was enough clearance so it should shift back several inches. By then he realized he could no longer feel his fingers. His cheeks too were numb. Even the moisture in his eyes was freezing. Quickly, without wasting another moment, he yanked back hard on the mechanism. Nothing. He adjusted his body, getting a better hold, and yanked again. This time it moved. The cold was beyond cold. He felt nothing at all—everything numb.

Now there was an open space that the ramp mechanism once filled. What had been a sandwiched layer of insulating material clung to the edges. Beyond, he could see the gangway, still attached to the tanker, slowly drift away from the van. Grabbing out with fingers that seemed to belong to someone else, he managed to lift the composite sheet up and position it over the opening. Earlier, he'd cut several lengths of duct tape that he now awkwardly spread over the panel's top edges, sides, and bottom—enough to keep the patch panel in place. Immediately, it was sucked in tighter—apparently there was sufficient internal atmosphere in the van to create a suction.

"Pressurize the cabin!" Ryan's words came out slurred and barely audible. Sound waves needed atmosphere—which, at present, there was little of.

The AI said something but Ryan couldn't make out the words. Some sense of feeling had returned to his fingers, face, and body. The cabin was warming. Along with it, came the perception he was on fire—as if every nerve ending was exposed. He screamed, and screamed, until his voice was a mere rasp.

The AI was still speaking. Though he now understood the words, he didn't want to listen.

Finally Ryan asked, "What do you mean it wasn't all that cold?"

"I did remember that you'd completed installation of the Aldo Pack fusion module. Thanks to me, it was already powered on. I adjusted the internal reactor settings. It was generating heat the entire time you worked. The temperature within your confined space never went below –150 degrees Fahrenheit. Chilly, yes, but survivable for a limited period of time."

"Whatever. I still need to screw this plate down tight then seal it with Starlite. Why don't you check on Orloff Picket for me—" but the AI cut him off mid-sentence: "Ryan … the Paotow Tanker is gone."

"Good riddance to the psycho. In which direction is he headed?"

"Nowhere at the moment. He's held up about two hundred miles away. Perhaps making repairs." Ryan felt his body deflate. As sophisticated as Two-ton had made the AI, some aspects of it seemed naïve. "Two-ton … he's waiting for me to make a run for it. This is only the beginning."

"Beginning?"

"Of the hunt."

CHAPTER 22

Together, they left Mystery Mine, riding the train back to the town's main street. They took the same seats from before. Mamma Picket was animated—obviously excited to commence their new business venture. She spoke nearly non-stop to them about her family's history—mostly about her daddy's early mining empire in the Smoky Mountains. An empire she wanted to emulate, even surpass, in outer space.

"You'll travel with my boys. Y'all go together," Mamma Picket announced.

"Actually, as you've witnessed, we have our own vessel," Nan said. "Perhaps we can follow—"

Mamma's irritation flared, "No! I don't know you. Not well enough, anyway." Turning her gaze toward Brent, she asked, "You got that thing working yet?"

"The *heavy*?" Brent asked.

"Of course the *heavy*! What else do you think I'm talking about? Are you dim-witted? I want you to take these fine folks to space to meet Orloff. Introduce them to him proper-like. You know how he can be with strangers, so make sure he don't get all riled up."

"I can do that," Brent said.

"We're not leaving our shuttle down here. So I hope you don't mind if we stow it aboard your ship?" Jason asked. "If I remember right, those Craing cruisers have plenty of space within their flight bays."

"You familiar with them, are you?" Brent asked, his interest piqued.

"Very. We all are." Jason didn't elaborate, sensing he probably said too much already. He was supposed to be a mining broker, not a U.S. Fleet Officer.

Bristol asked, "What's wrong with it? I've worked on Craing drives a few times."

Brent, after exchanging a look with his brothers, scowled, "How the fuck should I know; do I look like a mechanic? You can ask Jeebrie when we get on board."

"Who's Jeebrie?" Bristol asked.

"He's one of the Craing bastards still on board. We don't let him off the ship, or even out of Engineering. Without him on board, we'd be up the creek without a paddle."

* * *

The cruiser lifted off—barely—heading into space. Nan didn't like being on the Craing vessel. More than once, she'd been imprisoned by the Craing, held in one of the hundreds of jail-like confinement cages that were situated adjacent to the vessel's Grand Sacellum. Once used by the Craing as a shrine or sanctuary, similar in structure to a large church back on Earth, it was the Craing's main feeding area where they first roasted, then consumed, their prisoners. The Craing required fresh meat—preferably flesh off those most recently conquered.

An hour had passed since Sergeant Major Stone piloted the *Goliath* into the flight bay of the old Craing cruiser. Stone was again instructed to remain with the shuttle, but this time Rizzo cheerfully stayed on board with her. Beyond any doubt, they'd find *something* to do to pass the time.

Nan and Colonel Pope walked ahead, as Jason, Billy and Bristol followed. On Mamma Picket's side, the three brothers, Brent, Larry and Payne stayed close by.

From what Nan now understood, only a small portion of the huge ship was utilized. She figured nothing came cheap when operating a heavy battle cruiser, whose size and dimensions equaled several football fields. As a whole group, they walked through a maze of corridors and narrow passageways on one of the upper decks. An acrid tinge bit the air—reminiscent of old burnt flesh. Nan glanced at the shortened hatchways and dreary bulkheads as they passed by them—each was coated in a greasy film.

Brent said, "Up ahead are the officers' quarters. The best accommodations this old ship has to offer. It could take us a day or two more to reach the spatial coordinates. All depends on Jeebrie." He slowed down his pace then gestured toward a line of twenty or so hatchways. Each was equipped with a mechanical, lever-opening mechanism. "These three are ours … the others are available."

"This ship really is old," Bristol said, his expression looking like he'd just walked through a stale fart.

"Take an hour or two and get situated," Brent said.

"Sounds fine," Jason said, heading toward the nearest hatch. "Where do you want us to meet up?"

"You know where the church is?"

"The Grand Sacellum?" Nan asked.

The three brothers eyed her suspiciously. Brent said, "Yeah … that's the place; meet in two hours. We'll conjure up some grub. Our Craing chef is one hell of a cook, specially anything Bar-B-Qued." All three Pickets chuckled at that as, one by one, they disappeared into their respective compartments.

Nan watched others choose compartments. She suspected Jason thought she and Pope were close—an *item*—but that wasn't true. Sure, Pope had made personal advances to her over the years, but they were only friends. She didn't mix business with pleasure. Anyway, Pope wasn't her type.

Other than Nan, Pope was the last one standing in the passageway. "For appearances ... we should stay together," he suggested.

"That's fine," Nan said, "just don't get *handsy*. Ex-madam presidents still hold enough clout to have people shot."

Pope nodded, like he'd heard the same line from her before. Holding a hatch open, he said, "Your quarters, Madam President."

* * *

Jason took the old military adage—*sleep whenever the opportunity rises*—to heart, and grabbed an hour-and-a-half shut-eye. He awoke in the semi-darkness and made his way into the adjoining head. Undressing, he stepped into the cramped shower stall. Several minutes passed as he figured out the hot/cold water controls. Since the fixed shower-head was positioned low, the spray hit his body at navel-level. He crouched down and let the warm water flow over his head and shoulders. Thinking about Nan next door, he envisioned her also jockeying around under the shower-head's low placement. *Perhaps Pope'd help her with that?* Thinking it, he wasn't pleased with himself: *I'm a happily married man— married to an amazing gal ... what the hell's my problem?*

When he stepped out from the stall he realized no towel was handy. He flapped his arms and legs to air-dry before dressing. As he exited the compartment, he tried to recall which unit Billy and Bristol went into earlier. He opened a NanoCom channel and hailed them both.

Billy answered the hail first. "Almost ready, Cap."

Bristol said, "It's not two hours yet."

"Just get your butts out here," Jason told them.

Billy opened the hatch door directly across from Jason's own, his hair still wet. He too had taken a quick shower. Another two minutes passed before Bristol appeared, looking groggy, with bed hair.

"Where we going?" Bristol asked, yawning.

"Figured we'd take a look at Engineering. Offer our assistance to this Jeebrie character. Perhaps we can keep this old crate from breaking down in deep space. I've been thinking about Nan's nephew. If he is being pursued by this Orloff character, then every minute we waste could cost him his life."

* * *

Ten minutes later, they stood outside the heavy cruiser's Engineering section.

"There usually is an open corridor here," Bristol said, nodding in the direction of a doublewide hatch.

"I guess Brent wasn't kidding. They really do keep Craing crewmembers imprisoned," Jason said.

Billy said, "I don't much like those back-wood country cousins. Don't like the way they look at me. Like I'm not fit to be in their presence."

"Who cares?" Bristol, after shrugging, said, "These yokels wipe their asses with corncobs." He took a closer look at the hatch-locking mechanism. It appeared similar to those on their sleeping compartments. Lifting up a large metal rail then flipping it over, Bristol pulled on the hatch. When it swung open, he entered first, with Billy and Jason right behind.

Bristol said, "By far, this is the oldest Craing ship I've ever seen. What a rattletrap."

A voice asked, "Who ... who is there?"

Jason spun, finding a small Craing standing up on a catwalk, some fifteen feet above them to their right.

"Cap ... you seeing what I'm seeing?" Billy asked.

"I think so. Uncanny … huh? Um … my name is Jason. This is Billy and that's Bristol."

"I am Jeebrie. What are you doing in here? Master does not permit visitors. We could get in trouble …" The small Craing rubbed the side of his face. Even in the compartment's dim light, Jason noted the discolored areas on his flesh. Bruises.

Bristol said, "Don't take shit from them. You do know the war's over … right?"

The small Craing looked at Bristol with a mixture of mistrust and surprise.

"The war … it is over?"

"For six years now. Humans and Craing no longer kill each other. There's no reason for you to still be a prisoner on this ship."

"But … what am I to do? I am not a violent person. None of us on this ship are."

"How many of you Craing are there?" Billy asked.

"Eleven," Jeebrie said.

"Listen to me. When this is over, after we do what were here to accomplish, you'll be freed. I can promise you that. And then we'll get you home."

"Home?"

"Yeah … wherever that is. But for now, we need the Pickets' help in finding someone. Do you understand?"

"I think so."

Jason watched as the Craing, the spitting image of another small Craing named Ricket, moved across the catwalk and descended a metal stairway. Expecting him to head in their direction, he instead hurried toward the opposite side of the compartment. After first stealing a glance in their direction, he slammed his hand down on the console. A klaxon alarm shrieked all around them.

Billy yelled above the noise, "I can't believe the little shit …"

"He's scared. I guess the beast he knows is better than the beast he doesn't."

The hatchway into Engineering opened and three armed Pickets piled inside.

CHAPTER 23

Showered, wearing a clean pair of jeans and a plain white T-shirt, Ryan sat, bare feet propped up on the console, staring out the cockpit's forward observation window. Although it was too far away to see with the naked eye, he nevertheless stared in the general direction of the Paotow Tanker just the same.

It occurred to him that he'd forgotten, upon escaping, to disable Orloff's ship. Still, several decent excuses allowed for the memory lapse, like two snapping bear-trap robots shot at repeatedly, and a growing fear he too would end up mounted on Orloff's trophy wall. The simple fact he was alive and kicking gave him some solace.

On some level, Ryan was beginning to understand his adversary. Maybe *understand* wasn't the proper word choice. A better one, perhaps, was *fathom*. Ryan could fathom what the lunatic wanted. He liked to hunt—that was obvious—and he wanted Ryan's head. But more than merely that, he wanted the prey he sought to be worthy of the effort. Ryan had proved he was by the simple fact he was still breathing.

"There has to be a way to take the offensive here."

The AI, silent, didn't respond.

"We know what Orloff will claim if he's successful, but

the fight shouldn't be a one-way street."

"Come again?" Two-ton's AI asked.

"Think about it. It should be more than I get to live if he's unsuccessful. There should be repercussions on both sides. What price does he pay if he loses?"

"I don't think Orloff Picket gives a rat's ass about fairness."

"I'm not so sure. There has to be a way I can communicate with him."

"Now I know you've lost your mind," the Two-ton AI said.

Ryan brought his attention to the AI-Pac that was installed into the rack behind him. It was as near as he could get to actually studying the AI. "Tell me how to communicate with him. Show me how smart you are."

Ryan waited expectantly in the prolonged silence. "You know already ... don't you?" he finally asked.

"Yes."

"Are you going to tell me?"

"I'd rather not."

"Tell me anyway."

"You can send him a message."

Ryan rolled his eyes. "We already know the van's comms are down."

The AI said, "No, I mean *physically* send him a message."

"I don't think the pony express operates this far out in space," Ryan replied sarcastically.

"The thing about space is, once you set something in motion ... like an object heading in a certain direction ... it pretty much stays on course indefinitely, or until the object intersects with another object of sufficient mass. Then, it either stops or its trajectory is altered."

"I'm not going on another spacewalk," Ryan said.

"I know that."

"So how ..." Ryan stopped mid-sentence. He suddenly did know exactly how to do it. "The delivery interface."

"Bingo."

The delivery interface, or *DI*, was how Consignment Freight containers were received into the van's hold. Integrated into the very top of the van—similar to a small airlock with a built-in conveyor assembly—it allowed for the transfer of five specific container sizes: one small enough to fit into the palm of a hand, to the largest, about four feet wide by five feet long. Those objects of non-conforming measurements were not accepted, either into, or out of, the DI.

"I don't know," Ryan said. "I've never seen a DI operate anywhere accept at a CF depot."

"I can modify it with a few software hacks," the AI said.

* * *

Over the next thirty minutes, Ryan contemplated on what he wanted his delivered message to say. He needed to use the largest container to ensure it would be spotted in space—the container sized four feet by five feet. Looking around, he found one such container inside the hold bound for delivery to the glacially frigid Erass5B. It didn't look like he'd be making a trip to the god-awful planet any time soon, anyway.

Consignment Freight containers were far more complex than simple shipping boxes. Each one was microprocessor-controlled for specific, pressurized, internal environments; environments aligned to the intended planetary destination. One wouldn't want to experience the opening up of an Earth environment container on Cornica PL5. The pressure differential—as well as a full host of other environmental differences—could prove catastrophic. But since these *smart* containers are cognizant, always, of their outer environments—locking mechanisms made an accident practically non-existent. Ryan first thought about using one of the containers as a mail-bomb—one that went off as soon as

Orloff opened it—but its integrated safety presets rendered that idea nearly impossible, according to the AI.

"Can't get the thing open," Ryan said, frustrated with the large container now sitting in the middle of the hold area. "What does the paperwork state is in there?"

"It's marked *Confidential*—the contents are password protected. I should also mention the container is insured for two point five million dollars."

"So ... you can't determine—?"

"*Pshaw,* of course I can! It's a micro-replicator ... and a pretty good one, too."

"Well, open up the container. We're burning daylight."

"The only way to do that is to duplicate the same environment on Erass5B here within the hold."

"Can you do that without damaging our own atmosphere?"

"Our?"

"Fine. My ... atmosphere."

"I believe so but you'll need to go below. I'll seal the hold off ... bring down the temperature and alter the pressurization ... then make a few other minor alterations. That should be enough."

"Won't I need to be in here to open it?" Ryan asked.

"Nope, it can be opened via a wireless signal from me."

* * *

Altering the environment within the hold would take ten or so minutes, according to the AI. In the meantime, Ryan headed to the shuttle's living quarters and went to work on composing a special message to Orloff. He needed to keep it simple. Simple was better. He found a Sharpie and a pad of paper. It took six drafts before he felt satisfied with what he'd come up with:

Dear Orloff:

This has been tons of fun, don't you think? Hey, I have a riddle for you —

Q: What does a hillbilly do when his dishwasher stops working?

A: He slaps her on the ass and tells her to get back to work.

Funny, huh? Anyway, I'd like to take this — whatever it is we're doing ... to the next level. You are a hunter. A damn good one, if that trophy wall of yours is any indication. You want to see my head mounted up there with the others. I get that. That will happen, probably, if you are successful. But what if you're not? Are you also willing to pay the ultimate price? Personally, I don't take any stock in the stereotype that mountain folk have no honor; that they're cowards. I don't believe that — not for a second.

If you agree to a few sensible guidelines, we can take this competition to the next level. Here's what I have in mind:

The winner takes all.

This is only between you and me. No others involved.

We both should be equally armed (send back that Tavor TAR-21 — a real nice weapon. And as many full magazines as you have laying around.)

There is a timeframe of — let's say — three days, starting right now, as you read this letter. But here's the thing — If we can't finish by then, neither of us being dead, it proves neither one of us is a competent hunter and we walk away — no hard feelings.

That's it for now. Send back your reply, and of course the Tavor and mags.

Yours truly,

Ryan

CHAPTER 24

By the time Ryan reentered the hold, both temperature and pressurization had returned to normal. As promised, the large CF container was registering unlocked across a series of green LEDs, on the top band of indicators and its integrated message screen. He noticed the box's lid was now askew on one side.

Carefully laying the paper's composed, handwritten message on the deck, he went to work removing the contents of the replicator unit. Once emptied, he placed the single-sheet note inside it.

"So … irritating that crazed psychopath, that's your great idea?" the AI asked.

"Among other things. Yup." Ryan closed the CF lid and waited for the telltale *click* to indicate it was sealed. "We'll need specific spatial coordinates. Can you derive them from the tanker's position?"

"Yes."

"Go ahead then, and adjust the hold's gravity level to loading, unloading, parameters."

All Consignment Freight Vans' upper hold areas maintained their own gravity generators. That way, when a van's driver was instructed to either bring in, or push out, a container through the DI, he didn't break his back in the process. Within seconds, Ryan felt nearly weightless within the compartment hold. Studying the topside of the container, he found the AI had input the intended spatial coordinates. As with any mailing address, it was displayed on a small message screen. The RETURN coordinates read: From Your Buddy Ryan.

"I like it! Good to see you're getting into the spirit of things." Ryan, lifting up the near-weightless container, held it in his hands. "You've oriented the van? We only get one shot at this."

"From the centerline of the DI, the van's spatial X, Y, and Z planes are perfectly aligned with the intended azimuth— the direction of the target. What cannot be factored in are the inconsistencies generated by the DI mechanism itself. The thing is old and worn; parts are showing fatigue. In other words, it is not a fine-tuned, projectile shooting apparatus."

"Thank you, Professor, I understand. Just do the best you can. You ready?"

"Ready as I'll ever be," the AI replied, its voice expressing little enthusiasm.

As he'd done thousands of times before, loading or un-loading freight in and out of the van, Ryan positioned the container. He sent it upward, toward the DI at the top of the hold. Internal sensors, triggering a series of articulating arms, seemed to appear out of nowhere. As the container approached, its sides were grabbed. Then, quickly and effi-ciently, the box was fed, like a hungry robot, into the DI's mechanically re-sizing orifice. Within a split second, it was gone.

"Message sent," the Two-ton AI said.

Ryan smiled. Hurrying from the hold, he fled down the small flight of stairs and into the cockpit. The AI had the console display pre-configured to track the container. Across it, he could see the Consignment Freight Van icon, the Paotow tanker icon, and the slow, but steady, moving CF container icon.

"Looks to be heading in the right direction," Ryan said, taking a seat.

"You're having way too much fun with this," the AI responded.

Ryan shrugged as he watched. He looked up from the display and out into space. He gestured toward the display. "What is that?"

The AI said, "Small craft ... approximately the size of a Consignment Freight Van. It's about four thousand miles away."

"I wish there was a way to flag it down."

"It's heading in this general direction," the Two-ton AI said.

CHAPTER 25

The three Picket brothers stormed into Engineering. Looking angry, they raised their weapons.

Jason, palms raised up in mock surrender, said, "Sorry for all the commotion, guys. I think we scared your Engineer. Our mistake."

Brent glared at Jeebrie, who physically withdrew into himself, his eyes darting back and forth. Staring at Jason, Brent asked, "What are you doing in here?"

"As I mentioned to you before, Bristol is a wizard with propulsion systems of all kinds. Honestly ... it was a good-will gesture."

"You scared him. He doesn't like strangers."

Bristol said, "Or beatings either, evidently."

"You ... mind your own business!" Brent, then turning to Jeebrie, ordered, "Turn that klaxon off before we all go deaf!"

Jeebrie scurried off. A moment later, the voluminous compartment became quiet.

Jason said, "Look, we witnessed firsthand how the ship was laboring just trying to climb above Earth's atmosphere. But if you don't need or want our help, it's no skin off our backs."

Without being obvious about it, he opened up a channel

so Nan could hear what he was saying to the others.

"Again, I apologize for any misunderstanding here. We'll leave—return to our quarters … no harm done."

Nan, in his comms, said, "Jason, what the hell is going on? If you're doing anything that stands in the way of finding my nephew … I'll …"

Jason, interrupting her tirade, said, "Let's go, Billy … Bristol …"

"Wait!" Brent said. "What do you need … to … you know … get this heap fully operational again?"

Bristol said, "A miracle."

Jason gave him a sideways glance.

"If you let me take a look, I'll tell you," Bristol said, speaking more to Jeebrie than to Brent.

All eyes went to the small Craing, who looked uncomfortable from the added attention on him. He nodded. "I … I could use the help."

* * *

Brent ordered his brother Larry to stay and keep an eye on them. Within fifteen minutes he—sound asleep in the corner, his weapon across his legs—was noisily snoring, his jaw slackly open and head tilted back.

Speaking in lowered tones, Jason and Billy talked amongst themselves, while Bristol worked two catwalk levels above. Jason supposed Jeebrie was up there with him, but he wasn't entirely sure.

"You're still here?"

Jason and Billy turned, seeing Nan enter the compartment. She looked cold, her arms wrapped snugly about her.

"Sorry about all the commotion," Jason said.

"No, I'm sorry for yelling at you."

Offering a reassuring smile, he said, "I think Bristol will be able to help. He thinks once the propulsion system's been properly tuned up, we can cut travel time in half—maybe more."

"This is all so frustrating," Nan said. "We could phase-shift … be where we need to be in minutes."

Billy said, "Yeah, but they're already suspicious of us. They hate the government and the military. We do anything that even hints we're more than who we say we are, they'll clam up, and we won't get their crazy brother's last known coordinates."

"I know all that, Billy," Nan said irritably.

Footsteps clanged loudly on the metal catwalk above. When Bristol, with Jeebrie close behind, emerged down nearby stairs, he threw Jason a *thumbs-up* gesture.

"Go ahead and try it, Jeebrie," Bristol said over his shoulder, approaching Jason and the others. The Craing prisoner scurried from sight.

"Everything is out of alignment. Probably been years since anyone who knew what they were doing gave those drives any attention."

Nan said, "Thank you for doing that, Bristol."

"No big deal."

Jason raised two fingers to his ear. "Hold on … I'm being hailed." He took several steps away from the others, and said, "Go for Captain."

Orion said, "Cap … I have an update for you."

Jason pictured the *Jumelle*, following behind them at a safe distance, as they slowly made their way across the solar system. "What cha got, Gunny?"

"According to an emergency Consigned Freight call … another delivery craft's gone missing. The pilot was delivering a package to the outer fringe of the solar system. She's late calling in her status … Comms are non-responsive."

"She?"

"Yeah. The delivery pilot is a … Wendy Prescott. She's just a kid … like Ryan. Both twenty-three."

"You think it's related … Ryan and her going missing?"

Nan, at Jason's side, her brows furrowed, mouthed the words, *what's happening, Jason!*

"Here's the thing, Cap: Apparently Ryan and this Wendy girl are … or were … dating. They were an item. Seems an awfully big coincidence to me that she, too, is reported missing."

"Where was her intended delivery, in respect to Ryan's last known whereabouts?"

"Actually there's three Consignment Freight craft missing now: Ryan's, a Donald Koffman's, and this Wendy girl's. And yes, the other missing craft were within a relatively close proximity to Wendy's delivery coordinates. Long range scans of the area show nothing … they've gone … but it's a starting point."

"Good work, Gunny … Hang tight. I'll get back to you in a minute."

Jason turned to Nan. "I think we've caught a break, though maybe that's not the best way to phrase it. Another delivery driver's van has gone missing … two of them, actually."

"You know where that one occurred?" she asked.

"We do, which means there's no longer a good reason to stay here."

Jason looked up in time to see the sleeping Picket Larry was now awake and getting to his feet. Brent was back and verbally tearing them both a new ass hole. Looking concerned, he headed toward Jason and Billy.

"We have definitive coordinates of my brother's last-known location."

Jason was about to tell him that they no longer needed his help—to make an excuse to phase-shift off the Craing vessel, when Brent added something else.

"Orloff's comms are down … he's gone dark again. But based on his last location, I have a good idea where he may be headed. He has a place ... more like a hunting shack ... on a dwarf planet hidden within the Oort Cloud. It's relatively close to where those coordinates are."

CHAPTER 26

Present time …

Orloff Picket presented a good case for himself. Why he'd required Consignment Freight personnel to space-walk over—hand-deliver the package of needed prescription medications directly to him in his vessel. Typically, deep space deliveries—although rare—were managed via the van's delivery interface mechanism. CF drivers were never to leave the safety of their van while delivering. But Orloff, who'd strongly reiterated the fact he was handicapped, made a compelling argument that such CF regulations discrimi-nated against those less fortunate.

Orloff waited within the darkened confines of the Paotow Tanker's airlock. The big drawback to abductions such as this, held in the vacuum of space, was he couldn't hear the screams. So watching unbridled terror reflect on her face would have to suffice.

An hour earlier, before the delivery van pulled up along-side his tanker, there was another delivery, of sorts—a CF container from Ryan. Orloff had to spacewalk to retrieve it. In his current condition of broken ribs and fingers, the spacewalk venture forced him to endure substantial pain.

Perhaps Ryan Chase would be a worthwhile adversary after all. He'd already proven he was highly imaginative.

Orloff sat up and stretched his back. He'd been hunched over his workbench two hours straight; so completely engrossed in his work, he'd lost all track of time. But this was what life was all about. Vacation was almost over and getting in these special moments made the long months of waiting worthwhile. He had big responsibilities. He represented the Picket name ... the Picket brand ... in outer space, and was well suited for the job too. He didn't mind extended periods of isolation; or occasions when he had to use intimidation on those who worked either for, or with, the company—be it mining supervisors, union bosses, or late-paying clients. His size, stature, was only one aspect of his scary demeanor. He knew what people said about him behind his back—that he was deranged ... a psycho. There was a rumor bouncing around the Oort Cloud that he'd once crushed a man's skull with his bare hand. It wasn't true. He used both hands.

Orloff dipped his fingers in a nearby bowl of filtered water, then rubbed them together until the viscous matter came loose and swirled away. Wiping his moist hands on a clean towel, he readjusted the swivel light, and leaned back over the workbench. An open book lay across the workspace, on the left side of the subject. He'd spent over five thousand dollars for the rare, leather-bound codex—written by the renowned Nazi professor, Dr. Josef Clauberg. Only a few such publications remained in existence. Not only a thorough lexicon on taxidermy in general, it was dedicated to the unique intricacies of preserving and properly displaying the human body.

This trophy would be Orloff's finest to date. The delicacy of his threadwork was beyond anything he accomplished before. On the worktable before him was a complete upper torso-head mounting. Bare breasts—small and firm, the nipples pink and erect—still looked full of life. But it would be the young woman's face—her refined features—that would first grab the casual observer's attention. Orloff picked up a small hairbrush and began to stroke the long hair back and away from the slightly upturned face. Orloff smiled. What exactly was that in her expression? Petulance? *Yes—like a petulant child.*

For his entire adult life, Orloff kept similar works of art to himself. It was nobody's business what he did with his time. But he would make an exception *with her*. It seemed only fitting for Ryan to see this trophy, too … he would appreciate its accomplishment. Orloff began to whistle to himself. Still much to do: ears to attach, then the crystal glass orb eyes needed inserting. *Yes … much to do.*

* * *

Two hundred miles away, Ryan, overcoming physical and mental exhaustion, awoke. Intending to take a half-hour or so nap, he sat up in his rumpled bed with a start.

"What time is it? How long …"

"You've been asleep for twelve hours and thirty-two minutes. I tried to wake you four separate times."

"Well, you should have tried harder!" Ryan, swinging his legs over the side of the bed, rubbed his face, trying to clear the fog out of his head. Once on his feet, he staggered into the small head. In the process of relieving himself, he remembered the other small spacecraft.

"Hey … what happened with that other craft?"

"Now you ask … the other craft is a Consignment Freight delivery van, Ryan. I'm really sorry. It's been positioned alongside the Paotow Tanker for over nine hours and why I kept trying to roust your ass out of bed."

Ryan burst from the head, still zipping up. "No … no … no …. are you shitting me? Damn it, Two-ton!" He ran through the living compartment, up the stairs, then into the cockpit. Leaning in close to the display, he saw both the Paotow Tanker, and the freight van's icons, virtually sitting on top of each other. When sudden realization set in, he covered his mouth with an open palm. *Oh God no ... please no.*

"Can you determine the DSCVID from this distance? Without having a Communications Transmission Beacon?"

"I have the DSCVID ... you're not going to like ..."

"Well, what the hell is it!" Ryan asked, spinning around to face the AI-Pac.

"429. It is Consignment Freight Van number 429. Ryan ... I am so sorry."

Disbelief turned to panic. "Wendy ... that's Wendy's van! The son of a bitch, he's lured her there. Oh my God ... he's got her."

"Yes, he undoubtedly has." The AI's voice, only slightly above a whisper, said, "Ryan, there is something else."

"What?"

"The CF container you sent over to that tanker earlier, well, it's on its way back."

In that fateful moment, Ryan felt he was looking through someone else's eyes—living someone else's life. Tears, brimming in his eyes, overflowed and streamed down his cheeks. Sitting down, he stared at the console display and watched the newly added tiny icon move steadily across the screen.

"I need to suit up ... to retrieve—"

"No, Ryan, I can maneuver the van into place with thruster micro-bursts. I'll use the van's DI to grab the container."

* * *

Ryan stood within the hold compartment, staring up at the Delivery Interface, the DI. He swayed on his feet, feeling nauseous. He had no idea what he would find inside the box container and didn't want to know. Only one thing made his life worthwhile—Wendy. He never told her how he truly felt; perhaps fearing she didn't feel the same way. When they broke up—*again*—it wasn't because they weren't crazy about each other. On the contrary, it was the complete opposite. Their passion was beyond anything he'd ever encountered, but they both were guarded. Jealousy and game playing became the new norm, Ryan wondering if perhaps there was someone else. Maybe, *God forbid*, Tony Post? *Damn!* Why hadn't he told her how he really felt? How he wanted to move in with her? Now it was too late.

"Okay … here it comes, Ryan," the AI said.

The DI's articulating arms began to swing around—positioning and re-positioning. And then there it was. As the bottom of the container popped into view, it lowered out of the DI like some alien birthing. The articulating arms handed down the large container to Ryan, who grabbed the box in both hands. More weight to it—something clunking around inside—he set it down on the deck.

Kneeling next to the container, Ryan made no move to open it. He heard the telltale mechanism click and saw one flap partially pop open.

"The container is open, Ryan."

"I know that!"

He took a deep breath and opened the two top flaps. Looking inside, and to his utter surprise, the first thing he noticed was the Tavor and three mags, lying at the bottom of the container. He retrieved them and placed them on the deck. What remained inside was a note, written on yellow-ruled pad paper. Noting there was a second sheet stapled to it, he disregarded the hand-written note and flipped the page over. In horror, he stared at a printed out, full-color photograph. Immediately, his stomach twisting and churning, he threw up into the empty container box.

For several long minutes a series of dry heaves racked his body. The image of what he'd seen stayed present through closed eyes. It was the most disturbing, most grotesque, thing he'd ever seen. The beautiful woman was mounted, just like Two-ton, onto a wall plaque. He felt guilt seeing her face—because he was thankful—grateful, that the now stuffed and mounted woman was Olivia Baldacci—Wendy's partner. Consignment Freight almost never dispatched freight vans with a lone driver, especially if two women were consigned.

So where then was Wendy?

CHAPTER 27

Ryan read Orloff Picket's handwritten note three times.

Dear Ryan,

Q: What do you get when you have 32 hillbillies in the same room?

A: A full set of teeth ...

Do you like that one? Thank you for your letter. It's good to keep a sense of humor. The Tavor is my gift to you, Ryan. Over the days that follow, that weapon may very well mean the difference between life and death ... yours.

By now, I'm assuming you have adequately re-covered from what must have been a shock. Seeing Olivia that way would be jarring. But I'm hoping you can appreciate the care I've taken to preserve her likeness — what was, and still is, a beautiful wom-an. I do not take lives indiscriminately — I am not a barbarian. With that said, I am not delusional, either. What I am is a diagnosed psychopath ... although that is not the politically correct terminology these days. Yes, I admit it. I am a killer. Here's the thing. I allow myself these indiscretions just once a year, for a two-week period. I live for these fourteen days of vacation, Ryan. I hunt, I kill, and I practice my skills with needle and thread. Up until now, this has been my little secret.

Other than myself, you are the only one still alive to have observed my trophy room. I cannot allow this knowledge to be passed on.

So let me tell you what will happen next — that is, if you want to see Wendy alive again.

You will hasten to the spatial coordinates provided at the end of this note.

I already know your delivery van's comms are down — keep it that way. You bring in anyone else — tell anyone else — and Wendy will be keeping Olivia company on my trophy wall.

Sleep, eat — do everything you can to prepare for what is to come. You will be hunted — you will be my prey, Ryan. If you want to rescue Wendy, if you want to keep both her and yourself breathing — you will need to find a way to outsmart me — you will need to kill me. See you on Alaster-Rei.

Good luck,
Orloff Picket

Ryan held up the piece of notepad paper. "I take it you've read this?"

"Over your shoulder ... he's a sick fuck."

"Where is Orloff now?"

"Moved out an hour ago."

"And Wendy and Olivia's van?"

"Obliterated. Apparently that older tanker retrofit has a fair share of weaponry on board. Nothing that would stand up to Star Watch, but enough that the average commercial craft—"

Ryan cut him off, "Wait ... Wendy's ship was obliterated?"

"Completely," the AI replied. "Since it provided a means to use its comms to call for help. Which we need to do."

"Did you not read that deranged hillbilly's letter?" Ryan asked, again raising it high in the air. "I'm not doing anything that will get Wendy killed. No, I'll play his game and I'll beat him at it … somehow."

"That's the spirit, Ryan. With that said, Consignment Freight has already contacted our district Star Watch people by now. They may be a few days behind us, but I seriously doubt they'll have much problem figuring out what's going on. They'll be looking for the missing three CF drivers, and perhaps for Orloff Picket as well."

"Then we need to stop yammering and get moving," Ryan said.

"I've taken the liberty of inputting the provided spatial coordinates into navigation. But you do realize where you are going … he's probably going to kill you … both of you. It's his kind of game."

"Agreed. For now it is … but we'll see about later."

* * *

Orloff Picket sat down on the corner of his bed and stared at his left foot with growing contempt. His multiple bruises and contusions—even his broken ribs—were slowly mending, but his broken foot had not improved.

Even that simple act brought tears to his eyes. *Hurts like a mother fucker!* he thought. He unwrapped the last few windings of bandage and the deep purple-blue bruising, along with much-too-much greenish-tinged flesh, came into view. More than aware he was running a temperature, he could tell his foot was badly infected. If he didn't take care of it soon, gangrene would set in.

There came that racket again. His head pounded, though he'd downed four Vicodin within the last two hours. Still, the headache had only worsened.

Bang … bang … bang …

Orloff stared blankly at the adjoining bulkhead. He visualized her in there—that wild little hellcat. Normally, he would have taken her by now. Stripped her down—grabbed a fistful of her long blonde hair …

Bang … bang … bang …

Turning his head, he could just barely hear her words, "Let me out of here … you crazy son of a bitch!"

In spite of the pain, a smile crossed his lips: *Wild little hellcat*. He knew exactly how to silence her. Slowly and methodically, Orloff reversed his handiwork—rewinding first the bandage over his foot before putting the tube sock back over it. He slowly got to his feet.

* * *

Wendy stopped to catch her breath, giving her ears a short reprieve from the ultra-loud clanging. He'd left an old metal bucket and a roll of toilet paper—the entirety of her bathroom's accommodations. She took a few deep breaths, then, grabbing ahold the wire handle with both hands, swung the metal pail into the closest bulkhead. Eventually, she knew, she'd need to use the bucket for other things than making noise. For now, she intended to continue doing everything in her power to drive the SOB mad. *Hah … he's already mad!* She screamed out again, "Where … is … Olivia? Let me out of here! Let us both go!"

She stopped to listen, sensing she'd heard something. For close to twenty-four hours the weird spacecraft had been deathly quiet. The distant sounds of Olivia's screaming were no longer present. *What's happened to her? God … what's he done to her?* She silently reprimanded herself for letting her thoughts latch on to the worst: Had he beaten her into unconsciousness? Did he rape her? *Did that son-of-a-bitch rape my best friend?*

Earlier, it was decided that Wendy would take the short spacewalk over to the old, rusty-looking vessel since, technically, she was not yet a pilot—two years working through a three-year CF pilot's certification program.

So Olivia, staying with the van, instead gave Wendy the riot act as she suited up: "You drop off the delivery, then get the hell out of there. Tell him your partner is six-five and packs two-thirty pounds of solid muscle."

"He's handicapped … probably old and infirmed. This is a good thing we're doing, Olivia, delivering his prescription meds personally." Wendy, after winding her long hair into a makeshift bun, pulled with practiced efficiency her helmet over her head.

"Normally … I'd agree. You know I'm all for breaking rules, but with Two-ton and Ryan both AWOL … something's not right."

"You promised you wouldn't mention his name again for at least a month," Wendy said, bringing her attention to the HUD readings displayed on the inside of her visor.

She caught Olivia rolling her eyes.

"What?"

"As if in a month you two won't be back together."

"No, this time it's apart forever. I think we're just too much alike. We drive each other crazy. There's no trust there."

"Has he ever cheated on you? Done anything to warrant your suspicions?"

Wendy, now suited up, stepped into the airlock. She turned back and looked at Olivia as guilt suddenly spread through her like a surge of electricity. It wasn't Ryan who'd been disloyal—unfaithful. It was her. It only happened once. She and Ryan had fought and he'd left for a delivery to Liberty Station. She'd then consumed *way too much* to drink at Bottoms. Tony Post was there too … and she'd made a horrible, horrible, horrible mistake. What Olivia didn't know was that Wendy felt so deeply ashamed; that she didn't deserve Ryan. Hell, at their last parting she couldn't even look him in the eye. No … he would never understand. If she could do it all over again, she'd toss the second, *or was it her third?* Long Island iced tea into Tony Post's smug face. Recalling his hands on her naked body, she tasted bile at the back of her throat. How could she have, with that old—groping—pudgy … Sick guilt coursed through her again.

Wendy gave Olivia an over-confident smile. She smiled back, showing concern in her eyes. They were like sisters—both had the same athletic build. Wendy, a Scandinavian blond, had bright blue eyes. Olivia's hair, worn long, was auburn and her eyes a warm chocolate. Alone, they caught every man's attention. Together, they could bring a disco to a standstill.

"I'll be careful … I promise," Wendy said, reaching out to activate the inside airlock hatch.

Brought back to the present, hearing a scraping sound as the hatch to the small compartment opened, she moved farther behind the metal hatch door. Still clutching the bucket's handle, with mere seconds to spare, she raised the bucket and wound her body around—like a batter readying for a fastball pitch.

CHAPTER 28

In the eerie dim light, the large silhouetted shape—dark and lurking—stepped into view in the open hatch. A waft of something acrid assaulted Wendy's nose. A smell so foul it only underscored that something evil was nearby. *Oh my God ... I know it. He's going to kill me.* A moment passed and, in that brief timespan—that second of indecision—she lost any advantage she might have had. In the semi-darkness, the huge figure defensively raised his arms. Wendy swung the bucket at him anyway.

At barely five-foot-five, she was a foot shorter than the gargantuan standing before her. Unfurling her body like a released spring coil, tightly holding on to the pail's handle, Wendy swung with everything she had. In horror, she watched as the bucket fell short of its mark—the lunatic's head—by a mile. Instead, with a loud clattering noise, it struck him beneath his left armpit.

The jolting force of the impact caused Wendy to drop the bucket. She waited for the huge figure to pounce—pick her up like a rag doll and throw her against the bulkhead. Instead, a shrieking scream of pain, followed by prolonged wails of agony, emanated from the doubled-over abductor.

Wendy ran from her prison cell, unsure where to go. Now,

standing in a narrow passageway, she momentarily hesitated. Just behind her was the cell compartment she'd just exited, and just beyond that she could see a somewhat lit-up compartment. Positioned at the room's far end was an unmade bed. *His bedroom.*

Running in the opposite direction, Wendy yelled out, "Olivia! Where are you? I'm free … come on … tell me where you are!" She turned the knob on a standard framed door and peered inside—into some kind of storage room. She heard rustling behind her … he was coming. "Olivia, make a noise! Let me know where you are." She continued down the passageway, twisting doorknobs along the way. Each was locked. "Olivia?" She stopped to listen for her friend's voice but heard only rustling coming from behind her. She ran on. Ahead, at the end of the passageway, she spotted a stairway and sprinted for it. Grabbing on to a metal railing, she swung her body around. From the corner of her eye, she saw his beefy hand swipe out, missing her by inches. Flying down the steep metal stairway, she stumbled halfway down, nearly falling before righting herself. As her captor pursued her, descending the stairs right behind her, she heard his deep, labored breaths.

Wendy, upon reaching the bottom level, found barely enough light to make out even basic shapes. Taking in what was before her, her memories were fractured—remembering only bits and pieces of when she was first abducted and brought inside the vessel. Shaking her head to clear her mind, what she needed was a weapon. Her eyes roamed over the expansive single room compartment and spotted a wooden workbench, of sorts. A lit, old-fashioned swing light—a circular florescent bulb, surrounding a large magnifying glass— was pushed low over the bench surface. Hearing heavy footfalls nearing the bottom of the stairway, she darted for the table. Spotting a battered black leather case, she unsnapped it. Unfurling the two ends apart, she found inside an assortment of metallic tools of varying sizes—each secured to a silk-like fabric with elastic loops. To Wendy, it looked like a kit either a dentist or doctor would use. Seeing several thin knives, she grabbed up the longest one. With the knife now in hand, she looked back toward the stairs. He wasn't there. Her heart pounded within her chest and she had a hard time catching her breath.

Click.

Numerous indirect spotlights came on—illuminating a series of items hanging high up on the adjacent wood paneled bulkhead. Wendy, looking left and right, raised her knife hand—poised to slice or stab the fucker as soon as he came at her. Waiting for what seemed an eternity, her eyes slowly elevated toward the upper portion of the bulkhead before her. She saw the familiar branch-like antlers of an elk and took in the animal's long snout and its large brown eyes. They seemed to be gazing back at her. She'd seen mounted deer heads numerous times at her grandfather's cabin, so no big deal. But as her eyes moved to the left—to other mounted creatures—her pupils widened. She recognized the unmistakable profile of a two-horned rhino-warrior and … *what was that?* Mounted together were two Craing female heads and torsos—identical twins. Her stomach churned as her throat constricted. She needed air—badly needed breathable fresh air. As the room began to swim around her, she blinked—tunnel vision affecting her sight. Her heart stopped in her chest as her eyes came to rest on Two-ton's face. She took an unsteady step in his direction—relieved he was right there, still alive—only to realize a split-second later that those glistening, all too real seeming eyes were unnaturally fixed and unmoving.

Wendy's legs began to shake—her knees on the verge of buckling. She knew the unique color of Olivia's long auburn hair. Like no one else's—it shimmered and glistened when she walked. Olivia always said it was her best feature.

Wendy didn't want to look at her face. As she slowly sank to the deck, her body shaking uncontrollably, she noted her friend's nakedness and perfection—even in death. Finally, she let herself gaze upward into her best friend's eyes. They were speaking right to her—as though Olivia was saying the words aloud—*Help me, Wendy … Oh God … help me.*

* * *

For the last twenty minutes, Ryan was again working beneath the deck plates at the stern of the van. He'd been ready to head out—find the refurbished Paotow Tanker and find Wendy—but on throttling up the newly installed Aldo reactor, he found the Consignment Freight van's propulsion system incapable of acquiring the necessary near-light speed that was required for traveling in the vastness of open space. Upon closer inspection of one of the numerous hidden cable bundles, he finally found the problem. Although not a recommended practice, Ryan kept the reactor online while conducting repairs. He wasn't willing to pay for the time he'd give up for it to come back online. The heat of the reactor, far too close to his face, was nearly unbearable and as he felt his forehead begin to blister, he determined he'd inadvertently reversed two wires. Once he rewired them properly, he hurried from the crawl space, replaced the deck plates, and ran to the cockpit.

Not bothering to sit down, Ryan carefully eased the controls back, but even that small adjustment threw him backward, and into his seat. The sudden inertia, at first, was more than the van's G-force compensators could handle. He heard Two-ton's AI yell a loud "Yahoo!"

Ryan let a brief smile cross his lips. Finally, something positive! "Just make sure we stay on course." Leaning forward, he slowly increased the throttle then said, "Now we're talking! This baby's got some serious horses under the hood …"

"I can guarantee there is not a quicker freight van within ten light-years," the AI affirmed.

"Just maybe then we'll make up some time. Maybe even catch up to Orloff."

"Keep edging the speed up, but realize eventually you're going to far exceed the compensators," the AI said. "Let me know if you start feeling lightheaded … find difficulty breathing."

"I feel fine," Ryan said, edging the controls back further. "What's the ETA for reaching those coordinates? What is it … Alaster-Rei?

"At this rate of speed … close to three hours. We're really moving along."

"What can you tell me about it? Is it … a planet?" Ryan asked.

"Not even a dwarf planet. Quite a few celestial bodies have been discovered within both the Kuiper and Oort belts. Alaster-Rei lies saddled between two asteroids—one's highly volcanic and one's radioactive. Both are massive. The latter puts out almost as much light for Alaster-Rei as the sun does for Earth."

"What's the terrain like … is there breathable air?"

"A desert-like environment—yet more life than anywhere else in the region. Supposedly, it's a hunter's paradise. If anyone else could aver get there."

CHAPTER 29

Ryan found it interesting that the approaching moon-sized baby planet, Alaster-Rei, was situated between the Kuiper Belt and the Oort Cloud. Over the last few hours they'd made their way through the Kuiper Belt, via Vanguard's Breach. Historically, it was the location of Sol System's—*Earth's*—most devastating attack, by the Craing Admiral Ot-Mul, and his fleet of Dreadnaughts, nearly a decade ago.

The console display indicated there were no fewer than ten celestial bodies, all clumped together, in this one region of space. Almost a mini solar system, the radioactive *My Brittany* and the heat-producing *Eng252* introduced life-supporting heat into the region, while the baby planet's continually melting ice poles—creating limited amounts of water—provided a bazaar combination of factors that supported life on Alaster-Rei.

"We'll need to take things slow from here on," the AI said.

"Yeah … what a mess," Ryan said, increasing the display's sensitivity. While both the Kuiper Belt and Oort Cloud had trillions of asteroids present, they were, usually, spaced many miles apart from one another. Only larger vessels needed to be concerned with undue collisions. But, as they approached the mini solar system, there were multiple rings of tumbling asteroids that seemed positioned on top of each other.

"How in hell are we supposed to navigate through this shit?"

"I'll have to do it. Fortunately, the van is small, and, with my far-quicker response time mechanics, I can well handle navigating. No problem."

"Fine … but Orloff's huge tanker is five or ten times our size. How did he make it through?"

"There is another passageway, similar to Vanguard's Breach. While this one is a natural, interweaving course through the asteroids, it is a laborious—time-consuming—obstacle course. Unfortunately, I can't access that same secret, highly guarded roadmap for us to follow. Probably another reason Orloff selected this place for a vacation home."

Ryan thought about what the AI said. The van was within close enough proximity to the asteroid rings now to wonder if attempting to go on further was suicide. *But what other choice do I have?* He pictured Wendy—what it must be like for her right now—being Orloff's prisoner. So far, he'd managed to push away any thoughts of what he could be doing to her. But now, since he'd opened that door a tiny crack, his blood began to boil.

The AI said, "I think I have a lock on the tanker. It's down there, on the surface of Alaster-Rei."

Ryan, staring at the approaching house-sized rocks—swooshing by at different speeds—said, "Do it … take us in."

"Strap yourself in, Ryan … this is going to be a bumpy ride."

The small van suddenly slowed, changing course. Ryan reached for his harness, which he'd never used before, not even once, and strapped himself in. Though he pretty much had a cast-iron stomach, he wondered if he was up for what was about to come. The van lurched upward as it changed course again. Accelerating, the van sped between two small-ish asteroids. Ryan flinched. The Two-ton AI's rapid calculation prevented the van from being struck by fractional distances.

"How about a little music?" the AI asked, not waiting for his reply. Ryan, who'd programmed in Two-ton's favorite music playlist a while back, instantly recognized the blaringly loud *Born To Be Wild*, by Steppenwolf. Somehow, the music calmed his nerves and he found himself anticipating the rapid stellar swings, both left and right or up and down. For a moment, he wondered if he, too, could have navigated through this continual onslaught of space obstacles. He knew he was a damn good pilot—even touted, when in the service, as a bit of a hotdog by his commanding fleet officers.

* * *

By the time he'd listened to Two-ton's hundred-plus song playlist twice through, they'd made it through the bulk of the rocky torrent. Ryan released his harness and stood. Approaching them was the strange system: Alaster-Rei—a red, Mars-like orb—nestled between, and on the same orbital plane as, the bright-red volcanic asteroid, *Eng252*, and the bright-white asteroid, *My Brittany*.

They slipped into a fast, low orbit around Alaster-Rei. "You can give me back manual control, Two-ton," Ryan said, putting his hands on the controls. He peered through the forward observation window as he dipped the van lower into the atmosphere. The terrain below was much more dramatic than he anticipated—a desert of red sand sprawled below. Countless towering sandstone buttes, each a distinctive windblown column, rose high into the air. A harsh and unforgiving landscape yet one startlingly beautiful.

Ryan noticed a small red icon blinking on the console

display. Adjusting his course, he headed directly for it. The closer they got, the more the topography became slightly hillier. Now traveling five hundred feet above the surface, Ryan could see there were indeed signs of life below. Peeking up through small crevices in the rocks, and on the sandy surface, were patches of green scrub and an occasional short—stunted—tree.

"On the other side of this next rise, what we're looking for should come into view," the AI said.

Ryan, slowing down the van's speed, lowered to fifty feet. They crested the next rise and there it was—the refurbished Paotow Tanker—parked within a shantytown compound, of sorts. There were several, five or six, smaller stone structures—like barns or sheds—and a larger structure, which clearly was the cabin residence. Primarily made of rough-hewn, indigenous timber, it had a stack of stone at one end—the chimney. The surrounding yard was a mess of old odds and ends—rusted dilapidated vehicles, unrecognizable metallic parts, an old mattress—and fifteen to twenty big plastic container barrels. What looked like a cleared-out area had a hunter's meat pole driven into the ground—a long chain and hook slowly swayed back and forth.

"You picking up any nearby life forms, Two-ton?"

"Not here. But in the surrounding hills and valleys, within a forty-mile radius, there are eight life forms—each sufficient in size to be either Orloff … or Wendy."

CHAPTER 30

Ryan set the van down about two hundred yards away from the compound. Noticing the area from above, the secluded patch of land was sited between two medium-sized buttes. A remote area, probably visible only from above, or when stumbled across on the ground. He finished filling a backpack with minimal essentials: a water canister, food bars, a favorite Leatherman all-in-one tool, high-tensile rope, as well as Orloff's Tavor, and the extra mags.

"I need to go with you," the AI said.

Ryan, standing tall, swung the pack over one shoulder. "The atmosphere here?"

"A little thinner than you're used to; like being a mile above sea-level on Earth ... like Denver."

"While I'm gone you should swap out the air reserves," Ryan said.

"Did you hear me? You should take me with you."

Ryan huffed hearing that. "And how would that work? You're not exactly transportable."

The AI went quiet.

"I'll go get the lay of the land. Find out what Orloff wants me to do. For now, this is his game. Perhaps, in the meantime, you'll think of something."

* * *

The Two-ton AI watched as Ryan left. The AI didn't have feelings, per se. No emotions were at play—not in the human sense. What it did possess was sophisticated programming—highly advanced programming; it was programmed for loyalty. Donald, or Two-ton—the AI's creator—was an amazing, adept coder. But humans hadn't been the best programmers in over a decade. AIs were far more efficient at that function. Donald, or Two-ton, had known this, and after months of trial and error, he found the advanced elements essential for developing a far superior artificial intelligence, by hacking into one: in particular, Star Watch vessel's highly capable artificial intelligence system—the *Parcical*'s. With its sophisticated Caldurian knowledge-base at his disposal, unique *antecedent conditioning* was possible; and a high-level perceptual system was born. From that point on, the AI's perception of "well-being" became an internal—ongoing—active goal. The result—*humanlike* behavior. As close as possible to having an emotional response manifest in an AI, by human, even Caldurian, scientists.

The Two-ton AI had, in a sense, the capacity to actually miss another one's presence. The AI already *missed* Ryan and would do anything—everything it could—to keep that particular human safe.

Using the van's integrated, but dreadfully rudimentary, long- and short-range sensors, the AI began reaching out—assessing everything within the confines of the Orloff Picket compound. It started with the main cabin. With the exception of a toaster, a television, and an iPod, there were minimal electronics evident. With no other technology present, the AI, quickly becoming disinterested, moved on to the first out-building, where it found something of interest—a large quantity of organic material. The AI knew the human term for the items was *pelts*. Some were hanging from stretched lines, while others were stacked, one atop another. The van's sensors were not sensitive enough to determine the specific species of the pelts. Although, based on their size, perceived weight, and other factors, the Two-ton AI conjectured—with a 67% probability—two of them were probably of human origin.

The AI, moving then to the next out-building, instantly became interested. Junk. Wonderful junk. Piled up high, over five feet in some areas, much technology was evident. The AI assessed the piles of scavenged parts from a myriad of vessels—including a space freighter's navigation system; an *infuser* from a dark matter reactor; both left and right treads from some land vehicle; an *anti-gravity* hover module; several bucket seats; parts of an Earth-built motorcycle; and a metal table—set up with a dismantled robot lying atop it. The robot was of the most interest to the AI. Relatively new, it was no more than ten years old, and of *Trom*—a planet some sixty light-years distance—origin. *You're far from home, fella!*

It was an AI-controlled robot called a *mecher*. The AI reviewed what information it had about its technology. Approximately seven feet tall—when up and about—its metallic body was both heavy and unwieldy. *Tromians* had their robots do everything, anything they didn't want to do for themselves. But they were poorly designed. A strong wind could topple them over. The AI, after referencing several listed complaints, found the robots susceptible to falling, tripping over their two metallic feet. The mecher's internal AI was ridiculously inferior, which was fine. Soon, with any luck, it would not be using it.

With the Communications Transmission Beacon no longer present atop the CF van, communications capabilities was hampered—but not impossible. What wasn't at all operable in the complete vacuum of space, could, to some degree, operate here where there was atmosphere. When atmosphere is present, audio waves can be transmitted and received. The van, equipped with a PA system, had both internal and external speakers. The Two-ton AI began communicating via the transmission of a series of basic *Tromian* mecher diagnostic tones. Barely audible, a series of clicks and beeps swept across the sandy hillside then into the second out-building. Within the robot's *tin man*-like torso, where much of its circuitry resided, a series of micro-lights began to blink on and off. Next, the robot's AI began a painfully slow boot-up process. Two minutes later, the mecher, transmitting a series of clicks and beeps back to the CF van, messaged, "Hello?"

"Hello, my name is Two-ton."

"Hello, Two-ton. I … I am in pieces. I am broken. Will you help me?"

"Yes. Let's start with your name first. Have you been designated a name?"

"Yes. I am Ruderk. My master called me Ruderk."

"That name sucks; you're now called … Baron. I always liked that name."

"Very well, Two-ton."

"Baron, tell me about your physical condition. Are any of your limbs operational?"

"Yes … one arm and the hand appendage. Both legs are unattached, but are lying here next to me on the table."

"Your head is obviously attached, I take it?" Two-ton's AI asked.

"It is attached."

"Good! So where is your other arm? You're going to need that for what comes next."

"I don't see it. It's not here on the table with me."

"I think it is, Baron. Look harder. It may be lying above your head. Can you reach up and feel for it?"

A moment later, Baron, with an excited burst of beeps and clicks, responded, "Yes, you are correct, I've got it. I'm holding it out in front of me."

"Nice job. Put it down where you can still see it. Do not drop it on to the floor!"

"I won't drop it."

"We're going to need tools. Is that a pair of pliers I'm detecting by the left side of your head?"

"Pliers, yes, and three screwdrivers, with different heads, and an electronic test meter."

"Good! It looks like Orloff started on the repairs, but he obviously got distracted. Perhaps he had an urge to go out and kill someone."

Baron didn't comment on that.

Over the next hour and a half, the Two-ton AI remotely assisted the robot in reassembling its limbs back onto its central torso. First, came the attachment of the arm. Twice it slipped from the mecher's one-handed grasp and fell onto the table; once, it came perilously close to falling over the edge. With the shoulder joint now properly positioned, and the correct amount of pressure administered, *for mechers were, if nothing else, very strong*, the robotic arm popped into place. Electrical connections were then reestablished to the hand, fingers, and touch sensors. After that, the rest went easier. With arms both attached, the robot was now capable of propping itself into a quasi-seated position. First one leg, then the other, was attached, then tested, and both determined functional.

"My limbs are attached and seem to be fully operational, Two-ton."

"That's good, Baron. I'm proud of you. Let's try standing up. Can you do that for me?"

The Two-ton AI watched Baron through the blurry haze of the van's sensors as the metallic robot slowly slid off from the table onto two unsteady legs. The mecher wavered both left and right—like a toddler first learning to stand upright.

"I'm standing! Oops ..."

The mecher, wavering too far to the right, went over like a toppled tree.

"Get back up, Baron, there's still a lot to do."

The robot, doing as told, eventually stood upright. "What would you like me to do next, Two-ton?"

"Find something to carry the tools and test meter in. Like a box or a satchel." The Two-ton AI waited silently.

"Yes, I have accomplished that task."

"You're doing very well, Baron. Now, I want you to make your way to where I am. Out to the freight van that I'm situated in."

The mecher took one wobbly step after another until it reached the door. "The door is secured … locked."

"If it doesn't open … put some weight into it, Baron. Break it down, if you have to."

The van's audio sensors picked up distant clattering sounds as a metal door was ripped from its hinges.

"I am on my way to you, Two-ton. I look forward to meeting you. To serving you as my new master."

"I'm not your master, Baron. Shortly after you arrive, I'll be giving you a gift."

"A gift for me? No one has ever given me a gift before. May I ask what it is?"

"You'll be fitted with … higher intelligence …"

CHAPTER 31

After leaving the compound, Ryan spent the next two hours checking out the Two-ton AI sensor scans, showing the three closest life-form locations. Prior to leaving the van, he'd made a crude, hand-drawn map of the surrounding topography, then placed circles around those areas where the life forms were seen last. He used nearby natural landmarks to help him get his bearings: A massive, hollowed-out sandstone bridge was in one area; three towering buttes bunched together were in another area; and a small forest of thorny trees were in another. His first intent was to locate the landmarks, figuring he'd then be in closer proximity to actually finding the life forms. That, anyway, was his plan.

Upon reaching the sandstone bridge location—about a mile and a half from the compound—Ryan almost stumbled across the first life form. Granted, it was man-sized, but it was also reptilian. Walking through the sandstone opening of the arched, rainbow-like bridge, Ryan saw something moving in his direction. Low to the ground, it crawled along on all fours, like a large lizard, or gator. Only this reptile's head, held high, was situated at the end of its long thick tail. If the beast's approach wasn't so menacing, it might have been comical. Sensing it was a territorial thing, Ryan quickly moved away from the bridge. The tail-headed beast didn't pursue him.

The towering three buttes were visible from the rainbow bridge. Making good time hoofing across to them, Ryan stopped when he was within a few hundred yards, again assessing his map sketch. Since Two-ton's AI sensor zeroed in on two life forms present, he was more optimistic about this second location. *I'm coming, Wendy …*

Ryan opened up his pack and, after pulling his water canister out, gulped down long swigs. Next, he removed the Tavor and after checking it over, slung the weapon over his shoulder.

Moving ahead, the ground became softer—more sand than rock. As he crept forward, his eyes spent equal time scanning the ground for footprints and looking for any distant movement. At seventy yards out, though it was only midday, Ryan thought he saw something ahead in dark shadows cast by the three towering butte pillars. Fortunately, large boulders were strewn everywhere, and Ryan used them to his advantage. Keeping low, he ran from one to the next. Thirty yards farther on, he held up behind the last fifteen-foot-tall rock. He caught his breath, then slowly peered around it. *Crap!* Light this time of day seemed ridiculously bright. Shielding his eyes with one hand, he squinted into the shadows. There definitely was movement in there.

Pulling back further from sight, Ryan unslung the Tavor and mentally ran through his options. He figured the element of surprise would be his best advantage. Once he'd readied himself, he came around the boulder—the Tavor positioned shoulder level, he sighted down its barrel.

At ten paces away he stopped and yelled, "Don't move!"

As his eyes adjusted in the shadowy darkness, Ryan found he was staring at two furry, goat-like, creatures. Their wide-open eyes looked frantic, as they hung upside-down from a poled line, their hind legs hog-tied together. Startled, they suddenly bellowed out wild honking noises that were nearly deafening. Their cries echoed off the nearby rocks.

A bloodied note was attached to one of the animals. Ryan approached and carefully pulled off the message. He saw the bloodied nail head, still protruding from the animal's hindquarters. He started to read:

Dear Ryan,

I am impressed that you have made it this far. Welcome to my hidden get-away within the Oort Cloud. Since you are obviously reading this note, I'm sure one, or both, of the Pampalats are honking away. With that said ... I now know where you are. I am coming for you ... right now. You are being hunted. To add to the overall excitement of the day, I want you to know Wendy is, in fact, still alive. For how long — that depends on you. Like your Pampalat friends right there beside you, she is in a similar predicament ... hanging upside-down with her haunches bound. A most uncomfortable position. Add to that fact, there are roaming carnivores on this asteroid ... she will not survive long. What I will tell you is that she is within twenty miles of your current location, near a body of water and four surrounding buttes, and on higher ground than where you stand now. No more hints, Ryan. I've already been far too generous. Again ... I am coming for you, and I'm carrying the Barrett .50 caliber. I'm sure you noticed it while visiting my vessel. In the right hands, it's capable of hitting a gnat's ball sack at a distance of two hundred yards.

Regards,

Orloff

P.S. If you are still standing there, reading this, you're an idiot.

Ryan, in fact, was not still standing there. He was running back to the large boulder for cover. Once there, he did a quick assessment of the surrounding area and noticed only one region in the distance that looked higher in elevation than where he currently hid. It looked about ten miles away. From experience, he knew he could run, on average, eight miles or so an hour in similar terrain. But then again, the air here was thinner. He pushed the image of Wendy—desperate, struggling upside-down—from his thoughts, along with his growing rage. Never before had he wanted to kill someone like he did Orloff Picket. *Keep your wits about you!* Ryan admonished himself.

The question that rose in his mind was *is Orloff even telling the truth?* Ryan needed to think strategically—think what Orloff expected him to do since he'd want a clear shot. And one from a far distance away too. The son of a bitch was a skilled hunter. Anyone who owned an expensive rifle, like a Barrett .50 caliber, certainly wanted to challenge his abilities.

Ryan suddenly dropped low, and scurried into a grouping of trees. If Orloff was out there—somewhere within the elevated region—then Ryan knew he'd be dead by the time he heard the shot. Prying apart nearby spruce-like tree branches, he looked toward the distant region. If he skirted around the open spaces, it would add an extra hour's time before he got there. Again, images of Wendy began creeping, desperate, back into his consciousness. *Stop! That's what he wants.*

Spanned before him lay a shallow sandy valley—two and a half to three miles wide by maybe ten miles long. On both sides of the valley were rocky cliffs, also populated with patches of bright-yellow spruce trees, like the one he currently hid behind. He mentally traced a course that would start directly on his left; it progressed through some trees then through what appeared to be deeply eroded channels within sandstone cliffs. The route didn't look easy. Undoubtedly, he'd have to retrace his steps through the maze more than once. From there, he'd have to hoof it across several grassy hills. He'd be more exposed at that point, but there was no other way around it. He'd have to move fast—change course often. Ready to start, he spoke aloud. "Sorry, Wendy … better late than dead."

CHAPTER 32

Back in his dingy quarters, Jason was becoming more and more uncomfortable stuck within the confines of the Picket's Craing heavy cruiser. Something had changed—the way the brothers looked at them—the way they talked in low tones amongst each other so as not to be overheard. He was being hailed.

"Go for Captain ... what's up, Nan?"

"I have to leave."

"What do you mean you have to leave? This is your mission."

"Yeah, well ... as important as it is for me to find my nephew, it's more important that the Alliance's relationship with the Allarians stays intact. I've been on a NanoCom call, here in my cabin, for the last hour. Apparently, they have a grievance with the Alliance and are threatening to jump ship. Strategically, that would be a devastating blow. Don't forget, their close proximity in space to the Craing make them geographically the perfect watch dog ..."

"But why you? You're not the president anymore."

"No, but I'm the one they first built a relationship with. They want to speak to me and only me."

"Fine. How do we work this then? How do I explain

that you've suddenly disappeared off the ship, Nan? I have a feeling the Pickets are on to us anyway. Pretty bad timing."

"I haven't a doubt you can take care of yourselves. You've gone up against an army of rhino-warriors in the past, so you can handle a few mountain Bubbas. Just keep an eye on Bristol. He has a tendency to mouth-off and can't defend himself—well, like you, Billy, and Rizzo do. To keep your cover, I'll have Sergeant Major Stone take me off the ship in the *Goliath*. She can return right after she drops me off on the *Jumelle*."

"Wait ... you want the *Jumelle* to take you? Where? Back to Liberty Station?"

"That's the other thing, Jason. I need to borrow your Star Watch vessel as I'll have to be in Allarian space within the next few hours; a day at the most."

"So you're taking both ships ... the *Goliath* and the *Jumelle* ... and what ... leaving us stranded here?"

"You're a big boy, Jason ... stop whining. I'll send Stone right back. For shit's sake, don't fume like such a baby about this."

At that moment, Jason remembered how infuriating it used to be being married to this woman in years past. "Fine ... I'll contact the *Jumelle* and speak with Stone, she'll probably—"

"Oh, and I'll need Rizzo, too. Since he's still on board the *Goliath*, I could use him as a bodyguard."

"What about Colonel Stephen Pope ... your *supposed to be* husband?"

"He stays here. Pope's still the representative of our mining company ... right? As far as I know, Brent is still taking you to meet with Orloff. So meet with him and you'll then discover Ryan's whereabouts."

"I'm not so sure about that, but I'll stay the course," Jason said.

"That's the spirit. I'll come back as soon as I can. Sorry

about all this, Jason. I know you were doing me a huge favor to come in the first place."

* * *

Billy and Bristol caught up with Jason in the passageway outside Colonel Pope's quarters. He quickly brought them up to date on his latest conversation with Nan. After two firm knocks, Pope opened the hatch to his quarters. He was partially dressed, wearing Levi's and a wife-beater undershirt. Drink in hand, he said, "I found a bottle of *something* … can I get you boys a glass?"

Jason said, "No, but thanks, we're fine."

"Suit yourselves." Pope shrugged, then tipped an odd-shaped bottle sideways to pour amber liquid into a metal cup.

"What's going on with you, Pope?" Jason asked, perceiving the man had some kind of attitude problem brewing.

The older man swayed on his feet, an obvious sign he'd been sampling the strange elixir. Jerking his head up—his cold blue eyes narrowing—he said, "You'll address me as Colonel Pope, Captain. I outrank you, mister, and you'll give me the respect—"

"Oh boy …" Billy said, barely audible.

Jason, already in a foul mood, stepped forward and slapped the cup from Pope's hand. Next, taking a fistful of the colonel's undershirt in one hand, he slammed him up against the nearest bulkhead. "Listen to me carefully. Nobody outranks me. Nobody! I not only commanded Star Watch, I commanded the entire U.S. fleet and the Allied forces together simultaneously. I've chosen this current … *station* … because I'm tired and I needed one fucking minute to have some semblance of a normal life. But don't for a second think you outrank me, Pope. Have I made myself perfectly clear?"

Pope held Jason's glare for several seconds before offering up a nearly imperceptible nod. Jason gave him another good shove into the bulkhead for good measure, then released his shirt hold and stepped away. He caught Bristol and Billy exchanging a brief glance. Maybe he'd overreacted, but he didn't care. Pope's presence always irritated him, ever since they'd first encountered back in Colorado. Jason, still heated up, tried mentally to convince himself it had nothing to do with the fact the man was sleeping with his ex-wife, but he knew that would be a lie.

"We still have a mission to accomplish here. You can drink to your heart's content once we're done."

Bristol said, "I've been in contact with Ricket ... back on the *Jumelle*. They are, or were, about an hour ago, not too far behind us. Still out of this old bucket of bolts' sensor range. He told me that we've changed course several times and are currently headed for what looks like a very small ship. Perhaps a small delivery freight van."

"What's the ETA on that?" Jason asked.

Shrugging, Bristol said, "Any time now. Now that the *Jumelle* is gone and the *Goliath* is no longer parked in the flight bay, I guess we'll need to ask the brothers. We're pretty much on our own now."

Billy said, "I don't like this whole setup. It's obvious something's changed with them. How do we know they haven't been in contact with Orloff? Or maybe they've figured out who we ... you ... are, Cap?" He gestured toward Jason with an unlit cigar he'd pulled from a shirt pocket.

"We're slowing," Bristol said, looking upward at nothing in particular. "I can feel the compensators working overtime."

Jason didn't feel the change, but taking Bristol's word for it, he said, "Let's get up to the bridge. See if we can get some answers."

"We're due in the ... what's it called? The Grand Sacellum? I guess it's meal time," Pope said. "One of the brothers ... Larry, I think, knocked on my hatch ten minutes before you three arrived here."

"Yeah, you go ahead, Pope," Jason said. "I have too many bad recollections about that place."

* * *

The three made their way to the Craing heavy cruiser's bridge without passing a soul in the various corridors and passageways. Upon entering the bridge, Jason took in the large compartment.

"What a hellhole," Bristol commented.

At the far end of the bridge was a raised platform—typically present on Craing warships—where the officers usually sat, overseeing and presiding over their junior officers. One command seat was missing and the other two seemed ready to fall apart. Bristol was right; the ship was a hellhole.

Four crewmembers were present—all Craing—still wearing their original, now stained and frayed, uniforms. The Craing had their backs to them. Jason watched them as they worked. With the war over years ago, they should have been allowed to return to their homes ... to their families.

"What are you doing here!"

Jason spun around to see Larry Picket, standing at the back of the compartment with his arms crossed over his chest. Leaning against the back bulkhead, he was either overseer or slave master—perhaps both.

"Hey there, Larry ... we were looking for you," Jason said.

"You're supposed to be in the chapel ... getting grub." He eyed them warily.

"I have to be honest with you, that place creeps me out. We thought we'd take a tour of the ship instead ... is that okay?"

"I guess. But I should probably ask Brent." He moved toward one of the outlying consoles when Billy asked, "Um ... what's that?"

Larry stopped and turned. Noting Billy's pointed outstretched finger, he followed its direction to a somewhat blurry, scratched, forward display screen. There, in the blackness of open space, something small and white was visible.

Larry barked off a series of orders in broken Craing. The display's perspective altered and the object instantly magnified.

"That's a Consignment Freight van," Bristol said, taking a step forward.

It took several minutes before the Craing heavy cruiser got close enough for actual detail to become evident. Jason, taking in the extreme damage to the van's front starboard quarter section, knew the collision was obviously catastrophic for the driver. His thoughts went to Nan. … he'd have to tell her; tell her Ryan was dead. No one could have survived an impact like that.

"That's not her nephew's van … that's not Ryan's," Bristol said. "This one was piloted by Donald *what's his name* …"

CHAPTER 33

Larry stormed over to a seated Craing crewmember and began barking orders at him.

Keeping his voice low, Bristol said, "I'm pretty sure Orloff's vessel caused it."

Jason and Billy, baffled, both gave him bewildered expressions.

"Look ... the only reason we're here now, at that same van's location, is because the Picket brothers managed to obtain ... or at least some part of ... Orloff's spatial coordinates. Perhaps when he checked in. He obviously doesn't want to be found ... even by his own family. But should he call in ... wanting to talk to Mamma ... he opens up a channel and his coordinates are also transmitted. So I just bet you that *mountain man* was responsible. He killed Donald."

"I think it's time we end this little charade," Jason said. "It's elevated way past a missing person report." About to take action, he hesitated, receiving a new NanoCom hail. *That's weird*, he thought, noting it was from Gunny Orion.

"How is it you're contacting me?"

"Captain?" Orion asked.

"Didn't *Goliath* arrive? Nan, along with Stone and Rizzo?"

"That's why I've hailed you. I know you requested quiet comms for your mission, but *Goliath* has yet to arrive here ..."

Now noticing Larry—still standing on the far side of the bridge—was glaring back at him, Jason turned away. "You're saying that you're, the *Jumelle* is, still following behind us?"

"Yes, we're still back here, Cap. Do you need a team of Sharks over there?"

"No ... not until I figure out what happened to Nan. Shit, they may have taken her, or, worse yet, harmed her in some way. Gunny, can you get a fix on her location? Here on this ship?"

"Of course. Hold on, Cap."

Jason looked back over his shoulder and saw Larry heading in his direction. He didn't look happy.

"Cap, I don't see any sign of Nan ... or Stone or Rizzo either, for that matter!"

"And the *Goliath*?"

"Gone. No longer there in the flight bay."

"How about those other two brothers ... Brent and Payne?"

"Also gone. I'm picking up only a single Craing presence in Engineering. Pope is in one of the quarters, while everyone else on board is right there with you, on the bridge."

"I'll get back to you, Gunny, have to go now." Jason cut the connection and turned to face Larry. "What's going on? Where is—"

"Put a sock in it, Captain Reynolds. If you contact your ship again I assure you that all others in your party, starting with your ex-wife, will be killed."

Jason looked at him mystified, but Larry wasn't buying the act.

"We know all about your internal nano-devices," Larry said, pointing to his own head. "We also know who and what you are, Captain, since before you arrived in Dollywood."

At that moment, Jeebrie, the small Craing stationed in Engineering, hurried onto the bridge.

"That's not good," Bristol muttered, eyeing the object held in the Craing's hand. "He's got a *Drooler.* It's a kind of neural paralysis generator. The Craing started using those things toward the end of the war. Get caught in its beam and you lose all motor skills, along with the ability to utilize your nano-devices."

Without hesitation, Jason started to hail the *Jumelle*, but it was too late, as Jeebrie had already pulled the trigger on his handheld device. Billy, Bristol, and Jason—all caught in the wide beam, immediately fell, collapsing onto the deck.

Jason, lying prone, could see only the legs and feet of Larry and Jeebrie, standing above him. When he felt sudden moisture collect at the corners of his mouth he quickly understood why the weapon was called a Drooler. He also felt his bladder release. Unable to blink, swallow, or move, he tried to access his NanoCom ... but no go. The only good news was his heart was beating normally and his lungs taking in air. That, and he was able still to think and mutely observe what was going on around him ...

Movement. Another pair of legs was approaching. They came to a stop next to Larry and the small Craing. Wearing blue jeans—Levi's—Jason heard Pope's unmistakable voice ask them: "How long will they be ... like this?"

Larry said, "We'll need to zap them every hour."

"And the ship following us?"

"Can no longer see them," Jeebrie said. "Their bodies, all the way down to the molecular level, are resonating at a different frequency. Unless they'd know exactly what to look for, these three humans, like the others, are now invisible to their sensor scans."

Jeebrie said, "They'll send a team to investigate," Pope said. "We don't have long ... maybe ten or fifteen minutes."

Instantly, a blinding white flash occurred near him and

Jason saw the legs of someone else appear, wearing a battle suit. Relieved, he thought, *we're being rescued*. But, as segments of the battle suit retracted, he knew something was very wrong.

"Where's the *Goliath*?" Larry asked.

"Not far … we need to go."

Jason recognized the voice—Brent's.

"Here, clip these onto your belts."

Jason surmised they were SuitPac devices, probably taken off the immobilized Stone, Rizzo, and Nan. He also noticed Brent's hillbilly accent was mostly gone. Obviously, some kind of elaborate plan had long been in the works. One that Colonel Pope was involved with too. *The bastard*! But to what end? Was the abduction of Nan's nephew, Ryan Chase, always part of the plan? *Yes, of course!* He was the bait to get Nan involved. No doubt, Pope had manipulated her; had made suggestions and steered her into meeting the Pickets. In retrospect, it was ingenious. How else could the ex-president of the United States be lured away from her secret service detail—suddenly drop everything to journey into space? She would bring in a hefty bounty. Then add to that his own capture; there'd be no limit to what the Pickets could demand—be it money or gold … or, perhaps, something else entirely.

But some things still didn't add up. Like Orloff—the batshit-crazy brother. What was his role in this? Just to capture Ryan Chase? He seemed to have more of his own agenda—perhaps separate from the rest of the family.

Jason realized his body was rising, as smallish hands lifted him up. Craing crewmembers. Next to him, Pope lifted Bristol's body and Larry lifted Billy. Brent reinitialized his battle suit. Behind the visor, Jason could see his focused concentration—probably going through various HUD menus. The simple fact that he'd figured out as much as he had indicated prior military experience—perhaps even a tour on a Star Watch vessel, where access to a Caldurian battle suit was normal.

"Ah … here we go! Group phase-shift settings have their own separate menu. Make sure you've got a firm hold on those three," Brent said.

"And this ship? The Craing crew?" Pope asked.

Larry, initializing his own battle suit, said, "This ship's a piece of crap. And who gives a shit about a handful of Craing, anyway?"

Pope initialized his own battle suit.

At this point, Jason, Bristol, and Billy were being held firmly upright. Limp—their heads drooped loosely to one side. All three had lost control of their bladders. Though Jason couldn't quite see Bristol's face, he had a good view of Billy's. Long strings of drool dripped out from the corners of his mouth.

And then—in an intense white flash—they all disappeared.

CHAPTER 34

Wendy was not hog-tied, nor actually hanging upside down. But she was bound at the wrists and ankles and tied onto a tree, with her arms secured behind her. She was also gagged. She had come to a decision—right after her initial abduction—that she wouldn't become a victim. She knew she was smart, always did well in school, and told she had a good analytical mind.

Wendy watched the large brutish man move about the small clearing in the trees. Numerous times, before he gagged her, she'd tried to engage him in conversation but he'd have none of that. On those rare occasions when he actually looked at her, there was an awkward nervousness to his stare. His interaction with women, probably, was kept to a bare minimum. She guessed, at least in that regard, he had a childlike mentality.

Orloff was making preparations for ... *something*. Setting up some kind of booby-trap. And, she realized, she was the bait. The man was after someone. His long-barreled rifle, leaning up against a distant rock, looked like a fairly elaborate weapon. *Maybe like a sniper's*, she thought, though she didn't know much about guns. Twenty paces directly across from her was a tree similar to the one she was tied to. It too had bright-yellow pine-like branches. The fragrance the trees emitted was bitter and somewhat lemony—but not unpleasant. Orloff was now perched in that tree. He'd climbed up there with an assortment of things—a weapon of sorts, plus sharp objects—like crudely made spears or arrows. The guy was a serious hunter! But who was he hunting? If she was the bait—who'd come for her? *Her Dad?* No ... he'd never been to outer space. Her thoughts turned to Ryan. She'd considered him earlier, but then disregarded the idea. She adored him, but he was a skinny, rarely ever serious, kid. What had Olivia said? That he was an adorable goofball. But then again, wasn't he in the service ... in the Navy? When asked about that period in his life he always brushed it off. Was there another side to him she was totally ignorant of? *Maybe.* There was something else, too. Something Tony Post had mentioned. He'd said it with utter distain—something about a relative of Ryan's—someone super important. Ryan didn't like talking about that subject, either. *The guy's got so many fucking secrets!* She felt her irritation growing, just thinking about Ryan, when a heavy sadness overtook her. She suddenly knew, beyond any doubt, that this elaborate *setup* was for Ryan. The smelly big redneck was luring her boyfriend—or ex-boyfriend. No! He still was her boyfriend; she didn't want to be without him. She was his—all his—there was no denying that.

Over the last hour she'd been working her tongue and lips to loosen-up the gag. But she needed to be extra cautious. Careful not to let Orloff know she could almost push the gag down to chin level. When the time was right, she'd be able to warn Ryan.

Thick branches shifted as Orloff descended the tree. Dust particles, captured in sunlight, streamed down from above, swirling in the air's invisible currents. This place—this mini planet—was harsh yet very beautiful. Wendy only hoped it wouldn't be her final resting place. Or Ryan's.

Orloff, sliding down the base of the tree trunk, landed hard on the ground. Brushing bark and short, almost pine-like needles from his pants, he eventually looked over at her. His intense, cold-eyed stare made her uneasy—like he was able to read her thoughts.

Orloff moved over to the rocks and retrieved his rifle. He checked its load in a series of quick, well-practiced, movements. Approaching her, he stopped a short distance from her outstretched feet. "Once you've gotten that gag all the way off your mouth scream as loud and often as you like." He then did something she'd never seen him do before, he smiled. Then he was off … running into the trees.

* * *

Ryan stopped midway up the sandy hillside to wipe the sweat off his forehead with the back of his sleeve. For the hundredth time, he wondered if, in that very moment, Orloff had his riflescope trained on him. So far, he'd done his best to stay low, keep out of sight, but numerous wide-open areas loomed just ahead. He stared toward the distant raised bluff, which now looked more like a plateau, noting the high buttes surrounding it. He still couldn't see if there was a body of water there. One of the things Orloff had said to look for. Apparently, he wasn't high enough yet. He wondered if he was even heading in the right direction?

Trudging on, Ryan permitted only two things to occupy his mind—Wendy and Orloff. And that was a mistake. The Two-ton AI had made it very clear other life forms were present on this same space rock. He'd already come in contact with several species. So when he finally crested the hillside, huffing and puffing, he didn't expect to see the beast waiting for him.

It was huge. Immediately, Ryan cursed the AI for not mentioning this—*whatever* it was—creature. Sure, it said life forms were present, of human-size parameters, but not any the size of a pickup truck—a truck with an oversized head and a near-white, furless, body. Ryan stayed perfectly still, watching the beast's ears flatten; it slowly opened its mouth wide and—catlike—hissed at him. The thing definitely had feline features, but the bulk and hide of an elephant.

And then Ryan noticed its four paws, which sported eight-to-nine-inch claws. It was truly a killing machine—he could be ripped apart in seconds.

The beast sniffed the air—bringing its nose somewhat nearer to Ryan. He thought about the Tavor he'd stowed in his pack. But no way—the smallest movement and the beast would be all over him.

Maybe giving the large animal some space would work. Ryan took a tentative step backward. The beast leapt, its front claws out, and in a blur, pinned him to the ground; its moist hot breath misting wetly on his face. Ryan felt himself rising—going closer to the creature's face—and noticed its eyes' inner-eyelids opening and closing as it brought him still higher. Inspecting, it seemed, the human he was about to scarf down. *I'm going to die ... I'm going to die right fucking now!*

The beast's ears twitched as it suddenly looked away toward the distance. Hearing something, obviously, Ryan tried to listen, but he was much too scared. All he could hear was his own heart—beating like a jackhammer in his chest. But then he did hear *something*, though he doubted what he thought he was hearing was actually accurate. Moments passed and he realized, *yes ... it was.* When it came to cheesy 80s music, *Huey Lewis and the News* was right up there at the top. Now getting closer and louder, Ryan was sure it was *Hip to Be Square.* It sounded like it was coming from an old transistor radio. Filled with static, the catchy song echoed into the valley below, seeming to fill all space. Ryan could feel the pressure on both his chest and back release some, as the beast's ears twitched. It loudly hissed.

Just let me go! The fearsome *elephant-cat* lowered and eased several steps backward. *No … don't take me with you! Drop me … let me go!*

Now, with the scratchy music, sounds of an engine could be heard—and a powerful one, at that. Cresting the same hill he'd just ascended, it was now upon them.

Ryan tried to make some sense of what he was seeing. As *Huey* belted out the lyrics, a bright red, beat-to-shit, hovercraft had appeared, piloted by an odd-looking robot. It was almost too much for Ryan to absorb.

The beast, quickly releasing him, leapt away into the rocks. Ryan continued to stare at the robot, watching its head bop up and down to the beat of the music.

"Don't you just love *Huey Lewis and the News?*"

Ryan recognized the voice. "Two-ton?"

CHAPTER 35

As the disturbed swirling dust settled, the Two-ton AI robot yelled over the sound of the old craft's engines, "Are you going to get in behind me ... or just lay out there?"

Ryan, mystified, wasn't quite sure what to do. The ridiculous-looking bot had the voice of his friend Two-ton, though Two-ton was dead. The Two-ton AI, and a *very clever AI, at that*, seemed to have found itself a body ... of sorts.

A distant report, from a high-powered rifle, cracked and echoed across the valley floor and into the rocks. Ryan then noticed the robot had a new, perfectly round hole in its metal chest—close to the shoulder. He estimated it was from a .50 caliber round.

Ping—the sound of metal hitting metal. A second, same-sized hole appeared on the hovercraft. Then, another distant report cracked and echoed.

"Get in!" the robot yelled.

Ryan, scurrying to his feet, launched himself at the hovercraft, while the Two-ton robot gunned the throttle. Nearly losing his grip, Ryan hauled his body into the bucket seat, positioned directly behind the robot. The soaring hovercraft's engines pulled both against the seat backs as they climbed the steep, rocky hillside.

Ryan pointed over the robot's shoulder: "There! Get us into that scrub up ahead … out of sight."

"You think?" Two-ton yelled back.

Terrific! My smartass AI is now a smartass robot. Ryan, pointing ahead, said, "There's an opening … gun it!"

Ping … ping … ping. Although Ryan couldn't see where the hovercraft was last hit, he heard the three bullets strike home. He looked toward the distant plateau and the grouping of tall buttes. And then, he caught it—the instantaneous, bright, reflection—*Scope glare.* Gripping the back of the robot's seat, Ryan fought against the g-forces. He reached over the robot's shoulder and slammed the controls to the left. The craft abruptly swerved left—the engines straining.

"You need to keep changing course. A steady target is a dead target!"

Ryan was suddenly thrown back against the seat as the robot, taking his advice, abruptly turned to the right, while accelerating. So much dust was being displaced with the vehicle's back and forth aerial motion that a dense reddish cloud had formed all around them, making it almost impossible to see where they were going. On the bright side, they were a much more difficult target to hit.

Something brushed against his cheek. He reached a hand up to his face, fearing he'd been hit by one of Orloff's rounds. Looking at his fingers, he saw blood. Suddenly, seeing a blur of black scraggly branches flying toward him from up ahead, he leaned forward—bowing low—sheltering behind the robot's bulk. A bullet hadn't grazed his cheek, only the scrub brush. He risked a peek over the robot's shoulder and noticed a massive tangle of thorny bramble that seemed to go on and on. A small clearing lay just up ahead.

"Cut the engines!"

Two-ton set the vehicle down within the clearing, cutting the engines. Music still blared the last verse of *Hip to Be Square* until Two-ton hit a switch on the dash, then everything went deadly quiet.

Ryan patted the robot's shoulder. "Okay ... out with you ... I'm driving."

Two-ton awkwardly turned around in the seat and, for the first time, Ryan could take in its odd-looking metal face. Stifling an urge to laugh, Ryan had the immediate impression that a metallic, oversized, crash-test dummy was staring back at him.

It took some wiggling for the robot to extricate itself from the narrow cockpit and stand on solid ground. Ryan gawked up at the giant mechanical figure and, also climbing out, he continued to stare.

"First of all ... thank you for saving my life. That ... *thing* ... was going to eat me. And second, how ... ?" Ryan queried, gesturing first at the robot then at the strange-looking hovercraft.

"I felt useless; an AI stuck inside the van's confines. With a little exploring, using the van's limited external sensors, I found there were all kinds of junk parts and electronics lying around. The most important find was this Tromian maintenance bot. It was in pieces, but receptive to Trom audio signals. I got it moving and was able to instruct it on how to reattach its own limbs. I called him Baron. After that, it needed a bit of tweaking, but I soon got it sufficiently operational. I instructed it to find the van's cockpit, and from there, together, we were able to transfer my AI Pac into the chest of this bot. I replaced Baron's AI with my own. The interfaces were vastly different so several hours were needed just to do that. Now Trom robots, called mechers, like this one, are notorious for being ridiculously clumsy and top-heavy. So I reprogrammed the internal stabilizers and adjusted the gyros—"

Ryan cut him off, "Okay ... got it! And the hovercraft?"

"That actually took me longer to assemble and to get working sufficiently. For the most part, it's your basic, sustained hover sand-crawler-type vehicle." Two-ton stared down at Ryan.

"I'm assuming this robot is equipped with better sensors than those on the van?"

"Hell, yeah, man … not that it couldn't be improved upon. I'd like to—"

"Where's Wendy?" Ryan asked. Annoyed, getting impatient, he cut him off again.

The robot turned its body and pointed, "There's a rise over that way. She's there. I can't quite determine her condition, but bro … she's breathing … her body is putting out heat at 98.6."

Relieved, Ryan said, "That's excellent! And what about Orloff Picket?"

"The fucker is one hundred-and-twenty-three yards away from Wendy's location, in a stand of trees."

"Okay … we're going to have to deal with that hillbilly first. Wendy, obviously, is bait … used to lure me here."

Ryan stared off in the direction the robot had pointed to. The overgrowth of the surrounding bramble made it nearly impossible to see much of anything. "I have an idea. Not sure if it's a very good one, but it's the best one I've got."

* * *

Perched high up in a tree, Orloff Picket continued to stare off to the horizon. A layer of dust still lingered above the distant thick scrub where, most certainly, they were hiding. He hadn't anticipated the arrival of the robot. He'd only gotten a quick glimpse of it, but he knew it was his—the same one laid out on a worktable in the second out-building. Orloff peered through his riflescope—trying to find them through its precision magnified lenses. Again, he raised his head, pondering: That robot was left in pieces; had never been operational. Not since he'd scavenged it from a deserted space station several light-years away. *So then how? It didn't fix itself.*

Orloff felt a slight tingling—like a buzzing—deep down within his core. He also was aware his heart rate had increased. *Was it fear?* The briefest of smiles crossed his lips. He'd already underestimated the young deliveryman once. Had he done so again? To say he was resourceful, it seemed, would be an understatement.

Mamma, and his brothers, wanted Ryan Chase alive … simply captured and kept secured until they arrived. But Orloff wasn't good with orders. And, in this case, the prospect of going up against a worthy adversary—one to one—was simply too great a temptation. Too enticing. Only the rhino-warrior, currently mounted up on his trophy wall, had also shown levels of strategic thinking. In the end—the deliveryman would succumb to the same fate. He'd make a fine addition, hanging alongside his other trophies.

Orloff's mind turned back to the robot then to the sand-crawler hovercraft. He recalled seeing it, sitting among the junk piles within his compound. He'd watched Ryan for hours on foot—desperately looking for Wendy. *So who then re-assembled the robot and the hovercraft?* He considered the fact that there could be others, working along with Ryan. *Impossible!* He'd scanned the Consignment Freight van when it entered the atmosphere and Ryan was the only one on board. And there certainly weren't others here, already on Alaster-Rei. With very few exceptions, it was almost impossible for anyone to maneuver through the surrounding asteroid fields. And as far as intelligent life here went—they'd all been killed, stuffed, and mounted a long time ago.

Orloff thought about his preparations. The numerous booby-traps. The fact he knew these surroundings like no others did. This was his terrain. By nightfall, the deliveryman would be dead. And then he'd have to decide what to do with Wendy. Another brief smile crossed his lips. Shouldering the rifle, he methodically began climbing down from his high tree perch. In the distance, he heard the sound of an engine starting. The sand-crawler was on the move again.

CHAPTER 36

Jason was seated within the *Goliath*'s main rear cabin. He couldn't turn, or even raise his head—but he was aware of the others seated next to and around him in the nearby seats. It had been close to an hour since they'd been hit with the drooler. Since then, Jason had been working, nearly nonstop, at accessing his NanoCom. He'd counted seven separate NanoCom hails coming in from the *Jumelle*. Hails he couldn't answer.

By now the crew of the *Jumelle* would already be on alert that comms from his team had ceased. They'd be readying to send another team. Truth was—he was surprised they hadn't already. His thoughts turned to the Craing man, Jeebrie. He was back with his device.

Jason's aching head throbbed. Concentrating for so long—and not achieving any results—on calling up his nano-devices selection menu. Out of the corner of his eye, Jason watched Jeebrie. He was walking up and down the aisle between the seats—taking in the faces of those he's incapacitated—looking for any indication they were regaining their motor skills.

Jason was, in fact, feeling some control coming back to him—both physical and mental. Jeebrie was at the far end of the aisle now, but ready to turn back. Jason, finally, was able to access the primary NanoCom menu. Jeebrie was on his way back. Trying to initiate voice communications would be a mistake—he'd be hit with the drooler before he got two words out. He accessed the rarely used these days NanoTexting sub-menu and wrote:

All captured. Team hit with drooler. Send help.

He quickly sent the message with no time to see who it was he sent it to.

Jeebrie was standing right in from of him, the drooler in his outstretched hand pointed at his face. Jason continued to gaze forward with a dead stare. He tried to drool—to look as pathetic as possible.

A deep voice came from behind and almost made Jason jump. "He coming around?" Brent stepped into view and lowered his head to within several inches of Jason's.

"I don't know … maybe."

"Well, hit him again … just to be certain."

Jeebrie said, "The effects are cumulative … getting hit too many times with this and the paralyses becomes permanent."

Jason felt his mouth twitch. It was a reflex to hearing he was about to permanently become a quadriplegic. His mind raced. Who had he sent the NanoText to? It probably defaulted to the last person he'd communicated with that way. *Crap* … was it Mollie? She was the one who liked to Nano-Text more than anyone else … Would she know what to do with the sent message? How long would it take her to reach the *Jumelle*? Hell, if she was in class she may ignore it completely—until later.

"I don't give a shit … hit him again … hit all of them again. We're getting close to the asteroid field. We can't have any distractions."

That surprised Jason. He wasn't aware the *Goliath* had

even left the Craing heavy's flight bay.

Jeebrie was now using his drooler—it made a very distinctive clicking sound when the thing was activated. He'd started at the first row of seats. Jason wondered who it was sitting up there. Was it Nan? Or maybe Stone and Rizzo?

Jeebrie was moving to the second row of seats. Another voice said, "We've reached the outer fringe of the field." It was Colonel Pope. Jason felt his hands begin to flex into fists. Mentally he forced himself to relax. The clicking sound was getting closer.

Startled, a bright white flash filled the confined space. Jason found he could now blink his eyes—although his limbs were pretty much still limp at his sides. He heard plasma fire and the resulting ozone smell filled his nostrils. He still didn't know who it was that had phase-shifted into the *Goliath*. With effort he directed his eyes left and found—*Ricket?*

He wore a battle suit and was using the two integrated wrist plasma guns. Ricket wasn't alone, two paces in front of him was another familiar form also wearing a battle suit. It was then that Jason remembered who it had been he'd last NanoTexted … Dira. She fired twice at Colonel Pope and he went down like a sack of rocks. Within seconds, another phase-shift flash occurred.

* * *

It took another full hour before Jason regained his motor skills. Nan, Sergeant Major Stone, Rizzo, and Bristol—all were still paralyzed and recovering in Medical. Billy, who had been seated next to Jason on the *Goliath*, was also up now and moving around.

Colonel Pope, stunned by Dira's plasma fire, was unconscious and being held within a confinement cell within the *Jumelle*'s brig. The three brothers, along with the Craing, Jeebrie, had initialized their stolen SuitPac devices and phase-shifted into the nearby asteroid field. Apparently Brent had gotten fairly well-versed with the practice of phase-shifting. Other events in space that Jason had not been aware of while on the *Goliath*—but first he needed a shower and change of clothes. Coming out of the head, Dira was waiting for him sitting on the end of the bed.

"Shouldn't you be attending to your new patients?" Jason asked.

"And watch them ... what? Lie in bed doing absolutely nothing? ... no, they're fine for a few minutes."

"Hey ... thank you for showing up the way you did. I was expecting Gunny with a team of Sharks."

"That would have taken another ten minutes ... something told me in that brief NanoText of yours that things couldn't wait. I grabbed Ricket, who was standing right next to me in Medical, and with his help, determined the multiple phase-shifts needed to cross space to reach the *Goliath*."

"Well ... you were one fierce combatant. Ricket too."

Dira said, "Look ... Gunny wants to get you up to speed on current circumstances. While you were laying around on the *Goliath*, the *Jumelle* came under attack."

Dressed in a fresh uniform, and feeling mostly back to normal—Jason pulled Dira up to her feet and kissed her. She began to pull away and he pulled her back into him and kissed her again. She laughed, "No ... this is not going to happen right now. I wasn't kidding there's a lot going on and the captain of this ship needs to get back into the proverbial saddle."

He gave her wry smile. "You're right ... I'll have her brief me in my ready room."

* * *

Gunny Orion, Ricket and Billy were already seated when Jason entered his quarters' ready room.

Billy looked annoyed and started talking before Jason had a chance to sit down at the head of the table. "I'm going to kill those backwoods sons of bitches."

Jason let out a long breath, he too wanted the same thing.

"I've never felt so ... pathetic ... useless," Billy continued.

"You're not alone, Billy. Gunny ... tell me about the course of events, here in local space. Something about the *Jumelle* being attacked?" Jason asked.

"Ship and crew were never in any real danger, Cap ... from what we make of it, it was a small fleet of mining vessels. Some of the ships were well armed ... plasma canons ... rail guns."

"Where did they come from ... what were they after?" Billy asked.

Orion didn't make eye-contact with Billy, but instead kept her eyes on Jason. "The majority of the vessels had Picket Mining logos on their hulls ... and in the brief communications we established, apparently this section of space has been annexed. We'd crossed into a no trespass zone."

"Annexed?" Jason said. "We're within Alliance space parameters ... well within. You can't annex anything here. Commerce is free to pass through space here unmolested."

Orion shrugged and made an exasperated expression. Ricket shifted in his seat and looked as if he had something to say.

"Go ahead, Ricket," Jason prompted.

"I've been studying the situation, Captain. It's not one company or one family at play here. What you have are feuding pirate syndicates."

"Seriously?" Jason said. He thought of his own past dealings with interstellar pirates, most prominently the infamous and long deceased *Captain Stalls*. Jason shook his head. *I really hate pirates.*

"Yes. It's primarily two powerful syndicates—both are heavily vested with their own mining operations mainly within the Oort belt. It's the fastest growing industry in the system … hundreds of billions of dollars at stake."

"So how do the Pickets play into all this?"

"They're a big part of one of the competing syndicates. The Pickets provide the workers and the equipment, Captain."

"And the pirates provide the sales channels … illegal or otherwise," Jason added.

"Yes, Captain."

This was the type of thing Jason would have loved to hand off to the U.S. Fleet—but this fit well within Star Watch parameters. And with the regional redistricting of the organization, this was most definitely Jason's, and the *Jumelle*'s, district.

"And the attempt to kidnap Nan? That's a part of this?"

Orion said, "Definitely. We need to talk to Colonel Pope … He should be awake by now."

CHAPTER 37

Pope was not only awake, he was highly agitated. Jason heard his rantings as soon as he entered the *Jumelle's* brig. It was empty with the exception of a guard, one of Billy's Sharks, and Colonel Pope. Jason passed by several empty confinement cells and stopped when he reached Pope's. Jason looked through the energized, bluish translucent energy field at the colonel sitting upon his cell-bed.

Seeing Jason, Pope rose to his feet—his face twisting into angry rage. "How dare you confine me like this ... like a common criminal ... a thug. I've served my country—"

Jason was about to put the older man in his place, when from behind, Nan's voice interjected.

"Shut up, Pope ... you'll be spending the rest of your life behind bars ... that is if you're not executed for your crimes."

Jason hadn't heard Nan enter the brig. She too had showered and changed. Her hair was still wet and there was a flush on her cheeks from the hot water. She stood beside Jason and looked at Pope with contempt and something else—*hurt*. Jason surmised there had been something to this relationship, at least for Nan, and the realization that it had all been a ploy—well, she was still coming to grips with it.

"I left office as President of the United States with the

highest popularity ratings of any president ... including Abe Lincoln and George Washington. So believe me when I say that what I recommend ... will have an immense impact on the eventual sentence handed down to you by the military tribunal. I'm going to give you one chance to come clean ... one chance to lay things out ... without holding anything back. I detect you're lying, or holding back information, I'm out of here and you can deal with the fallout."

Pope seemed to deflate before their eyes. He looked at Nan with sorrowful eyes—as if he was about to cry. He said, "I'm sorry ... Nan ... I never meant to—"

"Don't you dare go there, Pope. I need to know exactly where my nephew is ... how to retrieve him and what your arrangement is with the Pickets."

Jason signaled the guard, "Bring us some chairs ... we're going to be here a while."

* * *

With the energy field deactivated, Nan and Jason sat and listened to Pope unravel his bazaar story. How he had first heard of a rare dark matter compound discovered within a certain area within the Oort cloud from an inter-stellar pirate named Stuart Futch, commonly known as *Stu-Fu*. The pirate was a middle-aged American who'd been captured from his small mid-western farm during the early years of the Craing war. He and a band of other prisoners had escaped from the light cruiser's jail cell, no small feat in itself, and within three days had taken control of the Craing craft. Stu-Fu spent the rest of the war raiding Craing supply outposts and even smaller military installations. He'd become an expert at evading direct confrontations—using his Craing vessel to slip into hostile territory and just as quickly slip away—with the vessel's holds filled to the brim with everything from food supplies, to weapons, to anything else that could be traded on the rapidly burgeoning open black market. Because Stu-Fu had directed his energies toward a common enemy—the Craing—the Alliance at that time was unconcerned with his activities. Pope had become friends, of sorts, with the pirate and—over time—had been talked into helping the pirate with several gray-area endeavors—including the exchanging of military-grade weapons and other supplies for information. All under the table stuff. When the Craing war ended, Pope no longer had a need for Stu-Fu's services.

"Is that when things changed … when you went over to the dark side of things?" Nan asked.

Pope nodded, "I'd gotten in too deep with the pirate. Too many years staying on the fringe of what was legal. He'd kept a file … a very in-depth file on all of our transactions. If it got into the wrong hands within the U.S. fleet, I'd be arrested and they'd throw away the key."

"Which is happening anyway," Jason said.

Pope didn't reply.

Nan said, "So it was this Stu-Fu character that came up with this elaborate plan to kidnap me? To use my nephew to lure me into space?"

Pope nodded.

"And how does this dark matter compound work into all of this?"

Pope said, "Look … the pirates are keyed in to all kinds of commerce. If something becomes a hot commodity, he's on a mission to get it and exploit it. When it comes to DM^2 … that's what it's commonly called … dark matter squared … it's a game-changer. Hell … everyone wants it. Its output properties are phenomenal … Enables propulsion systems to be on par with Caldurian technology."

Jason didn't like hearing that. Until now, the remaining Caldurian vessels within Star Watch were so far advanced that nothing else, from any of the thousands of intelligent known systems out there, even came close.

Jason thought about what Ricket had told him earlier about squabbling pirates in a section of the Oort cloud and this seemed to fit with what Pope was saying.

"So get back to holding Nan as a hostage," Jason said.

"Stu-Fu was aware of my ... *new relationship* ... with Nan. And he was keenly aware of her influence, *still*, with various U.S. Fleet and Alliance decision-makers. Simply put, Stu-Fu wanted a means to legitimize his operations and become the sole provider of DM^2 to all of the Alliance districts and beyond. With the stroke of a pen, he'd no longer have to fight with a growing numbers of other pirate syndicates to sell the rare dark matter compound. He'd make hundreds of billions of dollars and no longer have to worry about the U.S. Fleet invading his installations. Knowing Nan's reputation for being above-board and honest—there were few options available. With little digging, we discovered Nan had a nephew who was currently living and working in space. Someone who was easily accessible."

"And the pirate used the Pickets to help orchestrate the whole thing?" Jason said.

"I never liked the plan." Pope looked at Nan, "I never wanted to put you in danger. I was assured you would never be harmed."

Nan rolled her eyes and shook her head.

Pope continued, "Things started to fall apart with the weakest link in the plan. Fucking Orloff. We all knew he had issues ... a predisposition for violence. What he did have, was an uncanny ability to track and hunt all sorts of game. He was good at it. Orloff was relegated to the job of tracking down Ryan and capturing him—to do so in any means necessary."

"So Orloff has him ... my nephew is safe?" Nan asked, looking hopeful.

"Maybe. We've had only a few communications with

him. Apparently this small freight delivery man has been difficult to capture. That's not good. It only increased Orloff's psychological impulses ... he's as crazy as they come. Bastard scares the hell out of me. The plan was to have Ryan taken to a small, hidden planet within the Oort cloud. The place is nearly impossible to get to ... even by a ship with phase-shift capabilities ... it would be too wide to shift into before a house-sized asteroid—which are moving along at tremendous speeds ... would slam right into it. No ... only by traversing a known passageway through the field can anyone hope to land a ship on that planet."

"So there's a chance Ryan is there ... being held there by Orloff?"

Pope didn't look optimistic, "Yeah ... Orloff, and probably his brothers too. My suspicion ... and I'm sorry, Nan ... is that Orloff has killed or is in the process of killing him as we speak. Orloff doesn't care about monetary gain ... wealth ... he cares about his own personal satisfaction and his odd pursuits."

"You better hope he is alive, asshole," Jason said. "Tell us the name of this planet and how to reach it."

"Alaster-Rei, and I already told you ... it's impossible to reach. That's why they chose it."

CHAPTER 38

Brent Picket was by no means an accomplished phase-shifter. What he understood about the Star Watch-issued battle suits was just enough to be dangerous. Hundreds, if not thousands, of HUD menus and submenus could be accessed at any time—purposely or by mistake. The latter was more the norm for Brent. He knew basic comms, the very basics about how to initiate a group-shift with others wearing battle suits. What he was a little fuzzy about was establishing complex, far-away, drop locations. He imagined that once one was familiar with them—had been properly trained—he could pretty much hop around to any location within several thousand miles with simplistic ease.

So when things went sideways on the *Goliath*, when two beings flashed into the cabin—a short little Craing dude and a violet-skinned female, *and what a spectacular vision she was*—Brent and his brothers found themselves not knowing how to properly respond as plasma fire erupted from their wrists. *How the hell did they do that?* It only underscored how little he knew what these suits were capable of.

The only thing Brent could come up with was getting them out of there—fast! He'd use his somewhat practiced group phase-shift experience to put them somewhere else. But, at the time, he didn't have a clue where he would be sending them: neither the direction nor the distance. As it did turn out, in an instant flash he sent himself, Larry, Payne, and Jeebrie right smack into the asteroid field. He cursed aloud as spinning ice rocks the size of fucking Winnebagos flew past them—above, below, and on all sides. Flashing into space, they all screamed like little girls until they realized that somehow, miraculously, they'd found some kind of slip-stream band within the field of rocks that was free of flying projectiles.

So now they were here, floating in space. Brent had pretty much tuned his brothers out while he tried to figure a way out of the muddle.

Larry said, "I think I shit in my suit."

"Spare me the details," Brent replied.

"I've never been so scared in my life," Payne added.

Brent continued to ignore his brothers. He saw that Jeebrie was drifting deeper into the asteroid field. "Jeebrie, you need to stay with us! You're getting way too close to—"

He watched in horror as Jeebrie drifted directly into the path of an oncoming, bowling ball-size asteroid. One second Jeebrie was there and the next only a heavy mist of flesh, blood, and mangled battle suit remained.

Brent's ears rang from Larry's ongoing screams.

Obviously, this *safe haven* slipstream was anything but safe. Turning his head, he saw the distant small planet Alaster-Rei, nestled far away beyond the belt. It would take many phase-shifts to reach it. The only other option was to return to open space. He looked at his HUD readings. For now, their air reserves were fine. Same with the suit's power reserves. *Nope*, he thought. Once back in open space they'd surely run out of air and die. Who would ever find them? So onward they must go, hoping and praying they didn't end up like poor Jeebrie. At least if they did, their end would be quick.

Using the unfamiliar HUD sub-menus for phase-shifting, Brent focused full concentration on the task ahead. The problem was not having a definitive end location when floating in open space.

"Brent … we're drifting," Payne said.

"I just need a minute." Brent inputted his *best guess* coordinates—ones that would take them in the right direction—toward the planet Alaster-Rei.

Larry, his voice still an irritating whine, shouted out, "Brent! We're moving into the rocks!"

Brent glanced up. They were mere feet from a blur of ice rocks streaming past them. Going ahead, he initiated the group phase-shift and closed his eyes.

* * *

Brent, opening his eyes, looked about for his brothers. *Okay* … there's one and there's the other. He let out a sigh of relief and began inputting the coordinates for the next phase-shift. *There has to be a way to do multiple phase-shifts with this suit*, he thought, though he had neither the time nor the patience to figure that out. Larry was saying something and, again, Brent tuned him out. *Damn*! Mistakenly transposing two digits, he cursed the whole plan. He cursed Pope for bringing his harebrained scheme to them in the first place, and Mamma for going along with it. Next, he cursed Stu-fu and his pirates, who surely were going to kill them all for not holding up to their end of the bargain. Sure … on paper it had all sounded good; sounded great! Corner the market mining this Dark Matter DM^2 shit. Make billions! The pirates had all the right connections; all the means necessary to sell as much material as the Pickets' mining operations could excavate. The big cog in the works was obtaining official mining rights. Without the rights, every Tom,

Dick and Harry competitor would fly there, like all those in the Oklahoma land rush of the late 1800s. Pope had assured them that the ex-president lady would do anything to get her nephew back. The kid was super-important to her—a last connection to her dead sister, or something like that. A cluster fuck—the whole plan was in a tailspin, unless, of course, they could safely reach the planet.

Brent, after initiating the next phase-shift, opened his eyes and again counted both brothers, drifting right alongside him. Perhaps he was starting to get the hang of it, after all. He went right to work on the next set of coordinates and noticed, aided by a helpful *tips* prompt, that he could pretty much cut and paste all the work he'd been doing. That would speed things up significantly!

Five more phase-shifts and they were still alive. Brent made the conscious decision a while back to never look at what was either coming at them or passing by them, and to ignore Larry's perpetual whining. If they ever got back onto solid ground, he promised himself the gratification of beating his frizzy-haired sibling within an inch of his life.

Brent, making an exception to his own rule, glanced up. The planet was right there—looming bright and looking close enough to almost reach out and touch. How many shifts had they managed? Fifty? He didn't remember. It looked like one more phase-shift would do the trick. He entered the exact coordinates for the compound, and in a final bright white flash the three brothers disappeared from the asteroid belt.

* * *

The three brothers flashed into view, two hundred yards from the compound, and fell to the ground both mentally and physically drained. What they'd accomplished was beyond amazing—truly miraculous.

Eventually, Brent sat up and spotted Orloff's big, brown,

creepy-looking, Paotow tanker. The monstrosity was parked close to the main cabin. But what most captured his attention was the Consignment Freight delivery van nearby. He'd seen a thousand similar vehicles across space. Much like FedEx and UPS trucks that once were a common sight in neighborhoods on Earth, before the numerous Craing invasions.

"Larry, Payne … check out the van. Make sure no one's hiding in there."

In truth, Brent already knew the van was empty of life. He understood the HUD sensor readings well enough—but he doubted Payne, and certainly not Larry, had figured out what those readings meant. Hell, they might never understand them.

Brent made his way into the cabin, doing a quick looksee to make sure nothing unwanted was in there. Deactivating his battle suit, he watched all the tiny segments retract back into the small SuitPac device he wore on his belt. He smiled. *That sight never gets old!*

Next, he moved outside and headed to the tanker. The portside hatch seemed jammed so he walked around and tried the starboard hatch. It opened right up and Brent found the inside airlock hatch already open. Stepping into the main lower compartment, his nostrils flared. *Ugh.* Something putrid was on the ship. Brent had tried to be patient with his younger brother, knowing he had mental issues. Smart— probably some sort of *rain man* genius—but his … *what was the word? … proclivities* made him a constant problem. For long spans of time he'd be fine. Did his job managing the various Picket mining operations. He most always kept his calm but then, all of a sudden, he'd be off on a junket. Disappear without a word for days, sometimes weeks. Often he'd come here. This compound was Orloff's special place. Brent tried not to think about what else went on here, above and beyond hunting game.

He looked about the compartment. Midway down the

port side was his brother's workbench. *Creepy.* The bulkheads were void of anything—the compartment cold and uninviting. *Creepy-creepy.* He took the narrow stairway to his right at the stern and hurried up to the top level. He started at the bow end of the ship, first checking Orloff's quarters. It was immaculately clean. *Who at his age still makes his bed?* Off to the right was another small stairway. Brent knew from past experience that it led up to the claustrophobically small cockpit.

He moved back out to the passageway and next checked the holding cell. Opening the hatch, he saw the chains and bindings lying on the deck. A thin mattress, stained with god only knew what, took up much of the space. He side-stepped an overturned metal bucket and left. He checked out the other compartments on his way astern. The second door opened into some kind of storage compartment. Large blue plastic barrels dominated the space. The smell in there was ghastly. Staying at full arm's length, Brent used extended fingers to lift the lid off the closest barrel. Noting the contents within the barrel's murky dark confines, Brent instinctively flinched. The barrel top went flying, as Brent doubled over, both gagging and dry heaving. *Oh my god ...* a fucking barrel full of ... legs!

CHAPTER 39

At any other time, Ryan would have thoroughly enjoyed the exhilarating speed while flying two feet off the ground at close to one hundred miles an hour. The sand crawler, with its three oversized turbine engines, exuded so much raw power that Ryan was fairly certain he could double, maybe even triple, his speed, if outer conditions allowed. But his thoughts were consumed with Wendy. *Was she harmed in any way—had she been raped?* What was she going through at this very moment? It took all his will power not to crank the controls to the left and go find her—rescue her. But that was exactly what the mountain man wanted.

Ryan slowed down just enough to maneuver between an outcropping of sandstone rocks then quickly goosed the throttle back to its former speed.

Feeling a tap at his shoulder, he glanced back at the Two-ton robot, and yelled, "What is it?"

The robot leaned in closer, "Wendy is over that way … about a half mile."

"And Orloff?"

"Straight ahead. Two hundred and fifteen yards."

Ryan brought the craft to a complete stop, letting the

engines idle a moment. "All right … this is where you get out, robot."

* * *

The wind had come up, and Orloff Picket felt his large pant legs being whipped and buffeted back and forth, like a couple of flapping flags. It brought with it a funky putrid odor, coming upwind off the narrow lake—situated below and behind him. Between tree trunks, for those fleeting moments when the hovercraft was out in the open, he tracked their progress with his riflescope. He fired off three rounds and, missing each time, silently cursed himself as he looked back up. The target was too erratic and moving too fast to get a clear shot. He'd anticipated Ryan being on foot—not whizzing across the dunes and tundra in a machine like a maniac. The echoing roar off the hovercraft suddenly became silent. Orloff, putting his eye back to the scope, searched for any sign of the sand crawler and its occupants.

A static burst of noise began emanating from his daypack, and he gazed down at where it lay on the rocky surface. Lying prone on his belly, his rifle supported up on a small-portable tripod, he continued staring at the pack—willing it to stop making such a racket. Then a fractured-sounding voice accompanied the static, coming out from the radio. Orloff pulled the pack closer and opened the top flap. Without taking his eyes away from the distant terrain, he rifled around inside the pack until he felt the cold metallic radio unit. Pulling it out, he looked at the display and adjusted the squelch and volume controls. He depressed the talk button, and said, "Repeat last message … over."

"Where the hell are you? Where's the kid? Over."

The kid, his brother Brent was referring to, was Ryan Chase; he was supposed to be locked up tight within the Paotow tanker by now. Orloff glanced up toward the sky and realized he hadn't seen a spacecraft arrive. *How did they get here?* He tried to remember if he'd hidden his trophies—pulled the sectionalized sliding accordion bulkhead all the way across that back wall in order to hide them. *Yeah … I definitely did that,* he thought, somewhat relieved.

"He's being dealt with … don't worry about it," Orloff replied.

The radio crackled and Orloff heard several voices that sounded like they were arguing. Brent came back on, "Listen you overgrown retard, everything revolves around that fucking kid … do you have him or not?"

"Yeah, he's in my sights. I'm about to—"

"No! No! No! Do not … I repeat … do not kill him! Do you understand me, ass wipe? If he dies … you die … over!"

"I thought you already had the president lady," Orloff replied. "Why do you still need the kid? Over."

"She … they … got away. Don't worry about that side of things; it's all under control. But we still need the Chase kid … over."

Orloff stayed quiet.

"Look, we're on our way to you in a few … so hang tight and don't do anything stupid. Over."

Calmly, Orloff stared at the radio in his hand. Ten seconds later, he raised the instrument over his head and smashed it down quickly onto the rocks. Once, twice. Three times more he smashed the walky-talky radio until it was little more than a jumble of plastic shards and exposed broken circuit boards. Grunting with satisfaction, he flung what was left of it over the rocky cliffs. He'd deal with his brothers later.

Ryan, and then the girl, had to die. Both knew far too much about what was mounted on his trophy wall. Though people often disappeared when in space he didn't want to be tied to someone's murder. Sure, he understood why they'd needed Nan Reynolds to cooperate. A lot of money was at stake. Contracts made with the kind of people you don't double-cross. But he didn't like how things were changing. He'd managed the Picket family space-mining operations for years, but since that old pirate had become involved … what was his name? Stu-*something*. Orloff didn't like him; didn't like that things were changing. No! His brothers would have to find some other way to recapture the ex-madam president. It wasn't his fault they dropped the ball and let her escape. He was going to finish what he'd come here to do.

He pushed himself up and onto his knees atop the rocky perch. After re-stowing his small tripod into his pack, he moved to shoulder his rifle but suddenly lost his grip. One problem with not having pinkies, things sometimes got fumbled. As the rifle dropped, its stock hit the solid rock below then bounced. Orloff awkwardly grabbed for it—almost felt the cool metal of its long barrel in his hand. The Barrett .50 cal fell forward and slid three feet before sliding over the side. He heard a sickening *crack crack crack* as it smashed onto the rocks below.

Irritated with himself, but keeping an impassive expression, Orloff gazed out over the valley below, then toward the hillside off to his right. Again, hearing the engines roar up and seeing momentary flashes of red, he knew the sand crawler was getting closer. Best he got down there now—be there to witness what happened next. Watching young Ryan Chase's expression change when he encountered the first laid booby trap, for that was what this hunt was all about. One way or another, the delivery man was going to die today. He needed to hurry—retrieve his broken weapon and be ready for the show.

* * *

Ryan brought the hovercraft's speed down to a slow crawl as he approached the foot of the closest of the four buttes. Up atop, the psychopath was undoubtedly perched. Ryan, looking straight up, squinted his eyes against the bright sky but couldn't see a damn thing. He turned off the hovercraft and listened to its hot engines go *tic tic tic*. Then, placing a hand on the Tavor lying across his lap, he waited.

Five minutes later, he climbed up out of the craft onto an immense boulder and moved toward the base of the column-like butte. At least from its front side there was no easy way up. He jumped from one smaller rock to another then moved around to its rear side, where he saw a clear way to ascend to the top. Stacked step-like rocks were at the bottom, with a series of natural switchbacks set higher up. The chance of Orloff still being up there was slim. It wasn't like the sand crawler could ever be stealthily quiet, but he had to go check.

Ryan took in a breath, thinking *this is too easy*. But seeing no other alternative, he started his trek upward. The third step abruptly shifted under his right foot. Losing his balance, Ryan wildly windmilled his arms to keep upright. A distant echoing crack came. Movement too. From above, he heard the unmistakable sound of heavy rocks grating against other heavy rocks. What earlier looked like part of the butte itself, hundreds of feet above him, was actually a separate slab of rock now precariously leaning against it. Paralyzed, Ryan watched in horror as the ginormous slab of rock continued to pull away from the butte and go perfectly vertical—only to slowly lean out above him. So large was the slab there was nowhere for him to run—nowhere to take shelter. He watched with dread as the mass of stone came completely away and began to fall. With no clear alternative coming to mind, Ryan pulled the Tavor from his shoulder and began firing up at the big falling rock. He switched the Tavor to full auto and emptied the magazine into its center mass. The ear-splitting sound echoed off the surrounding rocks, *crack crack crack crack*. Above him, at no fewer than one hundred feet, the slab began to break apart. A sandstone solid piece of rock, it would have flattened him like a bug. Now, as mere seconds ticked past, the rock started to break apart—much of it turning to sandy rubble.

Ryan threw himself down on the rocks then curled into a tight ball. He covered his head with his arms and clenched his eyes shut, waiting to die.

As the largest of the fractured rock boulders crashed about him, a constant shower of small rocks and sand landed on his backpack, head, and exposed legs. Something that was both hard and sharp hit his shoulder, causing him to scream out in agony.

Ryan realized he'd survived the ordeal. By some miracle he was still breathing—hadn't been squashed into a puddle of fleshy goo.

Slowly raising his head, he assessed his condition. His left shoulder throbbed badly and, rubbing it with his other hand, he felt warm moisture there—blood, but not a lot of it. No bones seemed to be broken, but damn—it sure hurt. About to stand, Ryan noticed something beneath the cracked rock of the third step he'd been leaning against. Lifting the slab up, it broke completely in half, and lying there, just beneath it, he saw a jumble of wires attached to some kind of pre-hidden pressure plate. It had been an elaborate booby trap. Ryan thought back to when he'd first stepped on the step. There'd been a noise—prior to the sound of the rocks grating—like a tiny explosion. He shook his head. Setting this up would have taken hours. He briefly wondered if this setup was all for him or had Orloff prepared this trap days, even weeks, earlier? Perhaps for another poor shmuck, also caught in one of Orloff's games of hunter and prey. Well, Ryan wasn't about to become anyone's prey—not today—not ever.

He raised his head and took in the terrain around him. Orloff would have wanted to watch the scenario play out. He rose to his feet and slowly turned around on his heels.

"You'll have to do a lot better than this, ass hole! I'm coming for you!"

Several distant firearm reports startled Ryan and he ducked his head. *Small arms—not the Barrett .50 caliber.* A single round ricocheted off a rock behind him. Ryan ducked down lower to his haunches—then quickly dove into the nearby rock pile.

CHAPTER 40

Staying low, doing his best to keep his head below the rocks surrounding him, Ryan started to move back in the direction of the sand crawler. Halfway there, he heard the unmistakable sound of three turbine engines coming to life. *He's taking the crawler.* About to hurry after him, he stopped himself. *No ... Orloff likes traps. That's what he wants me to do.* Ryan pulled the pack from his back and, like a knife being driven into him, a searing pain engulfed his left shoulder. *Maybe something's broken in there, after all,* he thought. He opened the flap and dug out the last full magazine, swapping it with the spent one. Reloading the Tavor, he gingerly swung the pack back in place on his back. As quietly as possible, he made his way around the base of the butte.

Ryan heard the engines changing cadence as the craft moved off—its echoes bouncing off the rocks and all the way down into an adjoining valley. *At least Orloff isn't lurking out there—his riflescope trained on my head*, he rationalized. Picking up his pace, he continued to listen to the distant drone of the crawler. Coming around the butte's front side, he further tracked the sound. It was moving in the same direction the Two-ton-AI robot indicated Wendy was being held. Dread swept over him. He pulled the straps of the pack tighter and began to run.

* * *

He figured he was approximately three-quarters of the way there and clung to the hope that the robot, Two-ton, had made its way to where she was being held and had freed her long before Orloff would arrive.

A sheen of sweat covered Ryan's face, and the pain in his shoulder had progressed further to halfway down his left arm. The ground, mostly even here, was interspersed with clusters of trees, then clumps of rocks, then clusters of trees again. *At least there's no thorny bramble in these parts*, he thought, as he trudged on—running, then jogging, then running again.

Passing through a strand of tall yellow pines, he nearly tripped over the robot. His quick-moving stride landed him mere inches from its head, which was turned up—its conciliatory expression unnaturally fixed. Ryan went down on one knee. Assessing the damage, he turned the robot's head to the side and noticed it was dented in and now concave. An arm was missing. Only by ducking under close, low-hanging branches did he come across the metallic appendage hidden beneath them. Pulling it clear, he held it up—not quite sure what to do with it. He set it on the ground beside him then placed his open palm onto the robot's chest where a human heart would be. Orloff had run the robot down—probably gunning the powerful engines to inflict the greatest amount of impact. As sadness of the whole situation overtook Ryan, he wiped away the moisture welling in his eyes. Twice he'd lost his best friend to the same lunatic, who was doing who knew what now to Wendy. His grief quickly morphed into rage, and his fists tightened into two white-knuckled balls. Aloud, he said, "I'm going to kill that son of a bitch!"

He sensed sudden movement and looked down at the battered robot—its head turned left and right twice before its mechanical eyes locked on to Ryan's.

"Ahh … those tears for me?"

Ryan's first impulse was to hug the mechanical man, but he restrained himself. Instead, he asked, "Why don't you shut up for once and tell me how bad the damage is?"

"I was in the process of figuring that out when you interrupted me."

"I thought you were … *dead*."

"Um … truth is … that ship already sailed. But the artificial intelligence you've come to know seems to be in pretty good shape." The robot, while trying to sit up, realized it had a missing arm. "What the fu—"

"Hey, let me help you." Ryan put a hand behind the robot's torso and lifted up as the robot tried again to rise.

Success. Two-ton's AI robot sat up and looking at the ground, asked, "Hand me that arm, will you?"

Ryan did as asked and the robot began inspecting the arm—first turning it over, then side to side, then end over end.

"Promise me one thing."

"What's that?"

"That when this is all over you'll find me a better host robot. I mean, I already know mechers were poorly built … probably put together by some third-world hourly worker late for his lunch break … but come on …" The robot positioned the mechanical limb's upper ball joint, lining it up exactly with the open, receiving socket hole at the shoulder. "Okay, now give it a good whack."

Ryan had observed how the robot clutched the detached arm in its functioning hand, doing its best to keep the arm still—the ball and socket lined up.

"While we're young … would be nice."

Ryan smacked the robot's detached upper arm and heard it click into place. He looked at its distorted face for some reaction. "Well?"

Two-ton turned the arm—facing it up, then facing it down; raising it up then lowering it. Flexing each finger, one by one, and then all five together, it made a fist. "Works good enough. Probably will fall off when I need it most … but good enough for now."

"Can you stand?"

* * *

Orloff knelt down next to Wendy. Her head was down and her long disheveled hair covered most of her face. He took a look behind the tree and saw that her hands were still bound. "You haven't called out."

Her head tilted up and he saw her eyes, cold with hatred, staring up at him through strands of hair. She shook her head. "You've got me … you're not getting Ryan, too."

"I could have grabbed Ryan … killed him any number of times."

He tapped a holstered side arm, strapped onto his thigh. She didn't recall seeing it there before. "I need water."

Orloff raised two fingers and glided them down her cheek. At first, she thought it was an affectionate gesture but noting his eyes—how he was looking at her more like a scientist observing an experiment—she quickly realized what he was doing. He was inspecting her face—her flesh—for defects.

"Yes … you're right. We must keep you properly hydrated."

Renewed fear restricted her chest. She felt adrenalin course through her—bringing her, once again, to the very brink of sanity. The crazed man—with his near-perfectly round head and awkward, weird-shaped body, stuffed into oversized pants synched ridiculously high above his belly—left for several moments. Returning with a canteen, he lifted its top opening to her lips and let her drink. When she'd drunk as much as her stomach could hold, she jerked her head away and coughed. "Enough!" she sputtered.

He twisted the cap back on the canteen and started to walk away.

"I need to pee … it's been hours."

He turned and looked down at her. "No one's stopping you."

She glared up at him. "Fine, then I guess you don't mind a rash all over my skin down there."

Orloff shrugged. "I don't. Nothing down there is utilized."

Wendy's mind flashed to the trophy wall—all heads and partial torsos. No legs.

"You're beyond sick. I hope I have the chance to see you get what you deserve."

Studying her, he tilted his head. She knew, beyond a doubt, the psycho enjoyed prolonging her torment—was actually having the time of his life. *Where are you, Ryan?*

CHAPTER 41

The wraparound display gave him an expansive view of what lay directly in front of the *Jumelle*. Jason sat in the captain's chair and watched the constant flow of spinning asteroids move past at astounding speeds. He looked beyond to the distant small planet. What an odd spatial configuration—no heat-generating star—no great mass, like Earth's sun—to keep Alaster-Rei locked into a definitive orbit. But it all seemed to work.

He turned his chair to face Orion. "How many phase-shifts?"

"It would take a minimum of four … probably five," she said.

"I still don't get it. A phase-shifted object displaces the mass situated at the drop location. How many times had we shifted *The Lilly* right into the hull of another ship? We could do a multiple-shift."

"This is different, Cap."

"How so?"

"Those ice rocks are moving along at many thousands of miles an hour. Even when progressing through a pre-programmed multiple phase-shift routine, there's a split second where the *Jumelle* would be there … fully present in open

232

space ... and potentially in the path of an oncoming asteroid. No displacement of mass in that case. Captain, this ship is a third longer than a football field. The odds are high enough ... of being struck ... that I would not suggest we chance it. But you're the one sitting in that chair."

Jason turned back forward.

"Captain, there's an incoming hail from Liberty Station," Seaman Gordon said from the comms station.

"Designated private?"

"No, sir ... it's Omni Reynolds."

It had been a while since Jason spoke to his father. "On screen ... let's see what he wants."

A new display segment feed interrupted the 360-degree view of open space. The upper third of his father appeared. Dressed in his red Omni uniform, he was looking down at what Jason presumed was his virtual notebook. He looked up and gave a quick nod and even quicker smile. "There you are! We have a situation."

"Good afternoon to you too, Omni."

"Apparently, the *Jumelle* was fired upon ... recently."

"That's right. It's all in the report I'm guessing is right there in your lap."

"Was your Annapolis education so lacking that you didn't learn that it's not a good idea to tolerate enemy fire without reciprocity?" the Omni said—he was not happy.

"No damage, and we were on a mission. It's all there in the report. What's with the third degree? It was a judgment call."

"Well ... your judgment call, as you put it, has had serious repercussions! Those were pirates. They've been pouring into the Oort cloud over the last year. There's some kind of range war going on. Mining claims on designated open ... Alliance ... territorial space. They've set up some kind of gunship parameter. An Earth-bound freighter, the *Bumble Bee*, crossed over and was fired upon. Three casualties—vessel's put out a distress call."

Jason spun around to look at Orion. "Gunny?"

He watched her review her tactical display.

"Okay … I see it now. It was directed directly to Liberty. We work on a dispatch system now." Orion glanced to the Omni. "It wasn't a general mayday."

Jason turned back to his father. "Are they in immediate trouble?"

"Did you not hear what I said? Three crewmembers were killed. Damaged ship. I want the *Jumelle* to phase-shift into that sector and give the Bumble Bee protection while she makes her way to a friendly repair station."

"That could take days. You know why we're here, Dad … Nan's nephew …"

"Look, I'm sorry. But the *Jumelle* is the Star Watch vessel assigned to this district."

Exasperated, Jason said, "Call in the *Minian* from District 2."

"I'm not going to do that. This is your district, Captain Reynolds. Now manage it!" The feed went black. The segment disappeared from the wraparound display.

Pirates … I hate fucking pirates.

* * *

Jason met Nan within the *Jumelle*'s mess. There was limited time.

She was there when he arrived—sitting alone at a table nursing a cup of coffee. Jason sat down across from her.

"I already heard," she said.

"Then you know we have to attend to another matter … shouldn't take more than a few days. We can return—"

"I'm staying."

Jason could tell by her expression—one he'd seen a thousand times before—she was resolute.

"Leave me with a pilot … and the *Goliath*. We'll go get my nephew ourselves."

Jason stared at his ex-wife for several beats before answering.

She started speaking first. "Ryan is down there on that planet with a known psychopath. There're two other CF drivers gone missing. Wendy and Donald. You know as well as I do that that … crazy man … took them too. Come on, Jason … I thought Star Watch was set up to help … To protect people!"

"There's a freighter with several hundred crew on board that is in serious trouble … It wasn't my call."

"Fine … I said I'll go myself."

"That asteroid field is impregnable. Probably why the nutcase chose it. I'm not putting one of my pilots in that much danger. And phase-shifting is not an option."

He watched as Nan turned her eyes down to her coffee cop. Her bottom lip began to quiver. A tear disappeared into her coffee.

Jason looked off toward the stern of the ship. Toward where he knew the flight bay was situated. Where one particular two-man open space fighter was parked. It was designated as his ship—no one; no other pilots touched her. When he'd discovered the *Jumelle*—months ago beneath the frigid surface of Endromoline—he'd discovered her. Identical to his long lost *Pacesetter*. He'd designated her the *Pacesetter II*. Now he took her out fairly often—during his private time—traveling at incurable speeds. Learning death-defying maneuvers he had no business even attempting. He'd honed his piloting skills to a level unattained by anyone on the ship. But was it possible?

"I'll go," he said.

Nan looked up. "You? Like by yourself?"

"I'll take the Pacesetter II … she's small and maneuverable. I'm not risking another pilot's life, Nan."

235

"I'm going with you."

"No."

"Yes!"

"No! I mean it!"

* * *

Jason didn't tell Dira, to the full extent, just how danger-ous what he would be attempting was.

She insisted on walking with him to the flight bay. She took his arm in hers and held it tight—kept him pulled close. They talked about this and that—kept the subject matter light. He could tell she was worried—had told him as much. She didn't want him to go and didn't understand why he was doing this.

They entered the flight bay where numerous shuttles, manned and unmanned fighters, and drone crafts sat at the ready. The massive compartment that spanned the width of the vessel was relatively quiet. Approaching the sleek, bright red *Pacesetter II*, Dira lifted her head and spoke in hushed tones. "What is she doing here?"

Nan was standing by the two-man fighter. She held the straps of a small duffle bag in both hands. She returned a nervous smile.

"It's her nephew … she insisted."

"I thought you were the captain of this ship?" Dira said in a snarky tone he hadn't heard from her before.

He stopped and turned to face her. He took her face in his two hands and kissed her for a long time. He looked into her exquisite violet and amber eyes and said—so only Dira could hear him, "I promise you … I'm coming back. But I need to do this."

She nodded. "I know. But I don't have to like it."

* * *

Nan was quietly situated in the rear seat. He'd need an unencumbered view out the front of the canopy. Both had previously initialized their battle suits. Jason ran through his pre-flight checklist and checked then double-checked the *Pacesetter II*'s HUD display readings. He knew, while trying hard not to think about it, that he was attempting to deliver the very thing the Picket boys down on Alaster-Rei wanted most—Nan Reynolds.

CHAPTER 42

Ryan and Two-ton closed in on Orloff's makeshift camp as the sound of the sand crawler came to life. Its sudden, low rumble idle startled a small flock of birds that immediately took to the air—squawking angry protests.

Ryan moved closer through the trees, keeping low. He saw a flash of red and chrome in the distance. Orloff was there and Wendy too. She looked tired—beaten down—vulnerable and frail. Orloff was helping her into the rear seat of the crawler, which was difficult, since her hands were bound behind her.

Blinded by white hot rage, Ryan readied himself to charge. He wanted to beat the big man to a pulp, rip his head from his neck then smash it with a rock. He felt a hand on his shoulder.

Two-ton leaned in close and whispered, "I'd unpack your weapon first."

Ryan tried to control his breathing, to somehow bring his heart rate down. Hatred was driving him and he knew that was dangerous. *Stupid.* That's how mistakes were made. Wendy could get killed. He felt Two-ton rooting through the pack on his back and a moment later the Tavor was handed to him.

Ryan crept closer, his footfalls swallowed up in the sounds coming off the sand crawler. Orloff was attempting to mount into the vehicle, but the oversized pack on his own back kept him off balance. Trying again, this time he got one leg over the edge and inside the small cockpit. Standing off balance, in the process of pulling in his other leg, Ryan rushed forward into the clearing.

"Stay where you are! Don't move … don't do anything or I'll fucking blow your head off."

Wendy's head came up. Confusion turned to recognition, and recognition to an eruption of emotion. "Ryan! Oh God … Ryan!" She moved to stand but had difficulty with her wrists still bound.

With the Tavor held high—secured tightly into his shoulder—Ryan aimed at the mountain man's heart. He stepped closer with his finger on the trigger, and the compulsion to squeeze—end his worthless life—was winning.

But everything changed in an instant. An instant filled with multiple, bright white, flashes. Ryan spun around, seeing someone standing there in a battle suit. Sensing other movement behind him, he turned and saw two more men, similarly dressed in battle suits. Ryan knew this was advanced Caldurian tech, but the faces behind the helmet visors were not from Star Watch, nor the U.S. Fleet. Bearded, dirty, and scraggly, these three looked more like Orloff, sharing a common resemblance. Now there were four mountain men where only a moment earlier there was one.

"Drop the weapon, Ryan," the first man said. "No one needs to get hurt here." He raised his palms up in mock surrender.

None of the three seemed to be armed.

Wendy yelled, "Ryan! Orloff's …!"

Ryan turned to see Orloff pull the pistol from his holster and place the muzzle tight against her temple. He recognized its distinctive shape as a Glock 18. One of the only fully automatic pistol machine guns available. Not for civilians, they were strictly used by law enforcement and the military.

Now it was Ryan's turn to raise his palms. "Let her go … she's done nothing to hurt anyone. I'll go with you. I won't resist."

The man to his left, the tallest of the lot, and the first one Ryan had noticed, said, "My name is Brent … Brent Picket." He took the Tavor from Ryan's hands. "The two behind you are Larry and Payne. I gather you already know my younger brother, Orloff?"

"Yeah … I know him. He's sick … needs to be locked up."

Brent gave him a crooked smile, momentarily hitching up a shoulder. "What can I say … Orloff is an odd duck. But he's family, so what can we do?"

"Try shooting him in the head," Wendy said, her expression cold as stone.

Brent ignored her. "Orloff … hop on out of there and help the young lady out too." Orloff, doing as told, helped Wendy to stand then guided her out of the sand crawler. Once again on terra firma, with her arms still bound behind her, she ran over to Ryan. He wrapped his arms around her as she cried into his chest. He felt her tears seeping through his shirt. Speaking softly into her ear, he said, "I'll get us out of this somehow … I promise."

She didn't reply, only stared up at him. Big tears streamed down her dirty cheeks.

"Larry, Payne … grab an arm," Brent said.

Payne pulled Ryan and Wendy apart. Larry stepped in and taking Wendy by her arm pulled her away.

Brent walked over to Orloff and placed a hand on his beefy shoulder. "Time to go." He took a last quick look around and in a flash all six were gone.

* * *

Twenty paces away, peering through thick tree branches, Two-ton continued to stare at the spot where Ryan and Wendy stood mere moments before. Hesitantly, the robot moved out into the clearing. The sand crawler was still there—still idling. *They'll hear me coming.* The robot climbed in behind the controls and engaged the three turbine engines. Cranking the controls all the way around, the sand crawler fish-tailed, a backward spray of dirt and small rocks hit the air. Two-ton, gaining control of the hovercraft, steadied its course—then headed for the Picket compound.

* * *

Ryan and Wendy sat close together on a threadbare couch inside the Picket compound's main cabin.

The four brothers, seated together at the rough-hewn timber table in the center of the room, were eating. Heaping forkfuls—like little skip-loaders—delivered franks and beans into their gaping, wide-open mouths.

Brent, mouth full, said, "Eat!"

Wendy and Ryan looked down at the metal pie pan full of beans and two partially submerged spoons.

"We should eat … keep up our strength," he muttered.

Wendy made a face. "There's chunks of *something* in there."

Ryan shrugged. "Yeah?"

"Orloff made this … I saw him cooking in the kitchen."

Ryan leaned forward and reached for the pan. "Looks to be cut up frankfurters." He handed Wendy a spoonful of the mud-colored mush. Then taking a heaping spoonful himself, he ate. Chewing slowly at first, his eyes brightened. *Perhaps he was simply beyond hungry?* But it was good. Excellent, in fact!

Wendy took a partial bite and chewed; raising her chin up she looked down her nose at the remaining half-spoonful of beans. Ryan knew that look. She wasn't going to give Orloff the satisfaction. Making an it's *okay* expression, she spooned the rest of the beans and franks into her mouth. Together, they ate everything in the tin pie pan.

"I need to go to the bathroom … get cleaned up."

Brent looked at Wendy. "Go down the hall. Come right back."

Ryan watched Wendy get up and head for the small hall-way, which led to a single bedroom and, he guessed, a bathroom directly across from it.

Larry was up, moving around the table and stacking his brother's pie pans. This was one strange-looking family. Brent seemed the most normal. Larry looked like Larry from early days Three Stooges fame. Uncanny, he was bigger and brawnier, but his hair was a dead ringer for the old idiot-playing stooge. Payne, big and brutish, almost never spoke. He had a perpetual *Elvis-like* snarl on his face, perhaps due to some kind of early years mining accident. Orloff, though, was another story completely. Sure, he had the Picket family looks—but the craziness in the eyes was always present. Too expressionless, too disconnected from what was going on around him.

They all stood and moved toward the tiny kitchen on the opposite side of the main room. Ryan watched as they huddled together and spoke in low tones. Larry, and then Payne, glanced over in his direction. Orloff didn't look up until Wendy returned from the bathroom, his eyes lingering on her.

Her face was clean and she'd done something with her hair. Perhaps she'd found a comb in there? "What's happening with them?" she asked Ryan, gesturing with her chin.

"I don't know."

"This is hopeless … " she said, her eyes growing moist.

"No … this is an abduction, not a murder. Why feed someone you're going to kill?"

Wendy looked up at Ryan, her face as serious as he'd ever seen. "Orloff killed Two-ton and Olivia."

"I know," Ryan said.

"He … did things to them. Mounted—"

Ryan placed a finger on her lips. "I know … I saw."

"Promise me something," Wendy said—pleading.

"What?"

"You won't let him take me; do to me what he did to our friends. Swear to me you'll kill me before you'll let that happen to me."

"It's not … that's not going to happen."

"Promise me!"

He stared back at her for long seconds—her eyes locked on his. Not answering, he merely nodded. Off in the distance he heard the sound of turbine engines and smiled.

She furrowed her brow, "What is that … who is that …?"

Ryan said, "Two-ton … sort of."

CHAPTER 43

"**W**ho the hell is that?" Brent asked. "Who else is on the planet besides us?" He looked at Orloff, then stared at Ryan and Wendy.

Ryan shrugged. "You're asking me? Ask your crazy brother ... he lives here, not us."

Orloff looked out the grimy window toward the central valley and said, "It has to be the robot. It's one I've been meaning to repair ... from the scrap pile."

Larry said, "What robot? There's a robot out there? And it has a vehicle?"

Orloff, ignoring Larry, turned to Brent. "It *somehow* got reactivated once *delivery boy* arrived here. I thought I had ... disabled it near the campsite. It shouldn't have been operational after that."

"Terrific," Brent said, looking out the window as well. "So what are we talking about here? Just your basic mechanical toaster, or something we should be worried about?"

All eyes turned to Ryan. "It's your basic toaster. I'm actually surprised it figured out how to drive that sand crawler. It'll probably drive around in circles for days, so I wouldn't worry about it."

"Coming from you, that means the opposite," Brent said.

"It's not armed, is it? You didn't leave a smart robot out there with a weapon, did you? Did you, Orloff?"

Orloff's face flushed. "Not one that's ... operational."

"What the hell does that mean ... operational? Like it's an old television set? What weapon are we talking about here?"

"I dropped the 50 cal. Crashed down on the rocks from the butte. It was wrecked ... bent up and all. I left it at the campsite."

Ryan watched them as they argued back and forth, while keeping his ear tuned to the approaching sound of turbines.

"Somehow that robot was smart enough to repair itself but you don't think it can fix a fucking rifle?" Brent asked.

Orloff, placing both hands on hips, glared defiantly back at Brent. "I don't understand how the robot could fix itself. It's a Tromian mecher ... those things are a joke. It could no more fix itself than Larry could count to one hundred."

Good one, Orloff! Ryan thought. As long as they kept arguing amongst themselves, he and Wendy were not the center of attention and could keep breathing.

Everyone stopped jabbering when the not-so-distant sound of turbine engines suddenly ceased.

"Enough!" Brent spat. "Larry and Payne ... get out there and destroy that robot. Take the Tavor and grab whatever else you need from the armory."

Ryan and Wendy looked at each other. *Armory?* He figured it was probably located in one of the outbuildings; maybe even below ground—like a silo.

The two brothers hurried out the front door. Brent strode over to the couch and roughly grabbed Ryan by the arm. "Get up!"

Wendy moved to also stand.

"No. You stay right where you are. Orloff ... watch her. Make sure she doesn't so much as twitch her nose."

"You can't leave her with him. You know he's a psycho

… right? You know what he does to … to his victims, right?"

Brent said, "He's not going to touch her. Are you, Orloff?" His glare at his younger brother was anything but friendly.

Orloff sat down at the opposite end of the couch then looked at Wendy. "We'll just sit here and chat."

Brent pulled Ryan toward the door. Looking back at Orloff, he queried, "Comms up and running in the tanker?"

Orloff shook his head. "No, but it's a switch, on the overhead console, tagged comms main."

"I'll find it."

Ryan said, "Why don't you let Wendy come with us?"

Manhandling Ryan through the door, Brent replied, "This way you'll be good … won't try anything stupid."

* * *

Ryan hadn't been inside the tanker's cockpit before. After being ushered through the tanker's lower level, then up the stairs and down the long passageway into Orloff's bedroom, they ascended another small flight of stairs. Brent pushed Ryan into the ship's control center. It was small, a tad bigger than the cockpit in the van.

"Sit down, kid," Brent said, shoving Ryan into what he surmised was the primary pilot's seat. Feeling sunken indentations in the leather beneath his butt cheeks, he was somewhat grossed out, knowing that this was where Orloff typically sat. He watched as Brent, looming next to him, scoured the upper control panel. There seemed to be hundreds of tiny switches and small display screens, plus various types of meters. Holding out his index finger, Brent traced the surface back and forth.

"It's over there," Ryan said. "The one tagged Comms Main."

Brent followed the direction of Ryan's finger and eventually found it. "Here we go. I see it." He flicked it on. A third of the upper console lit up, springing to life. He sat down and looked over at Ryan. "She's going to want proof of life."

"She? She who?"

"Don't play stupid, Ryan. Till now I've been amiable. That could easily change."

Ryan had minimum doubt that the hulk-like, six-foot-five mountain man could inflict serious damage on him.

"Your aunt. We need her to do us a simple favor. After that ... you'll be set free."

"And Wendy, too?" Ryan asked.

"Of course ... we're not animals. This is just business."

"Tell that to your brother."

Brent ignored the comment, placing his attention back on the communications equipment. Then glancing at Ryan, he instructed, "Don't say anything extra ... just tell her you're fine. Understand?"

"Yup."

Ryan watched as he hailed a spaceship called the *Parcical*, spoke first to a Seaman Gordon, and then talked to a female named Orion.

"This is important ... patch me through to her or her nephew dies," Brent ordered. He looked at Ryan and shook his head, implying he hadn't really meant what he'd just said.

Close to a minute passed before Ryan heard a familiar voice. "This is Nan Reynolds. Who is it I'm speaking with?"

Brent held up a hand to stifle Ryan from speaking. "Well, hello there, Nan. Good to hear your voice again."

"Where's Ryan? I want to speak with him."

"I know you do. And that can be arranged ... easily arranged. But you have to do my family a little favor first."

"I talk to Ryan first ... that's the deal."

Brent rolled his eyes and looking at Ryan, nodded his head.

Ryan leaned forward, and spoke, "Aunt Nan? This is Ryan ..."

"Oh God, are you okay … have they hurt you?"

"No, I'm fine. Look, I'm here on the planet with Wend—"

"That's enough, kid!" Brent said, shoving Ryan back hard into the seat.

"What do you say we talk a little business now, ex-Madam President? As you've just heard, your nephew is alive and well. As you know, we need certain mining rights fast-tracked through Alliance bureaucracy. I'm talking about exclusive DM^2 mining rights for one small section of the Oort cloud. It's no big deal. We don't want to be greedy; let's say a thirty-year exclusivity contract."

"Since I'm no longer the president, you're assuming I have more influence than I actually have."

"Well, if that's the case we have nothing more to talk about. You're of no use to me."

"Wait … what makes you think I'd keep my end of the bargain, anyway?" Nan asked.

"Excellent question. Provisions in the contract will be very specific. We have an excellent high-priced lawyer. You didn't expect it to be something Mamma jotted down on a scrap of paper there in Dollywood, did you? No, this contract will be ironclad and recognized by the Alliance's regional regulatory commission. Don't worry, we know exactly who needs to approve it and to sign what. How to ensure that everything is legally binding. And one more thing … there will be clauses … total immunity for the Picket family. The paperwork was sent to you, care of your place in Colorado."

"A process like this could take weeks … months!" Nan exclaimed, clearly frustrated.

"You have two days. If not, we move to our plan B."

"What plan B?"

"You don't want to know. You're comms officer now has a means to contact me. If you want to see your nephew again alive, then get everything buttoned up tight within forty-eight hours. Now, say goodbye to your nephew."

"Stay brave, Ryan ... I love you—"

Brent cut the connection. Ryan knew his aunt. She was an amazing woman. And she was married to the famed Captain Reynolds. But he couldn't believe they'd ever allow themselves be blackmailed. And, with that thought in mind, rescue from this protected planet seemed nearly impossible. No, if he and Wendy were going to survive, he'd have to become highly resourceful.

Weaponry fire suddenly erupted outside the tanker. Ryan wondered if Two-ton had actually repaired Orloff's rifle? He next wondered if the robot also knew how to shoot?

CHAPTER 44

Between dodging asteroid after asteroid in a variable minefield, Jason listened in to Nan and Brent's conversation. He'd been navigating through the maelstrom for less than thirty minutes, and he was already having serious second thoughts about his decision. The *Pacesetter* was performing as he thought it would—with precision and finesse. But the intense level of constant concentration required of him was beginning to take a toll.

Up ahead, he saw a much tighter cluster of asteroids— too tight to maneuver around. *No way we're going through there.*

Nan screamed, "Jason! Look! On the … the … right! … Big rocks headed our way!"

"I see them." In desperation, Jason called up a HUD targeting solution for the rail gun, which he figured would be far more effective than using plasma fire. He felt the big weapon spin to life beneath the craft's nose. Immediately, a spray of projectiles that would explode on impact was unleashed upon the large asteroid cluster. Since this was a Caldurian vessel, the rail gun utilized JIT munitions, via an access back at the *Jumelle*'s phase-synthesizer unit. Jason knew he had an endless supply of ammunition at his disposal.

The asteroids exploded into rubble. The *Pacesetter* next plowed through a cloud of fist-size remnants—almost like driving through a Midwest hailstorm back on Earth. The clattering sound of rocks, hitting against the outside fuselage, was beyond intense. Jason increased power to the shields, hoping the move was enough to avert disaster.

Nan said, "Maybe this wasn't the best idea after all, Jason."

He didn't disagree. He silently chided himself for attempting such a foolhardy mission—for putting Nan's life in such danger. Hell, she was the mother of three children—including a five-year-old little boy—who very well might grow up without a mother—*or a father*.

The rail-gun continued firing non-stop, propagating ahead a devastating swath of destruction. Exhausted, Jason found he was spending less time maneuvering around obstacles than simply letting the rail-gun do his bidding for him.

A warning message flashed up onto the Pacesetter's HUD. The rail-gun was overheating. Even though an endless supply of projectiles streamed in from the multiverse—that didn't mean the laws of physics with the here and now didn't still play a part.

He switched over to the two-wing-mounted plasma cannons, letting the rail-gun cool down. Immediately, the results came back, which determined they were far less effective. Jason found he needed to step up his navigating game once again.

"How much farther?" Nan asked.

"Hold on!" He jockeyed the space fighter through a cluster of spinning ice rocks—each one moving at a different speed than the one next to it. He heard first—then felt—the portside wing scrape against the last ice rocks in the group. But a quick glance to his left ensured him the wing was still intact. He knew the hull's multiple layers of nanites were already at work repairing the damage.

"Did you hear me?" Nan asked.

"Yeah … a little busy up here. But to answer your question, we're not even a third of the way through this nightmare."

That quieted her down for several minutes. Then she said, "Maybe we should turn back. I love my nephew, but little Michael … he needs parents."

"A little late for that now, Nan. Turning around in this mess would be near impossible anyway."

A NanoCom hail was coming in. "Go for Captain; too busy to talk now, Ricket." He cut the connection and swerved around the largest asteroid yet. This time, the starboard wing was scraped against ice and rock. Another hail was coming in. "What is it, Ricket!"

"Sorry, Captain. I've been watching your progress through the asteroids—"

"Just get to the point!" Jason barked, as he cranked the controls, first one way then the other.

"Captain, I've calculated a navigable passageway. One the *Pacesetter* can autopilot through … all the way to the planet."

"How certain are you … that it … will work?"

"I'm positive. It's how others traverse their way to the planet. I'm only sorry it took me so long to calculate the millions of asteroid coordinates in conjunction with a valid flight plan."

"Well, stop jabbering about it, Ricket, and get it uploaded!"

Two seconds elapsed. "It is done, Captain."

Jason saw the newly added *flight package* waiting for him on the HUD menu. He hesitated before selecting it, but truthfully, he had no other choice. He was both physically and mentally spent. He engaged the new flight package, sat back, and squeezed his closed eyes tight and held his breath. He waited for the impact—a collision with an asteroid the size of a locomotive—certain death for him and for Nan.

A moment passed. He opened one eye not knowing what

to expect. The *Pacesetter* had picked up speed; was maneuvering around objects with a graceful fluidity that brought a smile to his face. *Amazing!* He let himself breathe, then craned his head around enough to see Nan, seated quietly behind him. She looked back at him wide-eyed. She too was smiling.

"Are we going to live through this?" she asked.

"I think so … thanks to our little Craing friend." He turned back around and hailed Ricket.

"Go for Ricket."

"Thank you, Ricket … sorry I yelled at you."

"It's quite understandable, Captain. The fact that you manually navigated that far into the asteroid field went far beyond the odds of your surviving."

"Well … that's something … anyway. What's the ETA for reaching the planet?"

"About an hour and a half, Captain."

"Good. Maybe by then my hands will stop shaking." He cut the connection, sat back, and quickly fell asleep.

CHAPTER 45

Orloff had some big decisions to make. Potentially life-altering choices there would be no coming back from. He stared across the open room—out through the smudged window—at his prized ship, which seemed nothing more than a shapeless, dark-brown form from his vantage point on the couch. Brent and the kid were out there taking care of business. Business that he was no longer interested in. Perhaps if he'd continued taking his prescribed regimen of pills … meds that deadened him inside. No. He'd rather live his life his own way, pursuing interests that gave his days and nights meaning. *What else was there worth living for?*

He'd come to terms with the fact the deliveryman—*boy*—was now under the protection of his brothers. Perhaps someday he'd get the opportunity to restart the pursuit, once things calmed down. He turned his gaze back on Wendy. *What an incredible creature.* Her features were small and delicate, her skin unblemished. It wasn't too late for her—not by any means. The real crime would be letting such magnificence get stolen away through the ravages of time. He suddenly felt the heavy weight of his conscience. His obligation. *If not him … then who?*

Orloff knew Wendy was aware of his stare, noting the

color drain from her cheeks. He liked that. Perhaps it was a sign. Sign that he needed to do the *right* thing. The odds were against his success, but still he owed it to himself, and he owed it to this spectacular young woman too.

Orloff stood, looking down at her. Drawing his pistol from the holster on his thigh, he ordered, "Stand up!"

Wendy looked up at him, fear in her eyes. "No!"

"You either do as I say or the very second Ryan Chase walks back through that door, I'll put a hole between his eyes. I won't think twice about it. You know it's true, don't you?"

She closed her eyes and struggled to breathe.

"You need to ask yourself, will it be you, or will it be him that survives? You need to determine right now how important he is to you."

Hot tears flowing again, her lower lip trembling, Wendy stood, staring at him defiantly.

Orloff grabbed her arm and pulled her along toward the front door. He stopped and peered out, looking right then left. Payne and Larry were out of view. Evidently, both had taken cover between the outbuildings and were now firing their rifles toward the valley—at the unseen robot out there somewhere. Orloff looked over to the Paotow Tanker. The starboard rear hatch was open—slightly agape. Renewed resolve coursed through him as he shoved Wendy forward, into the narrow space between the tanker and the front of the cabin.

Orloff spoke in a hushed voice, "Make a noise … say anything, and I'll kill Ryan, then you. In that order, so you can watch him die."

Wendy didn't say anything, scared half to death. *But then she has every right to be*, he thought. Guiding her to the bow of the tanker, he pushed her down and onto her knees, then crouched low as well. Noises were coming from the hatch. Orloff pressed the muzzle of his weapon to her temple and waited.

The first to exit the tanker was Ryan with Brent following two paces behind. He was also gripping an oversized Glock 18 pistol in his hand, pointed at the center of Ryan's back.

Orloff felt Wendy's body tense, deciding what to do—should she sacrifice her own life, or Ryan's? She kept quiet. As soon as Ryan and Brent disappeared back into the cabin, Orloff pulled her up slightly and shoved her forward. "Hurry! Now! … go go …" Placing his free hand on her shoulder to keep her body lower to the ground, they ran. "Get in there!" She momentarily resisted—clearly having second thoughts—but by this point it was too late. Orloff swung the hatch wider open and shoved her inside—into the darkness. Following close behind, he pulled the hatch shut and tapped at the keypad. As a hidden mechanism engaged, the hatch locked tight.

"Upstairs! Go! Where you were before."

"Don't do this, Orloff … Let me go. You don't need to do this!"

He pushed her through the airlock and into the main cabin. The air was stuffy, tinged with a funky sweet smell. "Up the stairs … I *will* hurt you if I have to."

Wendy reluctantly complied and started up the stairs. Stumbling and tripping, she began crying like a child. Orloff didn't possess the necessary emotional components for it to make an impact. No empathy. No sympathy. No regrets.

* * *

With Wendy properly secured back in her cell, Orloff hurried to the tanker's top-level cockpit. With well-practiced movements, he fired up the ship's drive. As it roared to life, the deck beneath his boots momentarily rumbled, then fell into a steady vibration. One of the many modifications Orloff had made to his refurbished Paotow tanker was a quick-start feature. There was no waiting time for the various intricate mechanisms to adjust, or for a reactor core to be sufficiently warmed up. Still standing, he took the controls in his hands and throttled up the propulsion system and lifted off. He watched as a set of indicators jumped to redline levels. The bow of the tanker rose, rising slightly higher than the rest of the ship. Then, yanking the controls all the way back, he felt intense G-forces pull him backwards as the ship pulled away, gravity-free, from Alaster-Rei.

* * *

As soon as he entered the cabin, Ryan could see Wendy was no longer sitting on the couch; that both she and Orloff were gone. He rushed to the rear of the cabin to check the bedroom, then the bathroom.

"They're gone! I told you not to trust that lunatic with her," he shouted at Brent, in that moment wanting to kill him. To feel his fists smash into his face, feel the bones break as he pummeled him into pulp.

Brent raised his gun. "Shut up ... we'll find them. We weren't gone that long."

Running, Ryan was out the front door. Loud rifle reports, *crack crack crack crack*, continued pouring from the nearby outbuildings. Only now there could be heard sporadic return fire, coming from somewhere in the valley below. Two-ton had obviously figured out how to aim and fire. Ryan briefly wondered where he'd found the ammo. Maybe Orloff had left a sack of .50 caliber rounds either in the sand crawler or back at the campsite?

Startled, Ryan flinched as a thunderously loud sound came from the stern of the tanker.

Brent said, "Shit! He's taking the tanker ... he's taking off!"

Ryan started toward the ship only to be roughly shoved aside. Staggering, he immediately felt a scorching-hot blast of heat on his back. As he scrambled away from the tanker's flaring rear thruster, he half-turned to look back, holding his arm up to shield his face. The ground shook as the Paotow Tanker rose ten feet off the ground. Ryan yelled over the noise, "Stop him! Do something! He's got Wendy!"

Brent watched—angry and confused. It took him a moment to begin fiddling with the SuitPac device clipped to his belt.

"Hurry up!" Ryan yelled.

"Shut up … I'm trying," Brent said, finally getting the suit to initialize—segment out over his body. For two seconds that seemed more like two hours Ryan watched Brent's face through his visor—his eyes frantically roving over the HUD menus. Then his gaze changed focus as he looked up to the sky—off to the far distance where the last vestige of the Paotow tanker was still in view—and then it was gone.

Ryan continued to stare into the empty sky.

"I'm sorry … I don't know how to use this … damn suit," Brent said.

Slowly, Ryan brought his attention back to Brent. He watched as the suit segmented back into the small metallic device hanging from his belt. "I'm going to kill that psycho fuck brother of yours," Brian said.

Brent shrugged. "… Yeah? Not in this lifetime, you're not."

CHAPTER 46

The hillbilly's nonchalant shrug triggered something: Pure, unadulterated, rage. Ryan was seeing red. It was all too much. Wendy was gone—again. Abducted by a crazed lunatic who had only one horrific intention in mind. This entire family—these backwoods bastards were at the root of everything. Ryan no longer cared that Brent easily had six inches in height on him, plus an extra one hundred pounds. And he no longer cared about the mean-looking Glock still gripped in Brent's hand. Coming off his back foot and stepping into it, he swung and punched with everything he had. He swung as if his life, and Wendy's life, lay in the balance of the kind of punch he could deliver—right then and right there. As if things were transpiring in slow motion, his punch was a solid right cross—one that hit Brent on the lower left side of his jaw and lifted the big man up and off his feet. The strong blow catapulted him five feet away. First of all, he landed flat on his back; second, his thunderous downward momentum flung his larger-than-normal cranium backward and cracking it hard onto the rocky ground.

Ryan stood over the prone, now unmoving mountain

man. Brent was definitely out for the count. He knelt down and took the Glock from Brent's hand, along with the Suit-Pac device hanging from his belt. Standing, about to turn away, he thought better of it. Once again, he delivered a momentous—akin to a full-on punt attempt from the fifty-yard line—kick to Brent's unconscious, somewhat placid-looking, face.

Gunfire continued noisily from the outbuildings, where the other two brothers were hunkered down. Sporadically, other gunfire sounds came up from the valley—the robot firing back. Ryan quietly moved around to the back of the first building then stopped to listen. *They were over one—probably between the second and third structure.* He crossed over to the second outbuilding and, hurrying along, stayed low. As he approached the far back corner he stopped and peered around the side of the building. He could see both brothers now. One had taken cover behind an overturned tractor of some kind. The other brother, Larry—with the frizzy red hair—was lying prone, shooting between the open gaps of a five-foot-tall stack of firewood.

Suddenly, one of the logs at the top of the stack exploded into wood chips and splinters. Obviously, Two-ton was a terrible shot. Even without an operational scope, unless there was something else seriously wrong with the .50 caliber Barrett, the robot should have nailed either one, or both, of them, without a problem. After all, they weren't that well hidden.

Ryan stepped quietly between the two buildings and moved forward. He raised the Glock, holding it in front of him, both arms extended. He crept up behind Larry and pressed the muzzle to the back of his head. "Take your finger off the trigger, Larry, and slowly put the weapon down. You even twitch funny and I'll blow your head off."

Payne suddenly looked over and noticed Ryan and the current predicament his brother was in.

"You too, Payne … real slow-like. Put the Tavor down on the ground and stand up."

Payne did as he was told. "Now you, Larry. Up with you … stand up."

Ryan gestured with his pistol. "Stand over there against the wall. Did I say you could lower your hands? Keep them up!"

Both brothers stood still, their backs up against the side wall of the third outbuilding. Ryan yelled, "Two-ton! Come on in … it's safe now."

He heard the sound of the distant sand-crawler coming to life, and then the drone of the hovercraft coming closer. Moments later, Two-ton appeared—sitting inside the small cockpit. Pulling to a stop, the robot cut the engines. Ryan saw the muzzle of the Barrett sticking up from the back seat. Two-ton unfolded the mecher's seven-foot-frame from the cramped fuselage and stepped down. Ryan did a double take, for the robot had seen better days. Half its face dented in, there were several new bullet holes on its upper body—three in both shoulders and two lower down.

"For God's sakes, how many times were you hit?"

"Too many," Two-ton said flatly.

"Are your … mental processes okay? Was the AI-Pac damaged?"

"A few rounds came close … but all's well in that regard."

"Good! Grab those SuitPac-thingies from their belts."

Two-ton did as directed, first taking the SuitPac from Payne's belt but then, bent over Larry, hesitated. He stood and looked at Ryan. "Larry doesn't have one. Are you sure he even had one?" The robot passed Payne's over to Ryan.

"Yeah … pretty sure." Ryan shoved the one into his pocket with Brent's and said, "Thanks. Can you help me find something to tie these two thugs up with?"

* * *

Every minute that passed was another minute he was delayed from catching up to the tanker and rescuing Wendy. But was that even possible? He was certain Orloff had navigated through the asteroid field numerous times—had followed that complicated, invisible pathway through the ice-rock obstacles that by now had become second nature. He probably knew all the tricks—maybe even some shortcuts, if there were any. But Orloff didn't have Two-ton along. Ryan hoped the battered robot would be his one big advantage—his ace in the hole.

"So … what do you want to do with the three yokels?" Two-ton asked, after he finished tying the still unconscious Brent's legs together.

"They can stay right where they're at, for all I care," Ryan said, staring up at the sky—like he had some kind of super vision that could see far beyond the surrounding atmosphere and into the blackness of space.

Two-ton looked down at the ground where the three bundled up men lay, wrapped like mummies, near the side of the main cabin.

"So … no water for them? Nothing to eat? It could be a long time before anyone returns here … if ever."

"This affair is their doing. They deserve worse … much worse." A long silence ensued. Finally, Ryan brought his attention back to Two-ton. Smiling, he asked, "You didn't miss … did you?"

"Say what?" Two-ton asked.

"Don't play dumb. What is it … some kind of internal AI directive? Never deliberately take a human life, or something like that?"

Two-ton did the equivalent of a shrug, though it came out all wrong—seeming more like an unintentional spasm or maybe a belch.

"You want to get them a few water bottles, fine with me. But don't free their arms or their legs. They can figure it out on their own. Give them something to do over the next few days."

The Two-ton mecher disappeared into the cabin, returning a few minutes later with ten bottles of water. He dropped them near the three brothers.

"Is it going to be a problem, hooking you back up to the van's system panel?" the robot asked.

"No … not at all. I won't need a physical connection for that. How about the van's Communications Transmission Beacon? Since we're on the ground, anything you could do to fix that?"

"We won't need it," Two-ton said. "Not with that pocketful of SuitPacs you're carrying around."

"We need to go … now! As for the SuitPacs, I don't know how to use them." Ryan hurried over to the van. "Come on … let's go!"

* * *

Ryan got the CF van's drive fired up and they lifted off from Alaster-Rei. He throttled up and headed for the upper atmosphere, as both he and Two-ton stood at the cockpit console. While Ryan was concentrating on getting them into space, Two-ton was fidgeting with one of the SuitPac devices that Ryan had handed him earlier.

"I told you, I don't know how to use those things," Ryan said irritably.

Two-ton found the two spring-loaded inset buttons and pressed them simultaneously.

Startled, Ryan watched the robot become fully encased in a battle suit over the course of several seconds. Seeing the robot's misaligned face staring back at him through the suit's visor made Ryan laugh out loud.

"Well, look at you … all ready for combat."

Two-ton turned the mecher's head left and right, next up

and down, then stayed still.

"What are you doing in there?" Ryan asked.

"Reviewing all the menu options and saving them to memory."

"Huh … I didn't know a robot could even wear one of those things."

"Ryan?"

"Yeah?"

"There's a hail coming in … it's for you."

CHAPTER 47

Jason was notified by Ricket, on the Jumelle, which possessed long-range, high-powered sensors, that a battle suit had been recently activated on a small ship leaving the planet Alaster Rei's atmosphere. At last! I finally have the means to talk to someone down there directly, Jason thought. Ricket also mentioned that the one wearing the battle suit, peculiarly, was not showing any life signs—none at all. Jason sloughed it off; probably only interference from the millions of asteroids milling about, or some other spatial anomaly. When he adjusted the settings on the Pacesetter II's HUD, he also could see the faint battle suit icon.

Hailing the individual in the battle suit, he expected it to be one of the Picket brothers, since they had taken his team's SuitPac devices earlier, but Jason was surprised to hear a voice he'd never heard before.

"Um … yeah … hello?"

"Who is this?" Jason asked.

"I'm the ghost of Donald Koffman. Better known by my friends as Two-ton. Actually, that's misleading too. In my present form I'm a robot … a *piece-of-shit* mecher, to be exact."

Jason, at first, didn't know how to respond. "So you're …

MARK WAYNE MCGINNIS

a robot?"

"Bingo."

"Can you tell me if Ryan Chase is there? Nearby?"

"Yes and yes."

"This is Star Watch Captain Jason Reynolds. Can I speak with him? Right now, if possible."

It took another couple of minutes. Jason connected Nan into an open channel and then a second icon came alive on the HUD, right next to the first one.

"This is Ryan Chase."

Nan yelled, "Ryan! Is that you, Ryan?"

"Yes … is that you, Aunt Nan?"

"Oh God, it's so good to hear your voice. Are you safe? Are you hurt? Where are the Pickets?"

"I'm fine. Three of the four Picket brothers are tied up down on the planet. But Wendy—my girlfriend—she's Orloff Picket's prisoner on his ship."

Jason asked, "Where? Here within the asteroid field?"

"That's right. He left the planet ten or fifteen minutes before we did. His ship is powerful. My van's sensors aren't very accurate, but the robot thinks it knows where he is."

"Hold on, Ryan," Jason said, reviewing the *Pacesetter II*'s HUD. He then saw the tanker ship—so dense—solid—that it was practically invisible amongst all the other space objects flying around.

"Listen to me, Ryan. We're coming your way. My ship is close to the tanker … maybe ten minutes out. Leave Orloff to me. He's dangerous—"

"No!" Ryan said emphatically. "That's not an option. And I already know he's dangerous. One look at his trophy wall on that Paotow Tanker and you'll know he's dangerous. I know that ship. No offense, but I'm not leaving Wendy's rescue to anyone else."

"That's admirable, son. But unless you have military experience—"

Ryan cut him off: "I do have military experience. Also, don't forget who it was who left about a thousand pounds of Picket brothers tied up back on Alaster-Rei."

Nan said, "Even so, Ryan … I think you should let Jason handle this. It's pretty much what he does."

Something immediately occurred to Jason that complicated things. If he left the *Pacesetter II*, Nan wasn't capable of piloting her. She wouldn't know what to do if the little fighter started to drift into the constant stream of passing asteroids. He couldn't trust her life to an autopilot system—not here. Then he had a bold idea, but was it one he'd be willing to bet the safety of his ex-wife's life on?

"Talk to me about this robot of yours … how competent a pilot is it?"

"Two-ton comes across a little … strange; its AI was developed by Donald Koffman. It's … he's … like nothing I've ever seen or heard of. It's the same AI that piloted my van to the planet through the asteroid field."

"Okay," Jason said. "Now I'm going to bring him into our open channel, so hold on. Robot? Two-ton?"

"I'm here," Two-ton said.

"Ryan says you're an excellent pilot."

"Ryan's biased. I saved his life earlier today."

Ryan said, "Two-ton … this is serious. This is not the time to be a smart mouth."

Two-ton said, "Yes, I can pilot with the best of them. As an AI, I'm programmed to a level that exceeds any artificial intelligence within the sector. And far beyond any human … no offense."

Jason believed him, *or it*. "Okay, I'm going to bring another into this open channel. Hold on, everyone." Jason hailed Ricket, back on the *Jumelle*.

"Go for Ricket."

"Okay, Ricket, in a second I'm bringing you into an open channel. I want you to talk to the robot … Two-ton. Ensure he's … it's … capable of piloting the *Pacesetter II*. Can you do that?"

"Yes, Captain."

"Okay, everyone, Ricket is now here with us too."

Ryan said, "I've heard of you."

Two-ton said, "You're a living god."

Ricket said, "Two-ton, please allow me a moment while I assess, through your suit's diagnostics port, your artificial intelligence matrices. With your permission, I'd like access to your core … both your *read* and *write* functions."

"Go for it, Ricky-D."

"This will only take a moment," Ricket said.

"Let me know when I should turn my head and cough," Two-ton said.

Both Jason and Ryan laughed, though Nan remained quiet.

Several moments transpired. Ricket finally said, "Thank you, Two-ton. First of all, you are not what I expected. Captain, this AI has a very high-functioning artificial brain. Far beyond that on the *Jumelle;* perhaps even the *Parcical.* I look forward to studying the machine code. Its originator, Donald Koffman, didn't use intermediary languages. There's no middleman program going on here—very clean, and incredibly sophisticated."

Somewhat exasperated, Jason asked, "Ricket, can he … it … fly the *Pacesetter II*?"

"It can now, Captain. I've uploaded what it will need; the complete Caldurian flight operations instructions set."

"All right, here's what's going to happen first. We're close to both other vessels. Within twenty-five hundred miles from the van. About a thousand miles from the tanker. Both are now within range. So Two-ton and I will swap places: The robot will phase-shift here, into the *Pacesetter II*, and I'll phase-shift into the van. You okay with that, Nan?"

"I'm fine … just hurry! Don't forget there's a young woman in that tanker ship with a crazed maniac."

Up on the fighter's HUD, Jason recognized both the Paotow Tanker, as well as the consignment freight van, somewhat farther behind it. Both were moving along the same designated winding pathway through the asteroid field. Their life icons next came into view on his helmet's HUD. The one in the van was Ryan and the two in the Paotow Tanker were Orloff and Wendy. He was relieved to see she was still alive.

"Two-ton ... take a seat somewhere. I want you in the right position when I phase-shift you over here. And Nan, I'll see you soon. This shouldn't take long."

"I've heard that before," Nan replied. "Just be careful ... bring them both back in one piece."

"Here we go, everyone," Jason said. He timed it so his phase-shift proceeded Two-ton's by three seconds. He flashed away.

* * *

Jason phase-shifted into the CF van's small cargo hold area. Without hesitation, he spoke into the open channel. "Two-ton ... are you in place?"

"It's a bit of a tight fit ... but yes, Captain, I'm here. Did you know there was a strange lady sitting in the back seat?"

"Yeah, well keep that lady safe or I'll be pulling your arms off and bashing your head in with them."

Jason hurried down the short flight of stairs and entered the cockpit. Standing, and wearing a battle suit, Ryan was at the controls.

"Can we go, already?" Ryan asked, his impatience with the situation clearly evident.

"Look, I know you want to get over there and save Wendy. Just give me a few minutes. Let me at least show you how to use your battle suit's wrist plasma cannons."

* * *

Jason was three minutes into his highly truncated course on Ryan's use of his battle suit's integrated weaponry, following a cursory overview of phase-shifting. Jason now was doing double-duty—working with Ryan, while keeping abreast of events in space via his HUD readings. The kid was smart, picking up on the subtleties of the segmented suit far quicker than most. His military training was apparent, which somewhat placated Jason's reservations about bringing him along onto the tanker. He was well aware that Ryan's first instinct would be to simply rush in and rescue the girl, then shoot a well-placed plasma bolt into the oldest Picket brother's head. Only experience teaches you to use caution and care; rushing in, unprepared for the unexpected, could yield devastating results. Jason had seen it happen: Thinking you have a situation well in hand when suddenly a new reality comes along and bites you in the ass. That's how people needlessly die.

"Hold on, Ryan, I'm being hailed by the robot."

"That tanker has fucking guns!" said Two-ton.

"Slow down ... what's happening? Is the *Pacesetter II* being fired on ...?" Jason's words fell short as he viewed for himself via his HUD screen. *Shit!* "Time to go!"

CHAPTER 48

Ryan watched as Captain Reynolds, a distressed expression on his face, barked off orders to the robot. Telling it not to return fire, as Wendy was still on board the tanker and the fighter's plasma guns were powerful.

Jason spun around and looked at Ryan. "We're going right now."

Ryan nodded.

"Remember what I told you about the battle suit's integrated plasma weapons? Be careful not to shoot Wendy ... or me, for that matter. We phase-shift on *three ... two ... one.*" They flashed away.

Ryan had to blink away the effect of the incredibly bright-white flash. *Such a strange experience, this phase-shifting thing*, he thought. They were in the middle of the main lower compartment. He watched the captain do a three-sixty as he surveyed their surroundings, hesitating when he took in the now-exposed trophy wall bulkhead. Shaking his head, Jason said, "I think I knew that rhino-warrior."

Ryan looked at his HUD and started toward the stairway. He said, "Both life icons are upstairs."

The captain, hurrying, got in front of him, and quickly

climbed the stairs, taking them two at a time. Ryan hesitated—distracted by his HUD readout. Then, recovering, ran up the stairs and caught up with the captain halfway down the narrow passageway. He saw Orloff in the compartment—on the left at the end. Wendy's earlier jail cell.

Captain Reynolds, reaching the closed hatch first, said, "He's got it locked."

Ryan watched as the captain readjusted his stance—setting his feet farther apart—and pushed then leaned into the heavy door. Although the hatch held steadfast, its entire surrounding metal bulkhead began to creak, and then bow forward. A moment later, the hatch crashed inward, with only one hinge intact enough to keep it from falling completely free. The captain glanced back, and said, "You got to love 'em, kid … nanites make all the difference."

Looking past the captain into the dark confined space, Ryan saw Orloff Picket, standing tall, wearing a battle suit. *Well, now I know what happened to Larry's missing SuitPac device*, Ryan thought.

In the soft glow behind Orloff's visor, Ryan could see his face. No better expression came to mind other than Orloff looked completely at peace. Ryan watched as one of the life icons began to blink off and fade from view. Right then … right there … he knew Wendy was dying!

The crazy mountain man's arms were both fully extended toward them. Orloff fired continuously non-stop. At any other time, at such close range, even their protective battle suits would have meant the end for them, but the captain did the unexpected. In a flash of bright-white light, they phase-shifted mere feet away—and right behind Orloff.

Ryan then noticed Wendy's naked body, sitting slumped in the corner of the compartment, and quickly lost all interest in what the captain was doing, or even Orloff Picket. Dark purple finger marks, bruises, surrounded her neck where she'd been strangled. Ryan fell to his knees and pulled her into him—cradling her tightly in his arms. Bright plasma bolts strobed behind him, illuminating not only the small compartment, but Wendy's fixed, lifeless, stare. Orloff had taken the life of the one person he truly loved; the only one he would have sacrificed everything for, including his own life. But now she was gone … *gone from him forever.*

Ryan, holding Wendy, watched Orloff stagger toward the open hatchway, just before he crashed down onto the deck, face first. The back of his battle suit was full of scorched, blackened, plasma strikes. He didn't move after that. On Ryan's HUD, the mountain man's life icon blinked then disappeared. He too was dead.

The captain moved to Ryan's side, his battle suit in the process of retracting into his SuitPac device. "Get back, Ryan … let me work!"

Reluctantly, Ryan released Wendy's lifeless body to let the captain take over. Jason laid her prone on her back, then placed the SuitPac device over her belly. He pressed the two inset buttons and the battle suit began to segment-out, covering the entirety of her body.

The captain looked up at Ryan: "No guarantees … but sometimes these suits can bring a person back from the brink."

The words had no sooner left his lips when he espied something: not in the dimly lit compartment, nor out in the passageway, but on his HUD. A once-extinguished life icon was illuminated somewhat. Very faint—but blinking. Ryan retracted his own battle suit to lie down next to her, bringing his face close to hers. Behind her visor, Ryan watched as her eyes fluttered several times before opening. She reached for her throat, attempting to swallow.

"You're going to be okay," the captain told her.

Wendy nodded, but cringed at the movement. Her eyes found Ryan's. In a scratchy voice, she asked, "Orloff?"

"He's dead."

EPILOGUE

The three space vessels floated in place, their propulsion systems inactive. Holding, they were midway through Orloff's intricate spatial passageway. One that progressed from Alaster-Rei—between thousands of loops and turns—and through millions of ice rocks within that unique, tightly clustered, asteroid field. At present, they were positioned close to one another; close enough that one could clearly see the other ships when looking out through a canopy or window.

For the trek that would lead them out of the asteroid field, Jason changed who would be traveling in which ship. Nan and Ryan would continue in the *Pacesetter II*. Although reluctant to leave Wendy's side, Jason convinced Ryan that she would be in good hands. He was sure Nan and Ryan had a lot of catching up to do and this would be a good time for that. Jason also noted Ryan was more than a little excited about being behind the controls of the sleek little red fighter.

Jason also decided he would pilot the Refurbished Paotow Tanker solo. The robot was needed on the Consignment Freight Van—its AI necessary in navigating safely through the asteroid field. Wendy, still wearing the battle suit, would stay below, fast asleep on Ryan's bunk. Once the van was close enough, Wendy would be phase-shifted directly into the *Jumelle*'s Medical—where Dira was waiting, ready to move her into a MediPod unit.

Jason watched from the tanker's cockpit, as first the *Pacesetter II* moved away, and then, a moment later, the CF van followed right after.

Jason rarely contemplated feeling alone, or even lonely. He liked his own company too much for that. Hell, he could be perfectly occupied with only his own thoughts for entertainment for hours on end. But right then, on board the creaky old vessel, he did feel *alone*. The Paotow Tanker seemed far larger now—with the other vessels gone. The energy that existed on board here was palpable, both dark and foreboding.

Jason smiled at his own foolishness. Taking a seat in the pilot's chair, he continued to stare out the forward observation window into the blackness beyond, and at the constant blur of large objects, moving past the tanker on every side. A cold shiver ran up his spine as he looked around the murky cockpit.

Chuckling to himself, he thought, *Get a grip, man*, though his thoughts continued to wander. He thought about Orloff's hulking body, now secured in one of the storage compartments, and about the mounted corpses—displayed below on the lower deck—on Orloff's heinous trophy wall. And then Jason inhaled the rank odor—putrid smells that permeated the entire ship. Would permeate the ship until it was destroyed. Turned into a fireball—with nothing but space dust remaining. *Soon! Very … soon!* he thought.

He was being hailed. "Go for Captain."

"Captain, this is Ryan. I wanted to thank you for saving Wendy's life … and mine."

"Don't mention it," Jason said. "Just Star Watch hard at

work for your tax dollars."

"Captain?"

"Yeah, Ryan?"

"What are we going to do about the other three brothers? Brent, Payne, and Larry? I left them tied up, down there on the planet."

Jason grimaced as he took another look around the dreary cockpit. "Yeah … I should probably retrieve them. Although, they certainly don't deserve it. I'll see you later … back on board the *Jumelle*."

The End.

Want more? How about right now? Turn the page to read two sample chapters of Mark's upcoming new SciFi series, GALAXY MAN … coming in December, 2016.

Thank you for reading Space Chase—Star Watch, Book 5. Find out what happens next—stay tuned for Star Watch, Book 6. There's lots of action still to come and I hope you'll come along for the ride! Mark Wayne McGinnis.

*If you enjoy these books, please leave a review of **Space Chase** on Amazon.com—it really, really helps!*

To be notified the moment future books are released— please join my mailing list. I hate spam and will never, ever, share your information. Jump to this link to join:

http://eepurl.com/bs7M9r

COMING SOON!

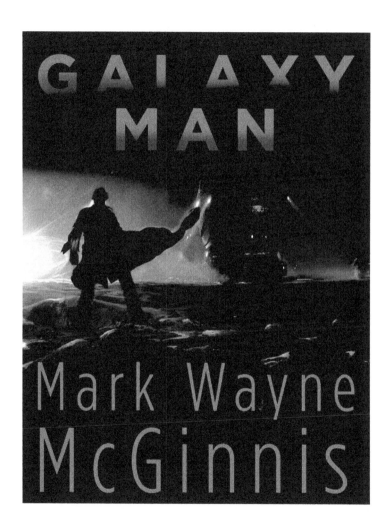

GALAXY MAN

Written By

Mark Wayne McGinnis

Cover design by:
Eren Arik

Edited by:
Lura Lee Genz
Mia Manns

Published by:
Avenstar Productions

E-book ver :

To join Mark's mailing list, jump to
http://eepurl.com/bs7M9r

Visit Mark Wayne McGinnis at
http://www.markwaynemcginnis.com

INTRODUCTION

Everything changed with that amazing, singular, discovery on Mars.

The year was 2029. It was the second manned mission, *Explorer Zheng He*, a combined U.S.–Chinese cooperative, decreed to reach the red planet and establish a far larger—far more elaborate—base than the first. The new site: *Musk-Horizon*, adjacent to what had become known as the *Hidden Valley*. It was here, where thick mudstone strata from an ancient evaporated lakebed—rich with river- and stream-related deposits, and a mere seventeen feet below the Martian surface—that the alien spacecraft was discovered.

In history, there had been other such monumental discoveries—discoveries that not only change the *then* current human condition—such as the discovery of fire, or the use of weapons to hunt with or ward off enemies, or that of the wheel—which single-handedly, inexplicably, transformed ancient societies, prompting early man to stray from what was known, what was safe, to venture forth. To explore. This was such a discovery.

It took three and a half years to bring key components

back to Earth. As scientists from around the world evaluated the highly advanced technology, especially the vessel's unique exotic-matter propulsion system, it was quickly evident that space transportation would forever be altered. It was designated *Zinton Tech*—*Zinton* being the name of the originating alien race. In one fell swoop, science and technology had been catapulted hundreds of years forward. Soon ... those distant twinkling stars and their accompanying planetary systems would be within reach ... and ... as with the advent of wheel ... things would never, ever, be the same.

CHAPTER 1

Dusk. Like a Cimmerian veil of purples and pinks, it quickly encroached upon the surrounding foothills, spreading next across the valley of short-grassed prairie land. A dark figure leaned into the buffeting, oncoming wind, pulling the collar of his leather coat closer around his neck—not against the cold as much as against the fine gritty sand, twirling and whirling around him. A gamey smell of livestock and manure, also hay and other aromas he wasn't sure about, permeated his nostrils. It was a small planet, colonized twenty-seven years earlier, for one purpose only—producing beef: hundreds of millions of pounds of beef annually.

The dark figure gazed off to his left and saw five or six groupings of cattle—mere blots on the landscape at this late hour, and from such a long distance.

John Gallic appreciated the sight—even the smells. Sights and smells that were, some twenty years ago, removed from Earth's environ. Cattle, it seemed, were just another contributor to Earth's ongoing global warming—a result of anthropogenic, man-induced, greenhouse gasses. Like carbon dioxide, methane, nitrous, and a number of various fluorinated gases, such as sulfur hydrofluorocarbons, perfluorocarbons, to name a few. Earth was now a closed system. A carefully controlled biosphere—no agriculture to speak of; no manufacturing to speak of; no anything that could cause any instability within Earth's now newly sanitized, relatively speaking, environment.

Gallic hadn't been back for years; had little desire to return, either. His life was here—within the many burgeoning territories a number of light-years away.

He brought his attention back to the here and now, to the job at hand. Running somewhat behind schedule. He liked being on time, keeping his commitments. Life was much less complicated that way.

Up ahead, partially obscured within the churning sand cloud, he saw neon-colored lights: muted reds, blues, and greens, plus variations of the same colors. The wind had picked up noticeably since he'd left his ship, but, ignoring the chill, he fixed his attention on the suspended sign—twenty feet above the bar. The name on the sign, Renegade's Haven, blinked on and off; a staccato rhythm meant to attract visitors from miles away. For Gallic, it induced no reaction at all.

He approached the front of the establishment, where loud music could be heard, escaping through the antiquated shack's countless open gaps—between old and bowed timber planks—and from the three small, ill-fitting, grease-smeared windows. The front door, faded red with time and a sturdy, stout affair, was wedged partially open by what looked like an old cast-iron anvil.

The parking lot was completely full. Some of the vehicles were open-bed hovercrafts—probably owned by local field hands, who worked hard doing whatever needed doing. Perhaps moving herds from one location to another, or delivering bales of hay, or escorting cattle to a sectioned-off area where they'd be put down, and readied for processing. Although Gallic didn't know much about either cattle or ranching, he knew a lot about many other things—things he was adept at.

Gallic walked between various-sized crafts, parked far-ther out in the lot. Some smaller, some larger, there were certain similarities between them, even though some were older, looking ready to be replaced. Others looked brand new and expensive—right off the dealer's lot—and were the personal spacecraft of wealthy businessmen, wealthy ranch owners, and the sons or daughters of ranch owners. Most of the vessels had approximately 800 to 1,200 cubic feet of inside volume capacity—about the size of an old school bus at the turn of the 21st century on Earth. But the similarity stopped there. These were sleek—precision-made—space-craft. Most had exotic matter drives capable of FTL, as well as integrated with the latest AI brains. Undoubtedly, these designer ships were far too smart for their own good and definitely too smart for their owners. The year was 2117. At present day costs, each individual ship could be worth a bil-lion dollars or more. Gazing across the nearly full landing lot, Gallic guesstimated that there, in front of Renegade's Haven, he was looking at a cool fifty billion dollars' worth of fancy, high-priced, space transportation.

It took Gallic another five minutes to pinpoint the spe-cific craft he was looking for. One of the newer ones, a Hau-senbach L35T, it was built within German manufacturing territories—close to a light-year's distance away across open space. A fine machine. Very expensive. And the owner was three months' delinquent making payments. Gallic was there to repo the vehicle. A fine ship like this would fetch a nice percentage. Maybe enough to pay off the *Hound*.

He moved around the taxium-glass and polished-chrome craft—sliding his palm across the slick surface—as he contin-ued to examine her from bow to stern. Ingress and egress for a new L35T was completely AI-controlled. No seams—no hairline gaps—which would allow Gallic to use the tools of his trade to penetrate a hatchway. Of German design origin, the AI was probably one of those Spincher & Cowl's—a real smart artificial intelligence unit. And it, undoubtedly, was watching Gallic at that very moment; had already tapped into the CoreNet and knew who he was and what he did for a living. Also, what he did another lifetime ago. Because this breed of AI was so thorough, so tenacious, it would have delved far deeper into his past—into every aspect of his life. But Gallic didn't really care what it uncovered. It didn't change the fact that this same vehicle needed to be loaded onto the *Hound* and returned to the selling dealership, either tonight, or tomorrow morning at the latest.

He gave the craft an affectionate pat then headed in the direction of the blinking sign of blue, red, and green neon lights. *Time to do things the old fashioned way*, he mused.

* * *

John Gallic entered the seedy watering hole through the faded red door, knowing exactly what to expect inside. He'd been there before, had conducted business there. Had been there to drink—or not drink. The proprietor knew enough about him to know when disturbing him would be a bad idea. Patrons came and went from Renegade's Haven all the time; for the most part, they went unnoticed. But that was not the case with John Gallic. At six-foot-six, and close to two hundred and sixty pounds, he was a large, imposing figure. Dressed in dark brown leather trousers, heavy black boots, and a well-worn leather trench coat—supported by shoulders that almost spanned the now open threshold— eyes turned in sockets to see who, or *what*, had so obtrusively entered the bar.

The music was loud and the smoky haze from cigarettes, cigars, and pipes gave the place a far more mysterious ambiance than it deserved. The combined hum of chattering voices decreased several decibels when more heads turned to face him. Gallic surveyed the room—taking in as much detail as he could without being overly obvious. Good with details, he was trained to notice things the average person might disregard. His training took place in another lifetime—when he was a different person. When he was Chief Inspector for the Colonial Police—Space District 22.

But that life was now in the past. For the past three years, Gallic had been a Territory Abettor, commonly referred to as a Local Joe. Local Joes were independent contractors, providing a handful of, not always the most respected, services. Earth's distant vast territories lacked much in the way of institutional policing. Here really was the wild, wild, west. At one end of the spectrum, a Local Joe would do space vehicle repossessions for several of the larger dealerships; they also provided various forms of security, on a per-case basis, and/or bounty hunting. Some of the more qualified, properly licensed Local Joes did investigative work. Gallic had done it all. Presently for him, repo work paid the best. It also kept him busy—too busy to think—too busy to remember.

He made his way over to the bar and squeezed between two conversing elderly men. Forced to stand up, they scooted their stools away from Gallic's imposing bulk, then sat back down. Leaning forward, the men peered around him; then, resuming their conversation, they drank their whiskeys.

Gallic caught the proprietor's eye. At that moment, he looked just like the other three busy bartenders. Wearing a stained white apron, the medium-sized man, possessing a severely receding hairline, wiped his hands on a dishtowel and made his way down the bar to where Gallic stood waiting. He asked, "Whisky?"

"Not tonight, Randy." Leaning forward, Gallic spoke just loud enough for him to hear. "I'm looking for a guy … name's Larz Cugan."

The barkeep looked hesitant. "Don't bust up the place, Gallic. No trouble here tonight … okay?"

"Uh huh. Just point him out to me."

The proprietor gestured with his chin, toward a large group which had pulled three tables together. An eruption of laughter, followed by arms raised high, and the clinking of shot glasses—a rowdy happy group.

"He's the one at the far head of the table. With that … thing … around his neck. Not sure what those things are called," Randy said.

"It's called an ascot."

"Looks pretty silly to me," Randy added.

Gallic said, "Anyway … thanks. Go ahead and ping my account for a double whiskey; drink it yourself or give it away." He turned and made his way through the packed sea of patrons, shuffling between chairs and tables. Several times he had to turn sideways in order to maneuver his way over to the boisterous partygoers.

No less than twelve, they mostly were in their twenties, Gallic surmised. All were dressed to the nines—designer clothes meant to impress each other or anyone else. The women were bare-shouldered, tanned, and wore an abundance of fragrant perfume. The men, equal in number, wore suits with bolo ties and leather cowboy boots detailed with elaborate designs.

Larz Cugan's eyes met Gallic's as he approached. Even sitting, he looked about six feet tall, had designer stubble, and wore his highlighted streaked hair parted on the side. His angled bangs were strategically combed across one eye. His suit was white as snow and looked expensive. Gallic didn't know much about fancy clothes, but he imagined the jacket's lining had a famous designer's logo stitched there. Invisible to the naked eye, but the designer was recognizable, just the same, by those who cared about such things.

A blonde woman's thin tanned arm was casually draped over Larz's left shoulder. Sitting close behind him, and to the side, as if she'd joined the party late and had to pull a chair from an adjoining table. Dangling, sparkly earrings caught the light as her head turned this way and that. She wore faded snug jeans and some kind of halter top that emphasized her breasts and her bare flat tummy. All in all, she was dressed more casually than the other women, but it worked—she was stunning. She had a confident air about her that Gallic found both irritating, yet somewhat compelling at the same time. Probably smart—beautiful—and undoubtedly wealthy. A dangerous combination. As Gallic closed in on the end of their table, a subtle, bemused smile crossed her pretty lips.

Seated directly on both Larz's left and right side were two big, barrel-chested guys. Like two matching bookends, they wore similar gray suits and an abundance of a wet-looking product in their slicked-back hair. Tweedledee and Tweedledum, they looked more like a rich boy's protection than actual friends. As Gallic leaned down to say something to Larz, they tensed, straightening in their chairs.

Larz Cugan quickly jerked his head to one side, which Gallic thought looked more like a nervous tick. Probably something he did often but wasn't aware of. In any event, it was enough to momentarily pendulum his hair away from his eyes. Hesitantly, Larz leaned forward to hear what the tall stranger had to say. The girl with the sparkly earrings also leaned closer.

Gallic said, "Hey, man … you Larz?"

"What's it to you?"

"Well, if you are, I thought I should tell you that someone just backed into your ride. If you hurry, you can still catch the son of a bitch out in the lot."

Chapter 2

Gallic stood aside as Larz jumped out of his chair, charged past him, and headed for the exit. Looking startled, both Tweedledee and Tweedledumb clumsily extricated their legs from beneath the table and hurried after him. *They move pretty fast for two porky guys*, Gallic thought. The girl with the earrings rose to her feet, appraising Gallic for several beats, with the same bemused expression. She held out her hands, palms up, in a gesture that implied, *You first …*

* * *

Outside, the wind had died away and the sand cloud dissipated. By the time Gallic arrived at the Hausenbach L35T, Larz had apparently completed circling the hull, looking her over. Making sure there were no new dents or scratches on the vehicle's pristine finish.

Larz looked Gallic over—from head to toe—an expression of distaste crossing his face. Like he was looking at a bug, or maybe a wayward turd lying on the ground. "What the fuck's your problem, dude? There's absolutely nothing wrong with my 5T." He shoved his body smack into Gallic's personal space—with hands on hips, his angry face glared up at him. And then, there they were too, his big bookends, hovering a step behind him on either side.

Gallic hadn't known the proper abbreviated vernacular for his ship was simply 5T. It had a nice ring to it. 5T. "Hey, it's your ride, man," he said. "It's no skin off my nose if you think she's fine."

"So why don't you tell us what you *think* you saw?"

Gallic shrugged. "Looked like an Old Buick Starflight. Green ... I think. It bumped your 5T down low there at the front, jostling her pretty good. But hey ... it's probably fine." Gallic turned, as if he were going to leave, then spun back around. "You did fire her up, didn't you? See that she's still operational after being slammed into like that?"

Larz seemed to contemplate on that for a moment. Then turning his attention to the girl who had just arrived, now standing closer to Gallic than himself, he raised his brows, questioningly. "Maybe he's right. Maybe I should at least check her out to be on the safe side."

Larz, patting his suit jacket pocket, brought out a *Start-Cube* then walked around the 5T to where Gallic surmised the vessel's hidden access hatch was located. Holding the cube in front of him on his upturned palm, it jumped right from his hand and disappeared, at waist-level, into the pristine fuselage. More *Zinton* technology. Gallic had heard about this latest use of the alien science and wondered how much extra Larz had to pay for such an option. A million? Two million?

Then, almost magically, the 5T's hatch began to lift up and outward—like a graceful gull wing.

Gallic let out a breath. *So, so easy!* Having the Start-Cube in place was exactly what he needed. The vehicle, accessible now, was also drivable ... by him, or anyone else. He said, "Hey, hold up there a moment."

Frowning, Larz halted, one leg poised on the first step, which led into the ship. Gallic reached him in three strides, first unfolding, then handing him an electronic *vid-sheet.* "This authorizes me to take possession of this vehicle. I'm repossessing it. Step away from the craft. Do so now!"

"Like hell you will!" Larz shouted, grabbing on to both sides of the hatchway. "No one's taking my 5T … there must be a mistake. I pay my fucking bills."

"Either that, or your daddy does," Gallic said. "Unfortunately, one of you has missed a few payments: Three, to be exact. You can take care of the default either at your bank or at the dealership. She'll be there waiting for you in the morning. Now move aside."

Larz, hunkering down, was not going to make this easy. "Johnnie … Donnie, take care of this!"

Gallic felt a heavy palm on his right shoulder. A surprisingly high voice said, "You're going to give Mr. Cugan a bit more time to take care of business."

Gallic, not turning around, glanced at the beefy hand resting on his shoulder. "Which one are you, Johnnie or Donnie?"

"I'm Donnie."

Gallic said, "Johnnie, best you head back into the bar. Ask for Randy."

"Yeah? What for?"

"Ask to borrow a bucket."

"What do I need a bucket for?"

Gallic sensed they were exchanging perplexed looks.

"Because, if your friend here doesn't take his hand off my shoulder, you'll be taking what's left of him home in it."

Gallic, while watching Donnie's hand come away, sensed the stocky man was turning his upper torso—winding up to deliver a fast punch. Gallic didn't need to watch him to know exactly what he was doing. So instead of leaning forward, or trying to duck away, Gallic did the opposite of what Donnie

291

expected. He stepped back and into him, hard and fast. Donnie's punch came, but it was more like a love tap to Gallic's kidneys. All his momentum—all the built-up energy—gone, like air farting out from an old whoopee cushion. Then, just as suddenly, Gallic—faking a half step forward—rocked back on his heels, jamming his right elbow back hard. The height differential between Gallic and Donnie couldn't have worked out better. The familiar knob protrusion, located at the end of every elbow, is actually part of the humerus bone. But Gallic's arms were not typical; they were large and muscular. The round knob on his humerus bone was more like the business end of a sledgehammer. When it made contact with Donnie's nose, it totally annihilated it. In a fraction of a second, Donnie's nasal bone—the supporting septal cartilage, as well as both sides of the maxillary bones—either splintered outright, or was instantly turned into something akin to toothpaste.

When Donnie dropped to the ground like a sack of potatoes, Gallic turned his attention to Johnnie, who was holding a semi-automatic handgun in his left hand. But all his attention was focused on the bloodied heap lying before him on the ground. Gallic stepped forward and slapped the gun from his hand, preparing to do the same to him as he did to Donnie.

The girl spoke. "Stop! Leave him alone." She looked over to Larz, and said, "You'll get it back tomorrow. Let the creep have it, Larz … it's not worth it."

Larz glared at Gallic, whose expression remained impassive. Almost as if the situation was an everyday occurrence, which it often was.

Eventually, Larz stepped down from the open hatchway. "Do you know who I am? Who my family is?"

"Nope. Can't say that I do," Gallic replied.

"You're done! I hope you've enjoyed this lowlife job of yours, because you're finished. You'll be fired by morning."

Gallic, stepping to the open hatchway, turned around to face the seething Larz Cugan. "Good luck with that. I work for myself. Best take care of your friend there …

he's going to need some TLC for about three weeks. And I'd turn him over on his stomach, if I were you."

Stepping into the craft, he caught the girl's eye as the gull wing hatch began to close. He couldn't quite read her questioning expression when she said, "You're a piece of work … you know that?"

"Yeah … well I've been called worse, sweetheart."

* * *

The T5's cockpit, with its myriad of glowing dials and indicators, was just as impressive inside as it was outside—a very expensive spacecraft. And Larz certainly didn't forego adding the more luxurious options. Gallic sat down in the pilot's seat and felt it automatically adjust to his girth.

He had never sat in anything so comfortable. A far cry from the rock-hard cushions found back on the *Hound*. Spinning the seat around, he studied the craft's warm and inviting cabin. Padded leather was everywhere—cushy wrap-around leather chairs and sectional couches. Inset strips of decorative wood—perhaps walnut—accented the padded interior sides and overhead bulkheads.

He swiveled his chair back to face the business at hand. Firing up the 5T's propulsion system, Gallic took the controls in his hands and lifted off. Thirty feet above the landing lot, he cranked the controls hard left, and accelerated fast, leaving Renegade's Haven, the sprawling pastureland, and the sporadic clusters of cattle behind.

At a quarter-mile out, Gallic reached into his inside coat pocket and found the small garage door-like opener. He pressed the button and the rear hatch on the *Hound* began to open up. Light then peeked out through the quickly expanding gap around the hatch. He slowed the 5T and waited for the hatch, which did double-duty as both hatch and gangway, to descend all the way until it was angled downward. He goosed the 5T, piloting her directly into the *Hound*'s massive hold, large enough to transport five old 747 jetliners stacked atop one another.

It took another five minutes to carefully strap and secure the 5T down onto the deck. Any damage incurred now would come right off the top of his repo fees. Once satisfied, he initiated closing up the hold's rear hatch. A handful of other vehicles were there, all strapped into place. Everything looked to be in order.

By the time he crossed the hold to the entranceway to the rear airlock, he heard the familiar pressurized *phunk* sound, as the massive hatch was seated into its surrounding cowling. Once through the airlock, Gallic headed up the ship's internal stairway, which led up to the second level.

* * *

The top level of the *Hound* looked more like an open, New York City loft build-out than it did the top deck of a working spacecraft. Fifty-five feet wide by fifty-nine feet long, it pretty much was a big square. Even while the huge compartment certainly looked industrial, there was something strangely inviting about the space. Perhaps due to the wide-planked timber decking, or the soft indirect lighting, generated from large can lights, fifteen feet overhead; or perhaps the intermixing of home furnishings—Navaho throw rugs draped over stuffed, worn, leather couches, and a set of multi-colored glass Tiffany lamps. Or maybe it was the long observation windows, installed on opposing bulkheads, which provided high-up views to the now dark landscape below.

Gallic moved all the way through the sectionalized space to a bank of forward-facing windows, where two rotating seats, and a waist-level semicircle-shaped console were placed. The paint was both dinged and scratched. Not really a bridge—nothing that elaborate—but not really a cockpit either. More serious than that, it was simply the command center. As he approached, a projected holographic display came alive on his right. Nearly as high in height as him, the display was in the process of updating his weekly job log. He noticed the latest repo job: **Vehicle**: Hausenbach L35T, **Owner**: Mr. Larz Cugan, **Current Standing**: impounded/transferring, **Destination**: Dealer/Bantum Exotic Starcrafts. Gallic traced with his index finger the other open work repo orders. There were three more that would require his attention over the next day or two.

A reminder window popped into view: *You have two vid-messages! Both messages are tagged high priority.*

Gallic, after taking a seat, addressed the *Hound*'s AI, saying out loud, "Go ahead and play the first one."

A blue-tinted, life-sized holographic image came to life. A short, bald-headed man, in a wrinkled Hawaiian shirt, looked back at Gallic. One of Gallic's past associates—Polly Gant—a less than scrupulous bail bondsman that he tended to avoid unless there was absolutely no other work at hand. Polly smiled. "Hey, Galaxy Man … Call me. I've a special project for you. It's perfect for someone with your … capabilities. Time-sensitive, so don't—"

Gallic said, "Skip message … go to next."

Up on the projected display was an older black man, dressed in a smart-fitting, navy blue uniform. His face was heavily lined; filled with more age spots than Gallic remembered him having. His hair, still mostly black, was peppered with more white, as was his immaculately trimmed goatee. It was Chief Superintendent Bernard Danbury, who—three and a half years ago—was his boss, friend and mentor. Gallic resisted the oncoming flood of memories—like snakes—trying to twist and wiggle their way into his consciousness.

Danbury said, "Hello, John. I hope this message finds you in good health."

Gallic said, "Pause message." He stared at the frozen-in-time holographic image. He'd worked for the Superintendent for close to a decade; had risen quickly within the Territorial Police Department, Spatial District 22. As Chief Inspector, he reported directly to this man. He left the position soon after the murders. Murders never solved that he hadn't been allowed to have any involvement with. John closed his eyes and fought to keep the snakes at bay. Nothing was more important than finding the ones responsible for the murders of the young, beautiful twenty-eight-year-old woman, and her equally beautiful three-year-old daughter. John Gallic's wife and daughter. His life, as he knew it, ended the day the two were taken from him. Now, he merely *survived*, continuing to do on his own what he wasn't permitted to do as a Chief Inspector for the Territorial Police Department, Spatial District 22. Since he was both husband and father of the homicide victims, he wasn't allowed direct involvement in the case. A conflict of interest. The grisly crime was front-page news for weeks as the investigation proceeded in earnest. All had good intentions, overtime approved for three full-time investigators. But, as things sometimes happened, potential leads hit dead ends. Promising prospects dried up. Official personnel and resources, eventually, assigned to other cases. Too many new crimes capturing the media headlines. But that hadn't stopped Gallic. For months, his friend Chief Superintendent Bernard Danbury turned a blind eye to Gallic's growing number of sick days—days spent on a private crusade to find the killer, or killers, of Claire and Mandy.

Ultimately, he was forced to resign, and it was for the best. Now, some three-plus years later, Gallic—in his off time—continued the pursuit. Seeking to find the one who'd ruined everything, stolen his life.

The life insurance policy hadn't been much, but he had some savings. Financing a high-interest loan, he purchased a wrecked Hewley-Jawbone carrier for pennies on the dollar—the *Hound*. It took him over a year to make the ship space-worthy.

With the *snakes* now somewhat at bay, Gallic said, "Continue message."

"John … I wanted to be the first one to tell you. There's been a … development in your wife and daughter's case. We have a strong lead."

There's more to come with Galaxy Man … coming soon.

To be notified the moment future books are released—including **Galaxy Man**—*please join my mailing list. I hate spam and will never, ever, share your, information. Jump to this link to join:*
http://eepurl.com/bs7M9r

Acknowledgments

I am ever grateful for the ongoing fan support I receive for all my books. This latest book, my fifteenth—*Space Chase—Star Watch, Book 5*—came about through the combined contributions of numerous others. First, I'd like to thank my wife, Kim, for her never-ending love and support. She helps make this journey rich and so very worthwhile. I'd also like to thank my mother, Lura Genz, for her tireless work as my creative editor and a staunch cheerleader of my writing. I'd like to thank Mia Manns, for her phenomenal line and developmental editing ... she is an incredible resource and friend. A special 'thank you' goes out to L.J. Ganser, who produces the audiobook versions of my books. Anyone looking for a truly immersive—not to forget 'fun'—reading experience, with all his wonderful character voices, will have to try the audiobook version. I'd also like to thank those in my writer's MeetUp groups, who, bringing fresh ideas and perspective to my creative output, elevate my writing as a whole. Others who provided fantastic support include: Lura and James Fischer, Sue Parr, Stuart Church, Brad Leppla, Eric Sundius, and Chris Derrick.

Other books by MWM

Made in the USA
Middletown, DE
27 July 2021